AKIN TO LOVE

In all her memories of this island lived a young man, a handsome painter who strode now into her thoughts, stepping from cobwebbed corners of her mind, drawing back a disused curtain and standing centre stage.

She smiled at the memory of him, recalling him, at first with affection and then pain, a pain so poignant and searing that swiftly, diligently she dismissed him.

The film script she had written was about him. Harry. He had been her first love. Once or twice that first evening during a break from learning lines she found herself alongside him, smelling the sweetness of him, recalling the touch of his flesh.

CAROL DRINKWATER is perhaps best known as an actress, particularly for her role as Helen Herriot in *All Creatures Great and Small*. She has also appeared in numerous films, television and stage plays. Her bestselling children's novel, *The Haunted School*, was made into an award-winning television series in which she starred. A film is also planned of her first novel for adults, *An Abundance of Rain*. *Akin to Love* is her second adult novel.

CAROL DRINKWATER

AKIN TO LOVE

CORONET BOOKS
Hodder and Stoughton

Copyright © 1991 by Carol
Drinkwater

First published in Great Britain
in 1991 by Hodder and
Stoughton Limited

Coronet edition 1992

Printed and bound in Great Britain
for Hodder and Stoughton
Paperbacks, a division of Hodder
and Stoughton Limited, Mill
Road, Dunton Green, Sevenoaks,
Kent TN13 2YA (Editorial Office:
47 Bedford Square, London
WC1 3DP) by Richard Clay
Limited, Bungay, Suffolk.
Photoset by E.P.L. BookSet,
Norwood, London.

British Library C.I.P.

Drinkwater, Carol
  Akin to love.
  I. Title
  823.914 [F]

ISBN 0-340-56459-8

For dear friends,
Doraine and George Tee.
And for Michel.
With all my love.

My very special thanks go to
Carolyn Caughey and Philippa Pride
of Hodder and Stoughton,
to Gina and Murray Pollinger
and to Jean Diamond.
For their faith and support.

"The characteristics of the white
youth which most alarm their
elders – the long hair, the new
dances, their love for Negro
Music, their use of marijuana, their
mystical attitude towards
sex – are all tools of
the revolution."

ELDRIDGE CLEAVER

"My salad days,
When I was green in judgement."

William Shakespeare, ANTONY AND CLEOPATRA

The telephone was ringing. Peter heard it in the courtyard. It seemed an age before anyone answered it. He dismounted and strode towards the old farmhouse.

Inside he found Penny. She was curled up on a cushion on the floor, staring at the flames of a log fire. Winters in Tuscany could be chilling.

"What are you doing?" He remained in the doorway. An instinct to keep his distance. Her mood seemed disturbed.

"Mmm, oh just . . . staring at my script."

"I heard the telephone. Did you get it?"

"Do you believe that a person can ever finally rid themselves of their past?"

"Confront it perhaps, little more. Why? Who was that on the telephone?"

"Ben." Sighing, she tossed the script aside and stretched her legs as though alleviating a cramp. Or to rid herself of news.

"Your agent? Strange for him on a Sunday. Thought he'd be on the golf course." Watching her, Peter crossed the room. He was on his way to the drinks cabinet, glancing at the clock. Almost six. Early for his tipple.

"Want something?"

She shook her head. "Gaza's directing the picture."

*　　　*　　　*

1

The interior of the Bentley smelt of soft beige leather shiny from usage, of walnut wood-polish and of Penny Morrison's musky Saint Laurent perfume. The actress was seated in the back running through her lines, attempting not to let her feelings overwhelm her. Excitement mingled with doubt; first day of shoot nerves. Penny knew the sensation well.

She glanced at her watch. She was growing agitated about the time. Her anxiety of course was unreasonable. Even with the unexpectedly heavy overnight snow-storms her flat in Lowndes Square was no more than a stone's throw from the film's first location; the Catholic church in Farm Street. Her make-up call had been arranged for six-thirty. It was only five to. Any disquiet about arriving late was illogical.

Momentarily calmed, she allowed her script to slide as though forgotten onto the unoccupied seat alongside her while she leaned away from it, left towards the window. Beyond the glass lay the dark and frosty un-born morning and a city still sleeping. Reflected there, staring back at her was an image of herself looking younger than her years. Her face was without make-up, scrubbed and moisturised; her hair was still damp and freshly shampooed. Penny in jeans, buried beneath a voluminous coat of calf-length suede stared at herself through generous hazel eyes. She was breathing deeply, steadily, seemingly poised, facing the root of her present nervous anticipation.

Meeting Jimmy Gaza again; unable to gauge how it was going to be. He would not trip lightly over her feelings, of that she was certain. No first-morning apprehensions about that.

*

Her heart was thumping, but to any stranger, such as the chauffeur she had noticed glimpsing her in his rearview mirror, she appeared composed and confident.

Snowflakes spiralled rapidly past her window. A swarm of white bees against a pewter sky. A flickering silent movie screen. She closed her eyes and held her breath listening to their whispered arrival. The wipers on the Bentley slid back and forth, a heavy steady rhythm echoing her heartbeat. Suddenly for no sensible reason the sound of them and the sight of the falling snow petals released her tension. They filled her with a childlike glee and made her want to giggle. If the driver had not been present she might have laughed aloud, leapt from the car and danced crazily in front of the new day. Her emotions were a seesaw of nervous energy.

He was watching her, the driver, sizing her up. What was he thinking? That she was smaller in real life, a bit on the skinny side and less glamorous?

"If you don' mind my sayin' so, you look different off the box. Always seen you with long hair," he ventured as though to explain why he had been staring, or simply to make conversation. "S'funny thing working with this limousine service, I've driven more faces than I care to remember. Rude bastards a lot of 'em."

"Really?"

"You seem quiet though. Keep yourself to yourself; not talkative."

Penny was feeling too jittery for conversation but not wishing to appear impolite she nodded and smiled. A feeble attempt.

"Cut it for the film have you?"

"What?"

"The 'air."

"Yes."

"Cryin' shame, if you don't mind my sayin' so. Long 'air suits yer better. Looks too boyish this way. I like my film stars to look like women. Gina Lollobrigida, now there's a woman."

Penny glanced at her watch once more, a reflex

gesture. Her lips were moving. Silently, nervously, she was repeating her lines.

"Don't fret yourself, Miss Morrison, I won't let this snow make us late."

"Pardon?"

"I said we're goin' to be righ' on time. First day. Gotta start yer right."

"Good, thanks. Yes, I was wondering . . . worrying." She smiled warmly at his eyes and the peak of his black hat reflected in the rear-view mirror before returning to her own thoughts, her own concerns, her other reality. The film ahead.

And the prospect of confronting Jimmy Gaza.

He would be there ahead of her. Of that she felt certain.

It had always been his habit to arrive on set way ahead of schedule, to pace out the creative space before any other member of the crew appeared, before the setting up of the scenes began. Like a lone figure standing on a stage in darkness before any lights had been lit, before any audience had been seated. It was a magic time, a time of powerful dreams. She had always related to that habit of his. His world of make-believe.

She held her breath, remembering him, recollecting fragments of their past.

That was how he had operated in the old days, way back, when they had worked together before. But even if he had changed, even if, a gigantic if, his ruthless obsessive energy had been tempered, Penny knew that today he would be there, waiting for her.

The first day of any shoot was always exceptional. The entire crew including herself was excited, expectant, nervous. The director's presence was essential. At this stage a film crew was simply an adolescent beast, all legs and arms, to be nurtured, moulded, created to his liking. It took patient dedication and skill. Jimmy Gaza prided himself on that skill. This morning counted, he knew that better than most.

She felt such reticence at meeting up with him again.

No not reticence, it was fear. Basic gut-aching fear. She was afraid of facing him again, of working with him again and of being close to him. He had been brutal. And this film, the film they were about to shoot, was a personal story, her story. That made her vulnerable. Might he have changed? In those early days he had been a king in Hollywood. Not so now.

The driver parked the Bentley across the way from Farm Street. Penny sat motionless for a few moments longer, summoning up her courage. The generator truck installed in front of them breathed and shimmied electricity powering all the caravans and buses like some mighty mother dragon. An as yet unfamiliar figure wearing round horn-rimmed spectacles, wellingtons, a yellow rain cape and a very intense freckled face, trudged with umbrella and over-fondled script towards her, to open her door and guide her.

She glanced about her. Had she miscalculated?

The snow was banking up high along the roadside. She caught sight of a couple of crew members further along the road shovelling great muddied-white clods onto the pavement. Clearing a path for unit cars, no doubt.

And then she spied him, at a distance of fifty yards or so. Without a moment's hesitation she had recognised him, the vigorous strut, the scruffy sinewy frame. Jimmy Gaza. He was beckoning to various folk, shaking hands, gesticulating animatedly, paying little heed to the descending weather. It would seem that every ounce of his gritty determination had remained intact. He appeared, dressed any old how in shapelessly baggy cord pants, wellingtons and a sodden three-quarter length suede jacket currently the colour of peat, rounding the corner of the breakfast truck with a viewfinder swinging from his neck like a huge chunk of jet jewellery. He was devouring a fried egg sandwiched in a toasted sesame bun. In all things Gaza's appetite was never less than voracious.

Someone must have informed him of her imminent

arrival, or he had been watching out for her, for he was heading straight towards her, stepping his way through the snow.

A confusion of thought and feeling rose up within her at the sight of him: anger, remorse, something akin to hatred, all born of their common past. Not surprisingly he had aged but she noticed too as he drew closer that his face had grown nipped, less red-blooded; if it had been someone else she would have said unexpectedly empathetic. Had the years been kind to him? She had heard not.

Not for the first time since she had been informed that it was to be he who would direct this picture had she totted up the time, calculating how long ago it had been. Ten years or twelve? Perhaps even a snitch longer. Twelve seemed sufficiently distant. She had been little more than a girl, twenty-seven perhaps at maximum, an eager, ambitious, naïve girl who had wanted almost more than anything in the world to be a film actress. Even now she baulked at the use of the word star.

As he approached she smiled, recollecting his power in those days, his black compelling intensity.

"Welcome aboard," he exclaimed extrovertly, taking her by the arm as she stepped from the car and the assistant with the umbrella relieved her of her script and beauty case.

"Here, gimme that." Gaza grabbed thoughtlessly, gaining possession of the assistant's brolly. He held it above her with an air of gallantry quite negated by his previous action.

"I'll take these to your caravan, Miss Morrison, shall I?" ventured the confused, suddenly roleless young fellow. She smiled her gratitude and with that the younger man sped discreetly away leaving her alone with her director. Alone, yes, although many eyes were upon them: crew members, occasional passersby, on-lookers, autograph hunters no doubt, and probably a fellow member of the cast or two.

"I think we gotta talk," he said, hauling her from

17

alongside the car.

"When did you get in?" she enquired coolly, as he ferried her directly towards her caravan, obviously seeking a private place, out of earshot of gossiping tongues. His arm was intertwined in hers, holding firmly, walking intimately close, smelling of tobacco and egg. She had forgotten that he was no taller than her, and she almost smiled now to remember how much pain he had caused her, way back then.

Almost smiled.

"Coupla weeks. I've been telephoning daily."

"Yes, yes. I was sorry not to have a chance to meet up with you before we got started. We fled to Tuscany. The house was crowded. Peter invited his children to visit . . . "

"Peter?" She felt the pressure of his grip tighten.

"My husband." The words were whispered, barely breathed.

"Your husband? Well, well." To anyone who might have been overhearing them their conversation was small-talk, amicable enough, almost old friends, but she caught the tempo of his underlying tension, his shield of sarcasm. "News in Hollywood must be slowing up. No one informed me of your divorce."

"Well, no, I'm no . . . Peter's . . . we live together," she laughed tightly almost haughtily, a nervous, bordering on skittish, energy rose within her. She was not yet able to let him in or to be at her ease. "Anyway," she continued, marginally more in control, "we got your messages but it was all rather hectic and we decided to stay on in Italy for a short while longer. In fact I left Peter there. Couldn't drag him away."

"Swell. And when exactly did you get back?"

In spite of his brusque approach, firing questions at her as though it were a grilling, she marked that he actually appeared pleased to see her, but then it was not he who carried the memories of humiliation and she wondered again what strange twist of fate had brought them together on this film, her story. A love story about

18

a young man called Harry.

"Mr Gaza!" Someone was calling his name, halting him on the steps of her caravan.

"Go ahead," he said, shoving the brolly at her as though it were something lethal. "Leave the door open. I'll be right back."

Inside the caravan she busied herself with the checking of her day's costumes. Full of nervous energy she slipped her feet into the tall, leather boots made especially for her while outside Gaza paced in the snow, talking, instructing, firing decisions at people as though he were assaulting them. He's even more strung up than I am, she measured, not without a certain pleasure.

Watching him outside now, a short aggressive energy, she was reminded of the first time they had worked together and of her final day on that unmemorable picture. She had spent twelve miserable weeks on location in and around Hollywood. *The Last Summer*, it had been a patchily written, torrid, film industry romance and her golden opportunity. The irony had not escaped her.

His parting words still to this day rang clearly in her head, just as though it had been yesterday.

"I know it's been tough for you, I know you hate me but one day you'll thank me. I've taught you how to survive, taught you a little of what you lacked, sang froid." She had merely gawped at him, hearing his pronouncement, unable to respond, bruised and resentful. "You're a fine young actress. You just need more guts," he had declared, offering the compliment as a consolation prize, brushing her cheek with a soulless kiss and carelessly shaking her hand while she had struggled to suppress her hurt and disappointment.

It should have been the last they saw of one another.

Both had known that the film would bomb, that either of them might not survive once it had been released and the critics had got hold of it, torn it to shreds. They would both need guts. He, she had thought then, would be no exception.

19

The film had bombed, a mighty overnight flop, but she had been persuaded to stay on in Hollywood. She had trudged around looking for work, found an agent and for a while she had believed her fortunes might change. By chance Gaza and she met up again. It had been at her agent's beachside home, a glitzy party. She had been down on her luck. He had been the one familiar face amongst a swirl of glamorous strangers . . .

It barely stood the recollection.

She heard his footsteps now ascending the portable stairs and she turned to greet him, breathing deeply, regularly, ready now to face him.

"You've got thin," she said weakly.

"You've been making it impossible for me to speak to you," he accused, silhouetted in the doorway, his suede jacket dandruffed with snow.

"That's not true," she responded curtly.

"We have to work together."

"We will, we survived it before."

"I want this picture to work, Penny."

"You think I don't!"

"Don't try to pay me back."

She spoke coolly, without emotion, without hatred or resentment. "I have no intention of doing that. I blame myself equally for what happened. I should have known there was no easy way."

Gaza took a step towards her, ice slurred the floor. His head was bent as she often remembered it when he was working, locked in thought, seeing no one apart from the characters alive in his head, seeking his way to deliver them to the screen.

Both in their separate ways had survived, he less successfully than she, but then he had had more to lose. He had been a master. She had been a nobody, a nothing in the industry until curiously, unexpectedly, opportunities had begun to occur, eventually. Other roles, other films. They met now for the first time in twelve years on an equal footing. He was the director but the story, the project, was hers.

"It was a long time ago," he whispered almost confidentially. "I don't have time left to waste." The pouches beneath his eyes underlined a sadness, and they hinted at a cruelty that had used to frighten her.

"I understand."

"Do you, I wonder?"

"Judge, don't patronise me please! I'm out of school now."

Without considering she had called him by his nickname and caught in his tired old eyes a glint of joy. It had touched him. It had been an accident of habit from way way back. She let it go now but it would not happen again.

Penny stood alone, her hands wrapped around a white polystyrene coffee cup in an attempt to keep them warm. The damp was seeping through her shoes and numbing her toes. The wind had left a biting chill in the air. Although the filming had not as yet begun she was feeling calmer, softened by her first confrontation with Gaza which she judged had gone smoothly enough.

Shooting had been delayed by the weather. She walked the length of Farm Street in search of a public telephone which would accept Telecom cards but seemed to be out of luck. Knowing she had time to spare, she set off for Carlos Place and the Connaught Hotel, ordered herself a palatable cup of coffee and booked a call to Italy. A coal-fire blazed in the hearth.

Outside it had ceased to snow. The sky above was a sheer bright blue.

"Your call is through, Miss Morrison."

"How is it going?" She heard the pleasure in his voice and was glad to appease his unspoken anxiety.

"Slowly. I'm setting off for Crete this evening. Want to be there ahead of schedule."

"Let me change my ticket. Close up the farm and join you there ... "

"Peter, it's important to me. I must do this alone."

"Well then, when the damn film's over let's get

21

married."

"I would make you a hopeless wife."

"Why for heaven's sake?"

"You know why. Marriage is not for me. It works like this, let's not spoil it."

"You should get divorced. You hide behind it. It's untidy, like clinging to some worn out sock."

"I'll call you from Crete."

All traces of cloud had been blown away by the wind which had now dropped, leaving in its place a glorious but crisp late morning. This had brought with it a stillness, an atmospheric muteness, that frequently accompanies such weather. Penny exhaled and watched her misty breath evaporate in space.

Cast and most crew members were standing around chatting, discussing the script, enjoying a fag and a coffee, trying to fathom out where they might have worked together before. At the same time as swopping anecdotes about past shoots, they were attempting to keep warm, to keep their spirits up and their adrenalin alive, while a few hot sweating lads from the props department shovelled and hauled the fast-melting snow into hillocks, out of sight around the corner onto the areas of the church gardens that had been pronounced 'off camera'. The general huddled mutterings assessed that it would be after lunch now before the camera finally got rolling, thereby costing them half a day's work right off although nothing official had as yet been announced.

Penny, made up now but still wearing her personal clothes save for the costume coat draped round her shoulders, roamed to and fro introducing herself, freezing but unwilling to sit keyed up and isolated in her caravan. She memorised the names of her new working companions and observed the general flow of things and in the midst of all this spared a passing thought for Peter. Words, emotions were always so much less accessible by phone, muddled and oblique. She knew how he hated being separated from her.

The director's assistant called an early lunch break and people drifted towards the catering van where they queued for plates and hot food and then disappeared to buses or comfortable corners in search of warmth, to eat and gossip. Penny had little appetite but she grabbed herself an apple and crossed the street towards her caravan, passing Gaza on the way.

"I'll join you when I get through all this." He was locked in decision making with the designer and director of photography. "There is something I gotta discuss with you."

She nodded and strode on, strangely disquieted by his comment, but the meal break came and went and Gaza never appeared. She felt a silent sense of relief.

After lunch the excitement began, people running to and fro, scene numbers were called and the first shot of the day, indeed of the entire film, was about to be rehearsed.

"Action," shouted Gaza, whose features were contorted with deep undisturbable concentration.

A hush descended. The filming had begun . . .

A light tapping on the door broke the silence in her caravan. Penny did not lift her head from her script nor budge from where she lay. She was wrapped in her costume coat, stretched out on a makeshift sofa-bed, attempting to keep warm. "Come in," she called cautiously, supposing it to be Gaza, and was surprised when she discovered hovering there the young second assistant with the freckles — known to her now as David — looking more discomfited than ever.

"Yes?" she smiled encouragingly.

"Miss Morrison," he muttered with shy excitement. "It's a wrap. We'll see you in Greece."

2

The house that Penny had rented in Crete was situated on a hillside towards the southern lip of the island and was estimated to be about thirty-five minutes inland from the village of Matala, the film's central coastal location. Penny's only prior acquaintance with the place was a series of overexposed photographs in a brochure, 'Island of Crete Holiday Homes', which had been posted to her by the production secretary several weeks earlier. 'Luxurious apartments' on the waterfront bearing more resemblance to building sites than homes she had rejected and had opted for the restored farmhouse, described in the blurb as 'Your get away from it all holiday. Romantic and Remote', believing that it would ideally suit the peace and tranquillity she sought during the stresses of filming.

Travelling by car from Iráklion airport up mountainous roads better suited to goats was guaranteed to be both tiring and arduous. As a gesture the production office had arranged for a helicopter to meet her from her Olympic Airways flight. This transported her the length of the island flying above snow-capped mountains and delivered her to a privately owned landing-strip in the Messara Plain where a local limousine firm had installed a chap who was waiting to drive her to her temporary residence. Limousine, she noted, was an overblown description of the motor waiting to ferry her up the mountainside. No matter, the driver was willing, smiling warmly, and knew without a moment's hesitation the address to which he was to deliver her.

The house, no longer a working farm, was uncontestably secluded. Nevertheless, as promised in the bumph, its setting was simply breathtaking. Penny stepped from the limo and was instantly embraced by an unmistakable stillness, an enticing quiescence, which exists nowhere to quite the same degree as it does in the mountains. In the desert one hears sand shifting, burning beneath the feet. Not so here. "Good," she whispered. "No one to disturb . . . " Huge unrecognisable birds swooped and soared in the ether above her. Nestbuilding. Silhouettes against an ineluctable sky which seemed almost within arm's reach. The light shifted, softening to a neutral ice blue. Dusk was beginning to fall.

"Your bags, Miss."

"Pardon? Oh yes, thank you."

The driver dumped her luggage outside the doorway and set off, explaining rather sheepishly that he preferred to reach the main road before nightfall.

The single-storey house had been erected at an almost unrealistic altitude, towards the crown of a cone-shaped hill. This was both a part of its charm and the cause of a disconcerting eeriness. Penny set to exploring. Even in the frosty evening light its view stretched out across hillock after hillock of terraced olive groves and to the north, north-west, just visible as a speck on the horizon, lay the ancient city of Phaistos which Penny remembered having visited by bicycle in her youth. To the west, best viewed from an expansive sun terrace (a more recent addition to one of the side walls of the original carcass of the house) was the shimmering hyacinth-blue of the southern Mediterranean, or more accurately the Gulf of Messara. A sweep of joy flushed through her at even this distant, evening sighting of it. Her memory of it was as remote in time as it now appeared in space. The house and its small garden were deserted, the main door unlocked. This didn't strike her as curious. There seemed little use for a key here. No one would be dropping by to steal or disturb. She and her taciturn driver had passed not a single other vehicle since turning inland off the main coastal road. The sole sign of human life had been three gnarled farmers riding side-saddle, single file, on their aged donkeys, returning home no doubt after a day's weary work in the fields.

The house with its thick walls had obviously been closed up since the previous autumn. The air inside smelt musty, of peeling plaster, vaguely damp. Several charred logs lay forgotten on the stone hearth. They gave off the scent of smoke long trapped in an enclosed space, a sweetish heavy scent. A single armchair faced the grate. Dust-sheets lay piled in a corner, bundled out of sight, partially hidden beneath the stairs behind the door which led to the ancient kitchen. The landlords could not have been expecting to rent it again before the spring. A film crew in March was a coup, a bonus to their annual income. But although magnificently situated, the interior lacked any texture of warmth, any expression of welcome or comfort. It had been, as so often with holiday rentals, furnished with nothing more than an assortment of idly chosen functional essentials. She sighed, a mite disappointed, deposited her suitcases in the living-room and set about a brief tour of the few other rooms in the place. Before it grew too dark she would be obliged to collect wood to build a fire. Both the house and the water were heated by it. She peered about in search of a torch but found none and cursed her own inefficiency. In her youth she would have thought to pack one.

Practical needs ruled out the early warning signs of sinking depression. She had three days before she was due to resume work. It gave her ample time to light log-fires, air the rooms, find somewhere to shop, telephone Peter and create for herself a temporary abode to return to and to work happily within.

On that first evening, alone, tired, dressed in working slacks and a heavy woollen sweater, she crossed to the window and peered out across the evening mist. It hung like pale-blue smoke around the hilltops. Her preoccupation with the reorganisation of the house had kept her busy and forced her to bury for the present an unanticipated surge of emotion. It came as a surprise and was curiously disturbing.

26

In all her memories of this island lived a young man, a handsome painter who strode now into her thoughts, stepping from cobwebbed corners of her mind, drawing back a disused curtain and standing centre stage. Like a figure who has been born again he beckoned to her, drew her towards him, seducing her as he had always done. She smiled at the memory of him, recalling him, at first with affection and then pain, a pain so poignant and searing that swiftly, diligently she dismissed him. In her newly created seclusion she cursed him, accusing him of being an intruder.

But he was of essence to the story that had brought her here. The film script she had written was about him. Harry. He had been her first love. Once or twice that first evening during a break from learning lines she found herself alongside him, smelling the sweetness of him, recalling the touch of his flesh. She was there once more with him, retreading paths of their past. The island, the view from the window, the trees, the scent in the winds, these things conjured him up, brought him to life with an ardour that the writing of the story had never led her in danger of doing.

She had felt so removed from him, so safe. True, until now she had never returned to the island but she had long since lost contact with him, Harry and his circle of friends. By the process of rechristening him, transforming him into a character on a page, no longer flesh and blood, she had believed that she had exorcised him. But as though he were returning to defend his corner in her heart, to reap his revenge on such a cruel act, she found herself wondering about him, where he might be, where they, the other characters in her story, were living now.

She had felt secure in the belief that it had all been so long ago.

Ches, the American musician was dead. So, of course, was Nikos the Athenian painter. But what of tantalising Helen and her son Ziggy, Harry's son too, and most especially what of Harry? It distressed her now to remember him – she had not been expecting that – the

27

times they had shared together and how very much she had loved him.

She was in Crete to film the story of these people. Harry, Ches, Nikos and Helen. Ghosts from her past disguised by other names, names that she had created for them. They — their faces, their personalities, their ages — had been arrested in time, fused with the spirit of make-believe.

The living people, who as far as she knew continued to live, were as dead to her now as the others who had died long ago. Dead or alive, they had become no more than phantoms floating occasionally through her memory, or so she had believed. The characters and their actions lived, not the original people. Characters could not harm her and so they had taken root, found a place in her present. It was she who had created them, given them thoughts, words and gestures. She who had cleaned them up, polished them and made them spotless, free from guilt and shame.

The reality, it no longer existed . . .

It was an undeniable fact that sections of her story had not ventured very far from the truth. The hurt and the joy were as it had been, so too the fear, the jealousy and the clinging guilt . . . that terrible night when Nikos was killed . . . She had forced herself to forget it but . . .

"Hello!"

A knock on the farmhouse door broke into her thoughts, intruding upon her and the crackling log-fire, her sole companion.

"Who's there?" It was pitch black outside. She had heard no footstep, no motor drawing to a halt.

Startled, she turned from the desk at which she had been working, in reality a tatty kitchen table dragged into the sitting-room and drawn up in front of the flames for warmth.

"I've disturbed you. I'm sorry."

"No, but you frightened me."

"Mind if I come in?"

"Don't be foolish, come in."

28

Gaza, the unexpected intruder, huddled like a tramp in a raincoat, stepped two paces into the room and smiled with contentment at the welcoming sight of blazing logs. "I see you've settled. It's cold up here." He was holding his script against his overcoat pressed close to his breast like a small shivering child with a hot-water bottle.

"What the hell are you doing up here? Trying to get away from me?"

She ignored his sarcasm.

"It's taken me the whole damned evening to find you."

"Then you'd better sit down."

He didn't heed her, didn't move. She shifted, disconcerted by his uninvited arrival.

"Why didn't you call me when you got in? I asked you to."

"I thought you were arriving tomorrow," she lied. "I considered going out again, trying to find somewhere . . . I have no phone here . . . but then I thought better to leave you, let you rest after the long journey."

"I need my strength, huh?"

"How did you find me?"

"The door was unlocked."

It wasn't what she had meant. The sparring had begun, creeping back one step at a time, noticed by both. She smiled at him uncertainly, his face shadowed by the firelight.

"Your driver drew me a map," he conceded. She was looking frail and worn in a chunky woollen sweater and bare feet. "You'll catch pneumonia on these stone floors. Where are your shoes?"

She glanced at a clock ticking on the floor at the hearth-side, where she had placed it earlier. It was a quarter to ten. Late in these parts for visitors. "What are you doing here, Jimmy?"

"I wanted to talk to you."

"What about?" She caught him glance beyond her seated, partially turned torso, to the table where she had

29

been working. He was peering at her script. Even with his glasses his eyesight could not have been sufficient to focus on the words, not from such a distance, but it made her defensive as though he were prying, attempting to read her mind. His unannounced, unexpected intrusion made her suspicious. Gaza was someone not to be trusted. Unconsciously she found herself turning the pages, closing the script, securing from him her memories, the secrets that had been resurrecting themselves within her.

"Lines not going well?" he asked, still standing, hovering above her seated figure, lingering like a flame not quite still.

"Yes, they're fine."

"You look concerned?" He crossed to the fireside, and then settled himself in the armchair, clearly intending to stay. "Want me to go through them with you?"

"You haven't come all the way up here to take me through my lines," she responded scathingly. "What do you want?"

Was it that he craved her company? Just like the old days when he had been hungry to have her near him, would not settle without her. After so many years his need, if that was what it was, perplexed her.

"I want to talk to you. I told you in London there are one or two things I want to discuss."

She removed her glasses – a recent necessary addition which Peter swore was due to her working, writing into the early hours with insufficient light – and laid them onto her makeshift desk. An inexplicable wave of sadness had descended upon her. Time forgotten, time past. Folk gone for ever, irretrievably so. Gaza had broken in on that. She realised that her irritation, studiously concealed, was caused by his intrusion, his barging in on her and her recollections of those times, of those old friends, her youth.

"You push yourself too hard."

"What is it you want to discuss?" she sighed, it flowed out of her as though she were exhausted. He was right, she was probably just overtired.

"The script."

"What about it?"

"This painter, you knew him?"

"What difference does it make?"

"What was his name?"

"Why . . . ?"

"I want you to think of him by his real name. What was it?"

"His name was Harry. Listen Jimmy, it's a script . . . "

"Yeah and I want to change it."

The incredulity on her face was sufficient. "But we've begun shooting."

"I don't believe a word of it," he pronounced.

"Change what? What are you talking about?"

"Hell of a past you seem to have had, mmm? Not like this girl in the script. She's squeaky clean, this girl, your young actress. It's a pain in the arse. Heroes, heroines if you prefer, they don't stick if they are without flaws, if they are simply appealing. I want to see the rot, the worm in the apple and her struggle to come to terms with it. Think about it," he said, rising from the armchair, car keys in hand. "And then tomorrow, you tell me what to change."

After he had left Penny placed a rusty old fireguard she had rooted from beneath logs in the yard earlier in front of the fire and crept with her alarm clock across the stone floors to the draughty lavatory at the back of the house. A few minutes later she was settling gratefully into her chilly sheeted, iron-framed bed. Even with woolly socks her toes were freezing. She would have to buy a hot-water bottle she was thinking as she lay tossing, sleepless, listening to the owls and the wind whistling through the olive trees. To the long buried spirits returning.

31

3

Penny's route to the coast, once the shaly descent from the farmhouse had been patiently navigated, was along a recently constructed bitumen road. It commenced well, seemed smooth-going even, until the car was forced to stop, brought to a standstill by a herd of unshepherded goats harnessed on great lengths of half-chewed rope. Her driver pressed the palm of his hand onto his horn and left it there for several seconds. The goats ignored him. He settled contentedly back and with his free hand lit up a cigarette as though preparing himself for a lengthy stay. Penny paid little heed. Her thoughts were focused on Gaza's visit of the previous night and his comment about her script. The goats lay in the road enjoying their siesta in the wintry sunlight. Once the first few drags of the cigarette had been enjoyed the driver craned his neck and hollered something derisory out of the window, a phrase that Penny vaguely recognised and knew to be indecent but one that she could no longer translate.

Shouting from the car window seemed to have been the only means of attracting their attention. Even then a great deal of patience was required. A little more idling then creeping inch by inch forward until the bearded creatures turned their imperious heads and stared with disgust, as though the impact of the driver's foul words had only now registered, before eventually deigning to budge. It was a slow process, but as Penny was not in any particular hurry this morning, one she found mildly humorous. The car sped onwards leaving the watery-eyed goats behind. They had distracted her, had reminded her how much in former times she had loved the unworldliness of this island.

Less gratifying was the new growth of architecture.

Blisters on the landscape, she pronounced them. Unoccupied, incomplete breeze block villas had been constructed everywhere, thrown together any old how. The closer they drew to the coast the more numerous these concrete shells became. Once spring-flowering fields were now chock-a-block with the countless warlike bunkers. Skeletons never to be brought to life.

And billboardings – an aggressive bombardment of billboardings either handwritten or printed – advertising hotels, cheap pensions and rooms to rent; zimmer, zimmer, chambres, rooms. It was a shock to Penny to witness the pulverizing hand of progress at work. And then from the rear of her locally hired car she spotted the sign she knew she had been waiting for.

It read: 'Matala 1k'. One more kilometre and she would be entering the village. Returning.

Penny could not help but be reminded of her first sniff of this coastline. An unfavourable comparison for the new scenery, the new mode of living unfolding before her. Her heart was beating so fast that it made her aware of it, strong firm beats. She glanced at her script almost not daring to look any more out of the window.

The actress flicked through the first few scenes and closed her eyes, transporting herself back to that callow year in her history, a time she had so efficiently erased.

Arrival by bus. 1972.

Bounding the last few steps at breakneck speed Penny plumped her rucksack onto the warm sand and her panting self at its side. She cast a sweated glance about her into the flushed evening sunlight, squinting the length of the virgin beach in search of a kiosk or small bar, some place where she might grab a cold drink, arrest her thirst, purchase a local beer, anything, but there was nothing. Harry had forewarned her. Here, at this inaccessible haven named for some unfathomable reason Red Beach – she prayed it might be for the glorious sight of blood-red sunsets splashed across the horizon – there were neither washing nor sleeping facilities, not even a source of fresh water. Simply the Mediterranean laid out in front of her glinting like newly minted money.

In the distance, towards a cluster of rocks, a handful of strangers were dotted here and there, lighting fires on the sand, busying themselves with preparations for their freshly caught suppers. Dusk was approaching. The climb had been more arduous than she had anticipated. She would wander over later and introduce herself but first she'd rest awhile, catch her breath and regard the ocean. Maybe take a swim. It had been an enervating day and a long hike. She flopped back against the sand, unpeeled her T-shirt from her perspiring flesh and rolled over onto her stomach looking towards the small mountain which she had just descended. Beyond it lay the village of Matala. She smiled and sighed. These last four days, she mused, had felt the happiest in her young life.

Every moment of them until this morning had been magical. But this place too, this deserted bay girdled by an amphitheatre of aromatic mountains would be an adventure. She would make it so. She would soon forget Harry. This bay was as idyllic as she had been promised.

She had set off from northern Crete the previous Tuesday morning. This place, Red Beach, had been recommended to her at the local youth hostel where she had been staying in Iráklion.

"Where ya headed?" a Canadian backpacker had enquired.

She had had no plans.

"I don't exactly know. Somewhere quiet. I just want to swim and read. No more sightseeing, not this trip, I'm worn out."

"You travellin' 'lone?" Trusting that he was not about to suggest that they hitch up together she had nodded that yes she was alone, and yes she was from England and if he was asking how long she had been on the road the answer was almost three months. Funny, she thought, how at every single youth hostel throughout Europe the conversation and the questions had been identical.

He whistled soundlessly and then nodded his head, grimacing like a goldfish. "Three months huh . . . Pretty lucky. You don't work?"

"I'm an actress," she had confided, not without a certain pride.

"Gee whizz, I never met a real live actress before," had been his response. He had looked so impressed that she had felt obliged to elucidate.

"Actually, I only finished drama school last summer. A couple of days later I did a screen test for a film and got the part. It was great. I couldn't believe it. It was only a few lines but it was my first film! I would have accepted anything. Then the leading actor got sick and the film fell behind schedule and they kept extending my contract. I earned quite a bit, saved it too . . . but I haven't worked since. I was feeling depressed about it so I decided to do a bit of travelling, visit Europe. I bought a student rail pass and later when I began to run short of cash I started hitching." Since childhood she had dreamed of visiting Europe.

Suddenly she was telling him — exuberantly chattering — tales of her solitary travels. "I've been to quite a few cities, seen some magnificent theatres, Paris, Berlin, Rome, Athens, Epidavros. Epidavros was great. I hid in the bushes until they closed the gates and then I crept back and slept on the stage. Under the stars on the stage, in my sleeping-bag. In the morning as the sun came up I practised my voice exercises and recited some of my poetry aloud. Sixteen thousand people it seats. You can hear a whisper anywhere."

The Canadian nodded. She thought he looked bored. Theatre acoustics was probably not a subject that interested him. And then he grinned and picked at his teeth with a match. "You know somethin', you're kinda cute an' mighty good-looking . . . If I hadn't been

35

heading off in another direction I'd 'ave liked to hang around with you for a couple of weeks an' have some fun."

Penny stared at him in amazement and then continued chattering. "Anyway, I've been on the road too long. I just want to find a beach, crash for a couple of weeks before flying home. I have a job in the theatre waiting for me when I get back. I have to be in Leeds by late September."

"Well, if you're looking for somewhere to hang out, try Red Beach down on the south side o' the island. It's pretty special. Not too many tourists know about it, only the cool guys. I've just come from down there."

"Really?" she said, smiling mischievously into her *horiátiki*, her Greek salad.

And so it had been. With nowhere more pressing to visit – and a local map that seemed to bear out the American hitcher's description – she had followed his advice and found the local bus which had trundled her the entire length of Crete, north to south. The journey had taken the best part of the day, stopping for a lunch only of yoghurt and honey and oranges, and bunches of freshly picked grapes from local vineyards. The entire island, much lusher than she had been expecting, was scented with the perfumes of citrus fruit and sweet, broken-skinned grapes oozing into the hot, late-August harvesting sunshine.

The bus had deposited her in the heart of a fishing village basking idly alongside the turquoise Gulf of Messara. It smelt of salt and heat, dead fish and Ambre Solaire; the birth of a resort.

This undiscovered village, a mere punctuation mark on her map, consisted of a bus station, a white church and one shop which Penny decided was as good a place as anywhere to begin. Peering into the cool cluttered darkness she glimpsed an aged sallow-faced woman, seated, buried beneath skeins of cotton and lace, imperfectly printed postcards, cheesecloth skirts, shirts and Ambre Solaire suntan oil, the perfume of which

36

pervaded the entire square.

"I'm looking for a hotel."

The hoary woman shook her head, proffered post-cards and lifted one finger which Penny understood as the price. One drachma. She refused. The cards were pressed towards her once more. "Not cards, hotel?" she insisted. The woman shook her head, placed the cards back onto the rickety mobile display beside her and returned to her lacework.

Outside in the heavy beating heat she surveyed the coastline. There were a few simply constructed white-washed homes dotted here and there, several more in various stages of construction, and three open-air tav-ernas, all situated alongside one another, smack on the clear sweep of beach. Clusters of empty wine bottles and vine-leaves dangled from their humble cane structures like gold trinkets worn by colourfully dressed gypsies. Each of the tavernas was closed and each displayed its own hand-designed sign, written in Greek and English, assuring potential customers of its intention to open again at suppertime.

Penny had circled the square and found herself back now beside the bright blue and yellow bus where she lingered, waiting patiently for her luggage. Judging by the sun – her watch had been ripped off in Athens – it was about four in the afternoon. She would have to find somewhere to spend the night unless Red Beach was within easy walking distance. Certainly the bus went no further. From somewhere behind her music started up, scratching strains of bouzouki. It came blaring like bag-pipes from the upstairs window of a small whitewashed house. On the steps of the cube-shaped house a quartet of women clothed in baggy black dresses and shawls sat huddled together. They looked like megalithic cock-roaches. Tight-lipped in the pulsing heat they fanned themselves, glaring impassively. Penny smiled. They glared and fanned. One of them nodded a cursory greeting. Penny grinned and headed towards them.

"Do you rent rooms?" No response. "Zimmer?"

From every conceivable spot geraniums blossomed: window-boxes, drains, square tins slapped with cobalt-blue paint, terracotta pots, doorsteps, lashings of colour, profusions of cascading, tumbling nail varnish-rich reds and pinks set in summer green. Stark contrast to the white houses or the stern black figures.

"Hotel?" she continued weakly.

An emaciated mongrel slouched into sight. One of the black figures shooed him away, thwacking at him with her fan. Penny returned to the bus. For a few steps the mutt trotted along behind her but realising the hopelessness of such effort slumped like a carcass to the baking ground.

Penny collected her rucksack from the driver who had by this time dragged it from the boot. "Which way is Red Beach?" she asked. He, not having understood her, simply nodded and smiled, exposing beneath a walrus moustache his lack of teeth. His skin was heavily ridged and resembled the lines of coloured sand on sale in bottles. She tried once more, "Red Beach?" He nodded once more, picked with a match at his few remaining teeth and tramped away towards one of the deserted tavernas. Penny watched his dark bent back recede and then swung around in search of inspiration. Where should she begin her scout about?

Mountains with great sandstone limbs embraced her, towering in every direction save for the sea. There was a light breeze blowing in from Africa which cooled her prickled features, nevertheless her skin itched. Every inch of her agitated from the dust and the bus fumes. She was thinking that her chances of renting a room here were looking pretty slim and stood dreaming of cool water with which to shower. Without a stroke of unexpected luck, it was going to be a night in the sleeping-bag.

And then from somewhere along the beach, a distance away, she heard the throb of pop music, recognisable pop music. It was John Lennon, he was singing 'Imagine', recently recorded yet already a familiar tune.

It must be coming from a private radio or perhaps a record player housed somewhere beyond her line of vision, she thought. Or might it perchance be a hotel? Hauling the rucksack from the track beside her onto her already dusty T-shirted back she set off purposefully in the direction of the music, humming the song as she stepped.

It was 1972. Penny was twenty years old. This was her first solo trip to the continent. Until now foreign travel had been two family package holidays to Rimini and La Costa del something or other crowded. More recently, during her years as a drama student, there had been no opportunity for travel. She had been obliged to work as a waitress to bolster a very meagre grant. Evenings and holidays had been spent serving up plates of veal and spaghetti in an assortment of north London restaurants and bistros.

But now she was independent, a young adventurer circumnavigating the big wide world. Feeling liberated and contented she turned beachside into a narrow alley, humming happily as the music grew closer, exhaling softly. It was already a relief to be out of the heat, shadowed by the walls of two stone whitewashed houses, one either side of her. Both fronted directly onto the beach and both, she soon discovered, had been rented to tourists for the entire summer, or at least for several weeks of it.

Two long-haired guys bleached and tanned and wearing nothing but sawn-off jeans, were sitting cross-legged on the sand strumming their guitars. A joint was being smoked and passed casually between them.

The second, accepting the elegantly hand-rolled smoke, turned to remark her arrival.

"Hello there." He was, she soon learnt, Ches the American . . .

*   *   *

Penny's driver thumped his horn with an angry impatient fist. He was also swearing, gone entirely was the smiling taciturn fellow of yesterday, but she was too stunned by the village to notice. Could this really be Matala, the same small fishing village that she had known so dearly? Even now, out of season, the place was a swarming mass of trinket shops, each identical to the next. Cramped arcades spilling with money changers and estate agents caused Penny to recall and comprehend Christ's fury in the temple. Cars were parked everywhere, skewed every which way. There seemed to be no rules of the road here. BMW motorbikes sporting every chrome accoutrement including German number plates terrorised the laneways, roaring to and fro like crazed bloated beasts.

"Is this it?" she murmured.

Her Greek driver, quiet once more, nodded proudly at the progress all around him. "I park here," he explained, "there's nowhere else."

"And the production office?" she asked, deflated. He pointed out to her the direction to walk, while promising to wait in the car.

Ahead stood rows of tourist buses offering visits to the renowned island ruins. Part of a two-day tour which included this village, billed as 'Matala. Home of the hippies. Visit their cave dwellings.' It was printed on the flanks of the buses. 'A part of the tour not to be missed', it read.

A part of the tour not to be missed, she reflected. So, our lives, our young community have become a late-twentieth century curiosity . . .

A village by the sea. 1972.

"I'm Ches."

"Hi," she had responded shyly. The other guy whose face she could not see paid her no attention. He continued to strum as though in serenade to the calm water. Someone within the house switched off the John

40

Lennon, creating a hot aromatic silence, diminishing heat and stillness, save for the gentle lapping of the water and the lugubrious chords from the guitar. The breeze was perfumed with herbs and hashish.

"You want some o' this?" the American proffered.

Penny dropped herself onto her rucksack and considered in her new grown-up world what she was going to do. She accepted the joint and took a drag. "I'm looking for a hotel, or a room. Somewhere to shower."

"Ain't no hotels here. Only place to stay is rent a house. But there ain't no rentals 'til summer's over. Some folks sleep in the caves but they're pretty disgustin'. Full o' crap and junk."

$$*\qquad *\qquad *$$

The film production office was up a dark and hazardously narrow flight of stone stairs above a recently fabricated boutique which was offering on sale local handcrafted leather goods. Handbags, wallets, thonged sandals, Penny had once owned a pair herself. Whiffs of cured goatskin wafted in through the upstairs windows, circulated the office and reminded her of sweet cow dung and childhood visits to dairy farms.

Penny introduced herself to the two girls who had been employed for the duration of the film and were responsible for telephone messages, typing of schedules and the general manning of the cramped and apparently disorganised space. As Penny drifted in wanting to make one or two fairly straightforward enquiries an air of tension caught hold of her.

"Anything wrong?" she asked casually. There appeared to be a minor crisis in progress which was being coped with by the plumper of the two, a dark-haired pubescent girl who was doing a great deal of shouting into the mouthpiece of an antiquated black telephone. Penny understood nothing of what was being said, realising that any Greek she had once learned had long since slipped away.

41

"Is there a problem?" she enquired once more, this time of the younger, the prettier of the two girls currently staring helplessly at her computer screen.

Without regarding her the girl simply shrugged. "A hotel is not finished. The roof has not been put on. People are angry," she explained placidly.

Penny nodded, overwhelmingly relieved that in spite of its inaccessibility she had after all plumped for the farmhouse.

"Have you seen Mr Gaza?" she asked, hoping for everyone's sake that it was not his hotel that lacked a roof.

"He hasn't arrived yet. Tomorrow."

"Tomorrow?" she quizzed incredulously. "But he flew in yesterday. I saw him last night."

"Tomorrow," confirmed the typist, turning to regard her companion who was quite obviously swearing foully at her telephone link.

There seemed little point in debate. She said her farewells, picked up a schedule and disappeared down alongside the goats' leather.

The wardrobe offices were mere steps away, along a winding lane yards from the outskirts of the original village. They were housed in what once must have been one of the fishermen's caves, overlooking the length of the beach.

"I remember this view," she said to no one in particular. "Yes, I remember it clearly." A seamstress smiled kindly, paying no real attention. "Of course it was midsummer then. The sun was constant. Weather changes perspectives."

After a discussion with the rather fraught wardrobe mistress – she being one of the crew members unfortunate enough to have been booked into the roofless hotel – Penny started out on a stroll along the beach, a fleeting pilgrimage, a reminder to herself of the magic and beauty that had once been Matala. The coastline was unchanged but the wind was blowing in short temperamental gusts. It changed the atmosphere, the personality of the place. Without the sunlight a dark-navy louring sky gave the rocky bay a dangerous air. She conjured up pirate ships anchored beyond the outlying promontory and supposed that decades, if not centuries before, these very same caves had no doubt housed smugglers and the booty from their skeck.

She had vaguely considered walking to the caves at the far end of the bay past the house that she and Harry had once shared but the wind was too strong. Squallish weather. It knocked her off course, making her steps tedious and difficult until finally she gave in to it, and subsided onto a rock jutting conspicuously from the sand.

The blustery air whipped at her clothing, throwing her scarf into her face, lifting the hem of her raincoat, drying her gloveless hands. It felt exhilarating. Quite suddenly, inexplicably, she was filled with an over-whelming upsurge of joy at having reconnected with the place.

She turned her watery windblown gaze about her, contemplatively surveying the once familiar coastline. It was simply not as she remembered it. This hugely pro-truding boulder for instance that she was now perched against — she had no recollection of it, and yet it must have always been there. It was not nature that had altered, the village certainly, but not its environment, merely the tricks of her memory reinventing the frame-work in which she had set her past. She wondered too what illusory deceptions her imagination had played with those friends, those events from her past.

A single sliver of sunlight which had been the sole source of brightness in the louring sky disappeared be-hind a bank of fast-moving storm clouds, causing the bay to darken noticeably. It was probably going to thun-der, or perhaps it was late. Penny had lost track of the day and glanced guiltily at her watch. A quarter past one. She had supposed it to be considerably later. She had time, even for lunch, realising that she was raven-ously hungry.

It was too cold to eat outside. The tavernas as she had remembered them were transformed now into pseudo-sophisticated fish restaurants, advertising freshly caught lobster and the best of the locally produced wines. She chose The Fish Bar, the restaurant that stood where once she had passed her summer evenings.

A check-clothed table in a deserted corner was where she chose to sit, by the window, to be inconspicuous, to overlook the water and the deserted beach. Her raincoat, should she want to escape swiftly, she placed on the back of her chair. The place was almost empty with an out of season desultory feel to it. Canned American folk music from the late sixties was playing through small speakers wired from the ceiling, a homage to the good old days, the swinging era when this village was alive and kicking, not merely a hollow tourist trap for coach parties.

She wondered where the patron might be. Who he might be. Was the music an indication that Spiros still ran the place? Or was she simply romanticising? There was no sight of any waiters, no staff at all. The only indication that the place was open were two couples seated at separate tables, each huddled and whispering, drinking beer, looking windswept. She might have been in Scarborough! The menu was written with chalk on blackboards nailed to the walls. Penny decided upon fish of the day and chips, no wine, and waited for someone to appear. A man's voice shouted to another behind the closed door of the kitchen. No doubt they would appear soon. Outside, the sea had become very choppy indeed and the sky miserably overcast. She looked about her to see if the name of the patron was written anywhere. Was it Spiros? Might he still own the place? It had been Spiros who had fed them that evening, her first supper with Ches and Harry . . .

A village by the sea. 1972.

The American wore a band around his forehead, hand-

44

woven, and threaded shells around his neck, both of which she noticed as she handed the joint back to him. Beneath the knuckles, the flesh on his right hand had been tattooed with the letters LOVE. Each finger a separate letter. On his left hand the word FEAR. His skin was smooth, dark, hairless as a baby's save for a minute scribbly patch between his nipples.

"You can shower here, if you like. You gotta sleeping-bag?"

She nodded.

"Bed down on the floor here then. It's illegal to sleep on the beach, 'cept over at Red Beach. Nobody bothers you there. Police can't be bothered to make the climb 'cept on days off to ogle the naked women. If you wanna hike it you can sleep over there. It's pretty beautiful but there ain't no water."

She swung round on her haunches to the left of her, scanning the mountain he was pointing towards, his handcrafted silver bracelet shaped like a coiled snake glinting in the sunlight. She reckoned she couldn't be across the summit before sundown. She was travelling with a torch but because she didn't know the path, setting off at this hour could be dangerous.

"It's too far. I'll take a shower here, if that's alright with you guys."

"Sure thing."

Penny rose and waited for him to direct her inside.

He made no attempt to move, simply eyed her with dilated, stoned pupils, surveying the length and the breadth of her. Her long-boned, loose-limbed body. She was too voluptuous for a dancer, yet so desirable. "Ask Sandy," he mouthed, "she's resting inside. She'll show ya about."

"Thanks, Ches."

Inside the house it was cool, dark. Strumming from the guitar filtered into the darkness. It took Penny's eyes a moment or two to adjust to the crepuscular gloom after the stark brilliance of the sunlight outside. The room – there seemed to be only the one on the ground

45

floor — reeked of joss-sticks, of candle grease and patchouli oil. The solitary window had been temporarily blacked out with a length of cloth, a printed skirt or something. A narrow dusty shaft of sunlight penetrated it. In this semi-darkness Penny could just make out a girl's figure, a slight form in a long flowing dress, outstretched, practically buried beneath a bank of cushions.

"Sandy?"

"Uhuh."

"I'm looking for the shower."

"Behind the curtain," a stoned or sleepy voice replied. Another American.

"Thanks."

Upstairs alone in someone's bedroom Penny stood lightly tanned and naked in front of a full-length mirror, cracked, angled against a wall. She was wearing a towel draped around her head like a turban and was pulling at her face searching for unsightly blemishes, but there were none. She always expected to find something. It was part of her constant insecurity, her inability to accept herself. She turned from the glass and strolled to the bed. Several strands of her long hair dripped loosely onto her shoulders as she began rummaging through her crumpled clothes still crammed inside her rucksack. She was in search of her hairbrush and fresh underwear. The door opened. Penny pewed with surprise, turning without thinking to regard the intruder at the door. She stood frozen in front of him, a lean young man several years older than herself. His sexuality startled her, made her conscious of her own nakedness.

"Hey, excuse me. Nobody told me I had a guest in my bedroom." And just as unexpectedly as the door had opened it now closed and the stranger, with a well-educated English accent she noted, disappeared. She slumped back onto the bed. She had supposed, if she had considered anything at all, that this was communal space, a kind of sleeping area for these hippies, just as the downstairs' room must be their living quarters. Now

46

for the first time she actually took in her surroundings.

Lying untidily in one corner of the room was a small pile of paperbacks. Curious to know something about him, she crawled from the bed and stretched to search through them. *The Catcher in the Rye, Steppenwolf*, a couple of other Hermann Hesse novels that she hadn't come across before, a biography of Picasso, a book on Zen by Alan Watts and *The Doors of Perception and Heaven and Hell*, by Aldous Huxley.

Beside the single bed on which she had been sitting – her wet hair streaming down her back dripping like a damp dog's – was a handmade table, constructed from young pine. Perhaps by the Englishman? On its surface were scattered several packets of green Rizla papers, a Greek cigarette packet with strips torn from it used for rolling joints, a dog-eared map of the island, one black comb, and a delicately engraved silver pill-box which Penny managed to lever open with her fingernails. Inside it were two very small corners of what appeared to be magnolia-shaded blotting paper. She had no idea what they were meant to be. There was also a large book, a hardback, some sort of manual. It lay open on the table, as though constantly in use. Loose tobacco shreds had been trapped between the inner spine and the tired open pages. Without losing his page Penny flipped swiftly through several of the earlier chapters. It had been well thumbed, this *Tibetan Book of the Dead*. She had never heard of it and found it bizarre reading matter.

Across the room, hanging from a metal coatrack nailed into the whitewashed wall, was his dressing-gown. Her fingers reached out and brushed it lightly – silk. She drew its luxury across her young face and smelt his male perfume: not displeasing. One multi-coloured towel hung next to it, several other plainer, soiled ones lay beneath, discarded on the floor with a couple of cheesecloth shirts obviously purchased in the village shop. Alongside this bundle of laundry was an extremely well-travelled leather weekend case. Its surface, now beaten and scuffed, had been plastered with travel stickers. Amongst them the Taj Palace Bombay, another, the Lake Palace at Udaipur in Rajasthan. Penny rolled back onto the mattress and balanced herself on her stomach, poised like an inquisitive snake to read his name-tag while idly massaging her hair. The damp towel was still coiled like a turban around her skull.

Written with a delicate script in black ink, she read: P. Knowle, Canterbury, Kent, England. Yes, she had accurately guessed at his accent.

Cautiously she stretched out a hand to open up his suitcase, but at that very moment there was a soft tapping at the door. One tap followed, moments later, by another. For an instant Penny remained immobile, startled like a rabbit caught in the glare of headlights, and then partially regaining her equilibrium she scrambled back towards the head of the bed, fumbling stupidly, guilty at having been caught snooping, grabbing clumsily at white cotton briefs and a baggy cotton shirt which she had only minutes earlier pulled from her rucksack. Hastily she pulled on the briefs, caught one foot in the wrong leg-hole before correcting it, cursed, wrapped the shirt around her and finally settled back against the pillow waiting for whoever it might be to enter.

The occupant of the room knocked again. "How about letting me in?" It was the same eloquent voice, known to her now as P. Knowle.

"Sure, come on in." Her heart was pounding from the panic but she was an actress she assured herself, she was charming and she could be cool.

"Dressed?" The door opened a crack and there, revealed, was P. Knowle, leaning against the woodwork. He grinned before entering, "Listen, I'm sorry about the intrusion. I would've left you alone up here but I just need to dump all this. My blasted work!" And with one motion he knelt to his suitcase, eyes averted, arms laden with sketches, brushes and pencils. "Can't leave them downstairs. Not with that tribe. They'll use the watercolours for filters!" Penny's stomach began to parachute. "I'm Harry," he said, turning to smile at her. "And you are? God you are beautiful. Ches said you were," he chuckled.

She returned his easy smile feeling relaxed now, the generosity in his face washing away her stupid guilt. "Thanks for letting me use your room."

He gestured that it was nothing and rose, leaving the case to close by itself. Gauchely, as he drew closer, she said, "I really needed that shower."

"Ches told me that you are considering spending a couple of days with us. That sounds like a fine idea." He reached the bedside table, hesitated, then pulled out a cigarette from the packet that Penny had registered earlier and he placed it lethargically between his lips. "Smoke?"

Penny shook her head, "I don't, thanks."

"Not even dope?"

"Well . . . yes . . . sometimes." It was more a lie than the truth. The number of times she had smoked hashish she could have counted on one hand. "I'd like to stay tonight, if that's alright. I was planning to go over to Red Beach but it grew late. I've been travelling all day . . . " She watched as he settled, perching himself on the corner of the mattress, whilst slipping matches from his shirt pocket. He dragged heavily on the cigarette. They sat silently, alongside one another, touching without touching, within fingers' reach of one another.

Penny felt her pulse beating rapidly beneath her stomach and began to fondle the towel on her head. She found him beautiful, his sculpted features as potent as some Florentine bronze, leaner, taller, more angular, less clean-shaven. His hair, almost shoulder length, hung loosely across one side of his face like a girl's. It was a nutmeg brown, blonded by the sun. She glimpsed his muscular flesh toasted from the summer beneath his clothing and glanced at his long paint encrusted fingers. The marble-blue of the watercolour was

49

repeated in his eyes . . .

"Is this your house?" Penny asked, for want of something better to say, fearing that the silence between them might betray her lubricious heat. The enclosed white-washed walls might amplify her heartbeat, her breathing, her desire.

He nodded. "I rent it every summer. I like to paint here."

"Who are Ches and the others?"

He paused, reflecting, took a substantial drag from his cigarette and then stubbed it out before answering.

"I met him in the village last summer. He needed somewhere to stay." As he spoke he leaned towards her. "You are very, very sexy," he whispered. He peeled away her shirt and stroked her undressed flesh with the palms of his paint-stained hands, shoving to the floor the untidy clutter of her clothes that had separated them.

Night had fallen. Light from a full August moon clearly visible from the bedroom spilled across the flat glassy sea. Penny crossed from the crumpled bed to the window and stood gazing towards the horizon. The Libyan Sea. Somewhere beyond, coloured by imagination, lay north Africa . . . Benghazi, Alexandria, Cairo, cities she had only dreamt of, Lawrence Durrell and André Gide country, but this was the furthest south that she had ever travelled.

From here on, she mused, everything was untrodden territory.

The room in which she stood creaked silently, the bed empty. Its perfume was sex and hashish. Harry had disappeared, she must have drifted off to sleep.

Laughter rose like smoke from the beach beneath her. Through the open window rock music was playing. It sounded as though there might be a party going on, a celebration. The tavernas that she had seen earlier in the day would be open now. Tourists and locals would be eating *horiátiki saláta*, octopus and red mullet beneath a ceiling of stars and empty wine bottles. She wondered why Harry had left without waking her. Suddenly she felt engulfed in pain, a tart unknown sadness, and a shyness about going in search of him and his companions. It was the first time — although not to be the last — in her young life that she had slept with a stranger and she felt an outsider, strangely out of step with the morality of her time. She was the novice in this southern Mediterranean community, this hip commune into which she had unsuspectingly wandered . . .

The shirt and bikini briefs that she had been wearing when Harry first touched her had been discarded somewhere amidst the crumpled bedclothes. She began searching for them. The towel that had covered her hair was strewn across the pillow, crumpled and damp. She caught sight of herself in the fractured glass, her disarrayed wavy hair, her young fresh skin, her dark searching eyes and she felt concerned, guilty and afraid. Tentatively she pressed her palms against her breasts, full wholesome breasts, rarely caressed, taut nipples, still warm from the stranger's touch, and suddenly she laughed at herself. She felt glowing, long-boned and vibrant.

She decided not to wear her shirt after all. Instead she chose a dress, violet crushed cotton, enhancing her tawny features. One that she had bought in Athens. It was cut sheer above her breasts with two tiny shoulder straps leaving her arms and shoulders bare. The night was balmy, she had no need of a wrap. The full skirt hung from below her bosom, waistless, to calf length. She slipped into it and when she was ready she checked herself once more in the glass. A scrubbed natural face, no make-up. She was feeling beautiful, vital. Nothing to be concerned about.

Her rucksack lay untidily on the floor beside the bed. Clothes, books, plays and maps had been scattered either side of it. Hastily she repacked it, lifted it to take it with her and then smiling foxily decided to leave it where it was.

The ground floor of the house, she had guessed accurately, was deserted, a bomb-shelter that had been occupied and then abandoned. She stepped out onto the loose sand and paused to enjoy the tarpaulin of stars above her. During her travels she had been sleeping in the open air and had learnt to appreciate the night sky, learning its various constellations. There were no clouds tonight, a steely marine starlight. Directly in front of her, shining as though solely for her, Hesperus, the evening star. No breeze now either. Only the brilliance of the moon shining onto the easy lapping water. Further along the beach to her right, in the opposite direction to the village, flickered the oil lamps of a distant taverna. She could hear no sounds emanating from there so chose to walk left towards the music which curiously sounded more muted downstairs in the open air.

Outside the second taverna she found Harry. Or rather Harry and Sandy and Ches. The second guy from the beach whose face she had not seen did not appear to be with them. It was Ches who spotted her and called out to her. Harry and Sandy were sitting with their backs to her. Harry casually resting his arm on Sandy's shoulder. A pang of jealousy ran through Penny like iced water, forcing her to slow up her pace, until Ches called out a second time and Harry turned to see her. He smiled and waved her towards them.

"Just in time to eat," he laughed as she approached.

He was wearing a white shirt, sharp against his tanned skin and in the flickering candlelight the effect on her was breathtaking. She was feeling flushed, confused, out of her depth. Cautiously, tactfully, uncertain of Sandy's role, she sat beside Ches, who shifted chairs, making room for her. It was then that she noticed that Ches was lame.

There were several empty bottles of retsina on the table. She glanced at their shadowed, candlelit faces. All three were quietly high. Sandy more extrovertly so. Harry poured some white wine into his empty glass and winked as he passed it across to Penny.

"I asked but you never told me your name. Is it a secret?" he grinned confidentially before summoning the waiter, "Spiros, *thélo mía boukála áspro krasí, parakaló!*"

"Penny Morrison. You speak Greek."

"Been coming here a long time. Got a whole history here," he laughed.

He seemed fluent and comfortable in the language. Penny resisted an urge to ask what that history might be.

Although it was late in the evening they had not begun supper. Fresh glasses, bottles and menus were delivered by the patron of the place. A handsome fellow in his late thirties whom Harry introduced as "My very good friend, Spiros, and inside, over there, Spiros's son Demetrius." Behind a bar serving drinks she spied a surly pubescent boy, perhaps thirteen, not much more. Spiros looked proudly towards his son and called out something unintelligible to Penny.

"Hey, Demetrius, you enjoyed your first woman, yes?" Harry and Spiros both laughed. It was playful, male and lewd. The boy blushed. Ches passed Penny a joint and someone switched on the rock 'n' roll.

It was impossible to know what time it was. Two-thirty in the morning. No one seemed to possess watches or clocks and anyway what difference did it make? Penny's head was lightly swimming, probably from the hash. She had hardly touched the wine. Even after several weeks in Greece she found the retsina unpalatable, it tasted and smelt like gasoline. She sunk back into the mattress and gazed towards the sky outside. The moon had crossed the bay and was not visible from where she lay. Somewhere beneath the half-shuttered window a party of wild cats had begun scrapping, or copulating.

The door opened and Harry crept in.

"Hi," he whispered, walking towards the window. Penny watched as he began undressing in the moonlight. The shutter cut a shadow across his torso. Naked, he turned towards her. Longing overwhelmed her, pouring out of her.

"We're going to get ourselves some real good lovin'," he crooned jokily.

They lay beside one another in the semi-darkness. She felt immeasurably happy. He rolled onto his side, cupped his head in his hand, resting on his elbow, and brushed her stomach with the fingers of his other hand. Tender intimate movements, the caress of a stranger painting her, discovering her, watching her with penetrating detached eyes. Between her breasts, circling her nipples, across her shoulders, her stomach, her forest of pubic hair and as she cried out and then cried again, on into her hot flowing cove.

*　　　*　　　*

"Your order?"

"What?"

"May I take your order?" Standing before her, holding pencil and pad at the ready was Spiros. But it could not possibly be! Apparently he had not aged a moment, not a day more than thirty-six, thirty-seven, slightly plumper than she had remembered him, hair cut differently yes, but physically almost unaltered.

"Are you alright, madam?"

The village had changed beyond all recognition, but this man . . . it was simply not possible. Her characters lived on in her imagination, fossilised and unaltered, but this was life. He stood in front of her now, flesh and blood, younger than she!

"Spiros?"

He regarded her, questioningly, puzzled by her.

"You're Spiros. I know you are." God knows, she thought, briefly for one miserable afternoon we consoled one another. We were lovers!

He shook his head. "Spiros is dead, madam," he said flatly. "I am Demetrius, his son. Do you want to order?"

"Demetrius! Don't you remember me?" she asked. He

stared patiently, brow furrowed, and then shook his head. "We have many people here," he offered by way of explanation. "Many tourists."

"Yes, stupid of me," she smiled and gave him her choice from the menu. Fish, chips, no wine.

Penny took the newspaper, yesterday's *Guardian* printed in Marseilles and bought in the village, laid it on the arm of the chair and crossed the room flinging her raincoat to the floor as she moved. Outside the wind rattled in the mountainous hills, whipping at the windows, causing them to sound like the whinny of unbroken steeds. She leant her forehead against the frame as if in need of support and gazed relentlessly, her body almost beckoning something, some invisible force, beyond the pine trees being blown like feeble sticks.

"How was your first day?" Peter would enquire if he were here. She wished he were, she felt in need of company. A longing enveloped her but she knew it was not for him.

"Think about it. And you tell me what to change." Jimmy Gaza's words echoing through her thoughts.

She sighed, crossing back towards the chair, lighting an infrequent Gauloise, pacing more, eventually settling herself on the carpet, stroking distractedly at her shoes as though at a pet, her thoughts confusing her.

"There's a storm brewing." She spoke the words aloud as though there were someone else in the room to hear her. "You seem upset, disturbed. What's happened?" She continued, talking to herself but all the while vocalising the thoughts. "Everything's changed ... Had you expected otherwise?" Her sentence drifted into a smoke-filled silence as she dragged on her unaccustomed cigarette. She stared with big eyes at the cavorting flames in front of her. Someone had stopped by to light the fire. Must have thought I was arriving today. She had found clean sheets in the hall. She glanced in a small oval mirror hanging across the room. The nape of her neck, her loose neat sweater, her strangely shorn head, all bent in reflection, caused her to look lost and broken like a confused schoolboy.

In need of someone to talk to she conjured up Peter, pictured him listening in the armchair, her sitting at his feet.

"I saw someone today, he didn't remember me, I knew his father . . . slept with him. I keep remembering the others, asking myself if my imagination has played tricks on me." And then with a force in her voice that almost terrified her – as though she were answering some inner indictment, a nagging argument – "I've lived with this past! I've sorted out the story and I'm afraid for it."

And Gaza's voice again, "You tell me what to change."

"I don't want to meddle with it!" she cried out. "It fits, harmonises with my truth. I don't want to dismantle that . . . Don't push me, Jimmy!" She caressed the brush of her hair with the palm of her hand, attempting to calm herself, to centre her strength and she smiled pathetically, a weak apology. "I hadn't expected it to affect me this way."

"It's a story, Penny. You wrote it," Peter would console if he were with her.

"Yes, I'm being . . . sentimental," she laughed brittlely, but then Peter had never been told; had never suspected the truth.

News had been travelling fast t...
villages that a film crew was in t...
ally, it was causing a certain am...
excitement. Bands of autograph hu...
mon sight now at the location base a...
prime target for them. This blustery...
exception. She signed her name on myr...
paper while David, the second assistant, talk...
with her her upcoming schedule.

"I'm afraid it's all going to be a bit roug...
Morrison," David apologised.

"I know, David, I wrote it!" she quipped, amused...
sometimes exasperated by his ever present earnestnes...
"And please call me Penny."

"Yes, Miss Morrison."

Their journey would be taking them inland high into
the mountains, way above and beyond the Samaria
Gorge. The going would be slow; it was expected to take
the better part of the day, travelling by jeep, arriving
early evening for supper and crew call. Most of the crew
had set off several hours earlier and Penny, along with
several of the other actors, was part of the last convoy to
leave the coast. All being transported by four-wheel
drives.

Outside the location base she caught sight of Chris
Grange, the young actor playing Harry. She had never
met him but had heard a fair bit about him, he was
considered up and coming. He was recognisable now
from his publicity photographs. She crossed the square
to say hello. It was his first leading role and she perceived the mixture of terror and voracious excitement in
his eyes. Not a bad likeness, she thought, applauding
Gaza's choice but her mind was elsewhere. She turned to

4

hrough the surrounding
e vicinity. Not unusu-
unt of interest and
nters were a com-
nd Penny was a
midday was no
iad strips of
d through

Miss

going?"
u that I
ult."

behav-

n his

way.

...ung

...hat

... it is, it won't
... We're tidying up the
... spring for you."

..., it's . . . " A discreet knock on the office door told her that it was time to be on the road. "I've got to shift," she said. "I'll call tonight when I get there, if I can."

Downstairs in the street, sheltering himself from the relentless wind blowing in from Africa, stood David, anxious as ever to see her into her car.

"I saw your photo in the local paper," he said, opening the door. "You looked great." She smiled at him, at his young freckled face which she found attractive, but her light-heartedness was an effort. Something was bothering her, distracting her from her work, a presentiment, heavy and nagging. Peter's welfare perhaps. She couldn't say for sure, but whatever, it hung louring like the rain clouds on the horizon and she could not come to grips with it. Settling into the jeep she peered out of the window, turned her head and looked back towards the bay. The choppiness of the dark-emerald ocean, the aroma of sea salt carried by the wind, the deserted brumous beach sullied by drift. Nature it seemed was distressed, dissatisfied, returning like a turbulent spirit bent on retribution.

"David," she said, almost as an afterthought before he had closed the door, "are you staying down here or coming with us?"

"Later, when I've cleared up here, before you start shooting I'll be there. Do you need something?"

"No, it's okay. I thought if you'd been staying . . . No, I'll see you up there."

Her eye lighted upon Chris Grange standing drinking coffee, he was watching her, appraising her with his cool dark eyes. "How's Chris getting to the location?" she asked. And before David could respond, "If he's ready and feels like it, ask him if he'd like to ride with me."

David hurried across the road to relay the invitation to the actor battling to keep warm in his full-length black leather coat. She waited while he received the news and was more than relieved to watch him ditch his polystyrene cup, grab his rumpled script and run towards her, smiling.

"Thanks," he said.

Within moments they were on their way. She felt a sense of relief, to be moving away from the ocean, from this village that she had once known so well. Memories of warmer days spent here were starting to torture.

"It's too far to travel alone," she said, by way of explanation.

They spoke little en route yet Penny felt calmed by the impulse that had driven her to invite him. She felt in need of a physical presence alongside her. It was curious, she possessed no real desire to speak to him, merely the need for companionship. Unobtrusively she slipped on her glasses and began to study her already well-thumbed script, occasionally studying him too, while Chris gazed from the car window.

They drove a while thus. Goats, hens, and inert reinforced concrete blocks, monstrous shells lying incomplete and neglected, flashed past their vision. The air smelt of dust and grit and early spring growth, a bizarre combination.

Penny pondered on how, outside the central village life, the island's progress gave the impression of having created little more than great barren strips of desolation.

"So you were here then when all this happened?" Chris asked suddenly. She glanced towards him, not immediately comprehending. "This story – *Akin to Love* – someone said it's true. Is that right?"

She faltered, weighing her answer. "Well, I was here for a while during the dictatorship . . . I wouldn't say . . . "

"And this character, my character, the painter, he really existed?"

"There was no one special painter," she lied, and then, "Not as such, but . . . there was a community of artists in the village . . . I knew several of them."

Chris grinned provocatively and for one brief moment she could have believed he was Harry. Chris's colouring was quite dissimilar and he, because he was too effeminate, lacked the soft-pedalled but fundamental strength of Harry, but fleetingly, just for a ghost of a second, she felt as though she had been beside him. Harry, with that piercing challenging look in his eyes. Harry, whom she had loved too dangerously.

A village by the sea. 1972.

When Penny opened her eyes she discovered Harry at the foot of the bed, sketching. He must have peeled back the sheets while she had been sleeping for now she lay uncovered and naked. His idle model. It pleased her. The sun streamed in through the window warming her sleepy skin.

Fearing to move, not wishing to disturb his concentration, she lay watching him. He hadn't noticed her wake up, immersed as he was in his sketching.

60

"May I see?"

He shook his head without speaking, and then added, "Later. When I've finished. You've got a great body. Are you a dancer?"

"No, an actress."

"An actress?" His pencil rested for a moment against the paper and he threw a glance in her direction. "I knew an actress," he said.

"Who was that?" Penny felt the vague stirrings of jealousy rise within her.

"Oh, a Greek actress. Beautiful lady. She's dead now." He said no more.

Harry worked on his sketch throughout the morning while Penny took an exploratory stroll along the beach. All around her she witnessed the morning arrival of the hippies, appearing like crabs from beneath their rocks, busying themselves with mats and towels spread out in rows or circles of fours and fives. She had been looking forward to exploring the caves at the far end of the bay, before they became too crowded, but as Ches had reported they were filthy, defiled by tourists' defecation and swarming with bluebottles.

Disgusted, she went for a swim, the water was cool and pellucid, and before it became too hot she paddled back to the house where she found Harry, still at work, drawing furiously, squatting beneath a slender tamarisk tree. She wondered whether she should collect her bag. Nothing had been mentioned about her staying another night.

Close by, three Greek fishermen, repairing their nets, perched against the upturned hull of a wooden boat. The nets were draped about them, shrouding them in spiders' webs. Their faces were as old as goatskins, seared by the sunlight. One wizened fellow was puffing at a small pipe and relating a long animated story, entertaining his companions who weaved and chuckled.

"Here," said Harry, offering her the drawing with a flourish. "It's for you. Come on, let's buy some lunch while the others are still sleeping." He took her by the fingertips, gathered up a small handcrafted leather satchel and set off with her in the direction of the main square and its solitary shop. Hurrying alongside him, attempting to keep pace with his long-legged easy gait, Penny sneaked an exalted peep at her unexpected gift, relishing the prospect of studying it later in the privacy of solitude. A first impression disclosed a supine figure, sleeping, sensuous, soft round curves with elegant enticing breasts (could this really be how he perceived her?) after the style of Matisse. He had titled it 'Penny Reclining'.

"I was planning to go over to Red Beach," she ventured, as they trod the shade between the dazzling white stone buildings, "but I could hang on for a few days . . ." She was glowing with a capricious daring inspired by the beauty in the drawing.

"Why not stay 'til Friday? I have to go to Athens on Friday. You can leave for Red Beach then."

"Tuesday," she thought, "three days to share with him."

They passed sweetly these days, sweet as the local Cretan honey. Penny had never experienced such happiness, such a tenderness. For, above all else, Harry was tender with her. He had recognised her innocence and cared for it.

Each morning they rose at dawn, creeping down the stairs past their companions, leaving them to sleep on. It gave them the early part of the day – the optimum part he claimed – for themselves. Before breakfast they swam naked in the pastel-blue sea when only the fishing boats were about. Afterwards they went shopping together for fresh salad and pitta bread, and when Harry wasn't occupied with his drawing and before the sun became too sweltering, they went hiking, scouting and exploring the countryside he loved so well. He sketched, or painted, for several hours each day. During those hours she never disturbed him, fearing to distract him. But once his working day was over his time was devoted to her.

"If you feel like it, before you head for home, you ought to visit some of the Minoan settlements," he suggested, "at least get to Phaistos. It's no distance from here. It's a pity we haven't time to go together. We have so few days."

It was the first mention he had made of their separation. And it had sounded so final.

"I have to visit somebody later. Want to come?"

She nodded gratefully.

"When I've finished my work then."

Later, as the afternoon grew cooler, he took her to meet a friend of his, Nikos Koumoulides, a painter from Athens.

"He's rather well-regarded in the city," Harry informed her as they trod the square, hand in hand, crossing towards the foothills on the outskirts of the village. "I met him in Athens a couple of years back and then bumped into him in a bar here. We became friends pretty much immediately."

The Koumoulides family embraced her with a red-blooded hospitality. Within moments of her arrival they had set out their photo albums, a display shared with fierce pride, and were offering her aniseed-perfumed ouzo, island olives, cigarettes which she refused and locally made goats cheese. When Penny asked them about their home in Athens, Nikos hesitated and then confided, with much melodramatic whispering beneath a bushy black, wheelbarrow moustache, that he had quit the capital forever. There was a watery sadness in his bloodshot eyes, a self-pitying regret. He had a kindly full-throttled countenance. Almost comically picaresque.

"I'm an Athenian, a true Greek," he announced with theatrical relish, "but I spit on my government." Here he actually played out a stage spit aiming it onto the stone floor beside him. "No artist can live safely on the mainland these days," he told them. "Not if he wishes to work honestly, to speak his piece with integrity. He must

63

please the dictatorship or keep his damned mouth shut. But here in *Kríti*, if I keep still they will not disturb me. I shall work here undisturbed until the junta has been overthrown." At this point he slapped the table in front of him causing photos to displace.

"I envy you your England. She's a free country," he pronounced. "You can be proud of your democracy, even your right wing government. Believe me, it's not so bad. Here, Penny, no actor can play in the theatre if he is not willing to become the mouthpiece of the government. Our actors, our artists have been gelded. What do you say to that?"

But even before Penny had been given a chance to respond, Nikos's wife, Melina, had chivvied him away, clapping her hands, shooing and reprimanding him as though he were her child. "Foolishness! Leave the girl in peace. Talk politics to your men friends," she had cried, or so Penny had loosely translated, for the woman had spoken in Greek. Harry and Nikos disappeared into an enclosed *avli* (their cluttered courtyard which reeked of vine-leaves and damp laundry drying in the sunlight) leaving her alone with the mother and her wide-eyed children whose language she could not understand but who stared agog and nodded approvingly. They sat stiffly on wooden upright chairs with rush-matted seats in a cool stone room, waiting for the men to return. All the while Penny was glancing towards Nikos and Harry. They were knocking back shots of *tsikoudia* (known to her as *ráki*), lost in further heated discussion. How she hankered to have been shooed out with them for inside there was little conversation and oh, she envied Nikos his intimacy with Harry who, lean and elegant, sat scribbling notes and drafting some sort of chart onto loose sheets of paper. He was rapt with attention only for his friend. She had been forgotten.

"You know," Nikos confided to her in challenging booming tones when they returned and had sat to drink yet another *ráki*, "your young Harry is the El Greco of southern *Kríti*."

The entire family including Harry laughed. Penny, abashed, had not even known that El Greco had been born in Crete.

On the Thursday afternoon, before dusk had settled, Harry and Penny escaped from the company of Ches and Sandy on the pretext of wanting to watch the sunset.

"It's a spectacular spot. Known," Harry promised her with a twinkle in his blue eyes, "to only a chosen few!" Isolated, hidden from the inquisitive stares of locals, they made love on a deserted beach, partially naked, water lapping over their clothes and bodies, until after sundown when all the stars had risen.

Penny felt as though she were in Eden, no other world existed for her. Only the nagging knowledge of the next day looming spoiled her sublime happiness.

"Why are you going to Athens?" she asked, loathe to mention his departure but gambling that the necessity for it had been replaced by a desire to stay with her.

"Oh, I promised Nikos I'd search out some watercolours. We both need them . . . " He was hesitating.

"Is that the only reason?" She hated herself for being inquisitive, for not just letting it drop. This was not cool behaviour. Besides, whatever it was he did not wish to tell her was probably better left unsaid. She would not want to hear it, but then again . . .

He slid his arm beneath her bare shoulder and kissed her gently on the mouth. "You're beautiful, you know that?" he whispered into the falling darkness while easing her unresisting limbs apart. "My Erytheia, I love fucking you." Before she could utter another word he was loving her once more and her body was being pressed into the moist yielding sand.

On Friday morning still sopping and salted from their early morning swim they sat together outside the house sipping Nescafé, watching the swallows. Neither of them spoke. Penny wondered whether their imminent separation was grieving Harry as much as her. Certainly as the moment had drawn closer he had become more withdrawn. Or was that simply her fancy?

"How long will you be in Athens?" she asked, calculating that if he had not returned to the island prior to her departure they might perchance spend one night together in the capital before her arranged flight to London. Perhaps this possibility had not occurred to him.

"A few days," he replied evasively.

How she longed to accompany him, but if he did not invite her she would not suggest it herself, her erstwhile daring had been sapped by a new uncertainty. She had learnt so little about him. They had become lovers but they were still strangers and this revelation disquieted her.

"Are you likely to be back before I leave?" Why was it she asking the questions?

And the answer crossed her mind darkly that perhaps these few days bore little significance for him, perhaps they had been exactly what she had been fearing, simply an amusement. Perhaps he was being guarded, not withdrawn, guarded lest she press him into some future commitment. Was that really all she meant to him? Nothing more. She wanted to matter more. She wanted these few days to have been as precious to him as they had been to her. And now because he offered her no reassurance she wanted to weep, to cry out and then she thought, but even if I am simply an amusement for him, nothing more, why must it finish? Why can we not continue to be lovers when he returns? I don't care! He can have my pride! If I am only a fuck, so what? Let it be! If that is what it is, I accept it! But let me have more of him. Oh God, don't let it stop now!

She sipped at her unpalatable instant coffee, clutching dangerously at her cup, knowing that her hands were shaking, attempting not to let it show.

"I'm not sure when I'll be back."

She was unable to read him, unable to tell. Almost as

though these last few days had never taken place.

Time was running out. He was taking the ten-thirty bus to Iráklion and an evening flight from there to Athens.

He cut two slices of bread for her and handed them along with the jam across the table. Penny shook her head, unable to respond, knowing she could not force a single mouthful. She stroked the back of his hand, attempting casualness, braving a smile. I'm an actress, she thought, he doesn't have to see how this is wrenching me.

"Hey," he smiled, caressing her chin, "cheer up."

She obviously wasn't succeeding and searched about for a jollier countenance, watching as he tucked into his bread and jam, feeling such a little fool.

"You want to walk with me to the bus station?"

From beneath the feathery fronds of the tamarisk tree she turned to regard him. He was dressed for travel – his departure was imminent – long jeans, cheesecloth shirt, sunglasses winking like a wise owl who had guessed at her secret, the weakness in her heart. Jutting from a small overnight bag slung across one shoulder were his precious rolls of canvas.

"Sure," she agreed, with composure. She had been waiting for him in the shade and during these twenty minutes while he had prepared his things she had showered and calmed herself. She was feeling in control.

They walked alongside one another silently holding hands.

"Will you leave for Red Beach today?" he asked, eventually.

He doesn't want me here when he gets back, she thought. "Yes, I thought I'd head off pretty soon. Before the sun gets too hot."

He glanced towards the sky. "You're better to wait 'til later. If you start to climb now it'll be midday before you hit the summit. It's baking up there. When you do go make sure you take plenty of fresh water with you. There's nothing the other side. Just beach and ocean."

Penny nodded tightly, feeling her newly gained composure sliding away, out of reach.

The bus was at its station just a few miserable yards ahead of them. Nothing remained to delay him. A lump which felt as cumbersome as a boulder wedged itself in her throat. She lowered her eyes, welling with cursed tears, and gazed stupidly at the sandy street beneath her, while Harry busied himself with his satchel, tossing it onto the front seat before shaking hands with the driver who was enjoying an al fresco cigarette. They greeted one another companionably in Greek. She was estranged by the clipped sentences, blindly waiting for him, and then he returned his attention to her, cupping her tanned face between his still paint-encrusted fingers, lifting her eyes to meet his.

"Take care," he whispered, and kissed her hard on the mouth. "We've had a great few days, don't you forget them," and he stepped onto the bus.

There were no other passengers. The driver checked his watch, shared a passing joke with Harry and started up the engine which straight away excreted black clouds of foul diesel fume to choke her emotions.

"See you soon," Harry shouted, throwing her a wink as the bus pulled away and Penny stood idiotically waving, doing her damnedest to nod and smile. But she knew they had not exchanged addresses. How could they see one another again? And in that moment she remembered P. Knowle who came from Canterbury in Kent! She had been so bowled over by him on that first evening that she had never thought to mention the name tag, and the idea now of never having acquainted herself with his identity, after everything, caused her to weep miserably. Bereft in the deserted square beneath the unrelenting burn of the sun. And later with her swollen eyes, gathering her bits together, trembling, rushing to be gone, before the others awoke and found her wretched . . .

"It's a great scene, the death of the Athenian revolutionary, very tragic. But you know, it's the painter's role in all of it which really excites me," confided Chris Grange. She noted, not without a certain scorn, that he was an overtly ambitious young man, hungry to carve his niche in all of this. No more of course than she! He was currently attempting to engage her attention, while clutching at the strap above his head as the jeep which transported them both skirred full-tilt round a hairpin bend.

"Mmm?" she crooned, surfacing back into the present.

"I have been wondering, asking myself, whether it wasn't the painter who tipped off the police that night."

"Tipped off the police?"

"Someone must've."

"Whatever makes you believe that?"

"It adds another dimension to my role."

She laughed mockingly. "Why should anyone do such a thing?" She was knocked sideways by his suggestion, by his extraordinary leap of imagination, but he had not perceived that. He was not as perceptive as he thought and besides she had become far too accomplished at concealing her emotions. "They all believe I've got the hide of a rhino," she had once confessed to Peter. "Thick-skinned, that's how they perceive me. It's only you, my sapient friend, who sees and knows me!"

Even that was a falsehood. Peter knew the truth no more than the others.

Rolling to and fro now, rising with the height of the pines and the elegant cypress trees, peering back down into the valley slashed out of mountain rock beneath them, like a sabre wound, a great searing gash of nature, circling for balance like oil in sockets, they brushed up against one another, balls bobbing in water, hanging on for dear life as the jeep, almost defying gravity, scaled the mountain face. And as they ascended, drawing ever closer, she wanted to confide to Chris Grange, "You move too hurriedly, young man. We are not there yet." Instead she simply smiled her rueful, winning smile which caused him to say, "Reading too much into the text, that's what you're thinking, isn't it? Directors are constantly yelling at me, keep it simple, Chris!"

Penny nodded, a comprehending response.

"It's easy for you," he continued. "You've done loads of these." She peered at him curiously. "Films, I mean. Ever do any theatre?"

It was the question that, earlier in her career, had most infuriated her but today it no longer grated. "Yes," she said simply. "I did a fair bit in the early days."

"Where, which theatres? Which was the first? Recount to me your first theatre experience."

She laughed, an abrasive explosion. Actors, she thought kindly, with our unceasing need to compare agents and past experiences. "Too long ago," she teased, "to even remember."

But she had not forgotten . . .

5

Leeds, northern England. October, 1972.

Penny Morrison cast an inexperienced and unimpressed glance about her. This room to let in Mrs Hardcastle's theatrical digs was really much too tiny, considerably smaller than she had gleaned from the wording in the newspaper advertisement. Frankly it was little more than a shoe-box, decorated with a *feuillemorte* raised flock-wallpaper with a colour tone so sombre that it merely accentuated the room's size and gloom, and would no doubt heighten Penny's feeling of claustrophobia during the winter months to come.

In one corner, alongside the sunken single bed, a gas meter had been fitted. "It takes them new ten ps. No foreign coins, if you please," the landlady warned.

"Yes, I see." Penny spoke politely with a smile fixed across her face. On top of everything else she had the distinct impression that she detected gas leaking, but in fact after several more intakes of breath she realised that it was Mrs Hardcastle's cooking. Good old English cuisine. Waterlogged cabbage would be her guess. And indeed, escaping like choke damp from the kitchen below and drifting sneakily up the stairs were mixtures of cooking odours and various other clues to this woman's domestic life. They permeated both the room and the upstairs landing. Through the floorboards they wafted: greens, Harpic and bacon fat.

The general feel of the place was hardly snug. Truth to tell it was pretty bleak, but at four quid a week what more was she to expect? She turned to Mrs Hardcastle, the landlady, who stood like granite in the doorway, and smiled her acceptance.

"It'll do fine," she said cheerily.

"Right then, good. One week in advance, if you please, Miss Morrison." The woman held out her great square hand calloused by scrubbing.

Penny dug into her cloth shoulder-bag, purchased in Greece, and pulled out three pound notes and two fifty-pence pieces. Almost the last cash she had until pay-day. The notes crinkled as the waiting palm folded around them, a private embrace, and they disappeared into a pinny pocket.

"And from here on, I expect to be paid every Friday evening before you leave for the theatre to do your performance, or you'll be out on yer ear the next day. I stand for no nonsense, and just for the record, this is a decent house. I'll have no actors' hanky-panky here, if you follow my drift." And with that the stout pinafored Mrs Hardcastle turned on her heels and disappeared, heavy footing her way back down the stairs into the dingy hallway and out of sight into the cabbage-sodden world of her scullery.

The word 'actoor' rang in Penny's ears for several seconds after Mrs Hardcastle had made her exit. It had been spoken like a judgement through thin curled lips, drawn as though she were smelling something malodorous or referring to something obscene.

"Probably her own cooking," thought Penny, lifting her suitcase. "What a bloody welcome."

Alone for the first time in her new room she fastened the door securely, not wishing to be disturbed and dumped her suitcase onto the bed. She had a 'Welcome to the new "actoors"' meeting at the theatre at twelve-thirty. It was a fifteen-minute walk down the hill past a housing estate and across a busy intersection. The time now was eleven-forty. She could begin her unpacking.

Penny had set off from London at dawn and had driven her rather tired old mini through the beating rain along a motorway jammed with roadworks. Such a journey made the prospect of walking to the theatre appealing. The exercise, even in this damp, would be invigorating. In any case her starter motor was playing up. She unlocked her case and spun like a child in the centre of the room gazing about her. This was to be her home until early February. It might be spartan but it was only the beginning.

"After this," she declared, "there will be other jobs, better paid jobs."

A single wardrobe carved from pine stood in the corner beside the door. Penny turned the key and wrenched it open. The interior smelt musty, of unaired wood and mothballs. A pair of wooden shoe trees lay forgotten in the dust, a long mirror had been screwed to the inside of the door and three metal coat-hangers swung like dead men from the iron rail. Penny stared hopelessly at them and with a deal of resolution she returned to the bed to unpack her suitcase. Thick sweaters, a windcheater, several pairs of denim jeans, rehearsal clothes and thermal underwear – bought for her by her insistent mum to whom, no doubt, before the season was over she would be eternally grateful judging by the ungenerous size of the gas-heater.

She unloaded several foolscap scripts sent to her by the theatre, to be learnt for the forthcoming season. Nestling in between them was her pencil drawing from Harry – 'Penny Reclining'. She drew it lovingly from between the pages and held it in her right hand, turning it towards the ungenerous source of light, feasting her eyes over it, stroking it. Not for the pleasure of her own image but for the memories it carried with it.

"Oh shit!" Penny breathed.

Subsiding back onto the bed and stretching herself out across a pink embroidered candlewick bedspread she pored over it, as she had on so many occasions since her return to England. Every curve, every line, even an indistinct smudge, reminded her of its charismatic craftsman whom she had been unable to forget. Despite not seeing him again her memories of him had lingered, her craving for him had grown more acute, taunting her as though it were an addiction. It stung her to think of him and yet she seemed unable to let him go.

She recollected how, during her stay at Red Beach, she had twice hiked back over the mountain to the village and, without daring to venture too close to Harry's house, had searched for him, beseeching whatever forces might be at work to orchestrate a chance encounter. It was during one of these excursions that she had spotted Ches and Sandy shopping in the square. It had been the village market-day.

She had called out to them, longing to engage them in conversation, not for the purpose of renewing her friendship with them but solely to hear news of Harry. Where was he? Had he returned from Athens? Why hadn't he crossed over to Red Beach to see her? Please, she thought, invite me to the house, let me feel him close again, smell him, let me be amongst his possessions even in his absence. But they had merely told her she 'was getting tanned and looking great', they had said what 'great times' they were having and that the village was even better because all the tourists were heading out and 'wouldn't it be great here when winter came'.

"And Harry?" ironing the desperation out of her voice.

"Aaw Harry. Guess he's still in Athens," Ches had told her languorously and then Sandy had drawn his attention with a cry. She had spotted something.

"Hey Ches, look at the colour of those tomatoes! Wow, aren't they great!" And they had hurried away forgetting her, oblivious to her sadness. Ches had reappeared briefly, limping towards her while Penny had been choosing grapes.

"Hey Penny there's a guy, Don, hangs out at Spiros's taverna. He's got some magic mushrooms if you're interested. Blow your mind."

"Thanks Ches." She had smiled bravely.

"Good to see ya, Penny."

"Yes, and you, Ches."

She had observed the pair of them for a few moments. Sandy laughing, jumping, shrieking excitedly, fair-skinned, so frail. Very sixties, very Californian. An emaciated gypsy child in her long flowing dress and waist-length light-red hair. She had been waving aubergines and cucumbers into the sunlight as though she had unearthed gold nuggets, riveted by the fruit, stoned out of her mind; Ches, kindly, a cripple at her side, watched over her, superintending her emotional pandemonium. Penny had ambled away towards the baker, bought a loaf, gone in search of water and prepared to head back over the mountain before nightfall. She had been leaving the next day, flying back to Athens en route for London.

Leaving without sight of Harry. P. Knowle. He had gone. Just as incredibly as he had walked into her life he had disappeared again and it smarted that she hadn't understood why.

She rested his drawing on her bedside table, propping it against her alarm clock and promised herself that as soon as she had earned sufficient money she would have it framed. She glanced at the clock supporting it. Time to leave for the theatre.

Winter came early to northern England. One interminable day of drizzle followed upon another. Northern dampness and rheumatism seeped like drains through the mining-town community. Pitch evenings, black as the local coal, together with a raw biting wind whipped into Penny's bones, sharpening her lonely existence but never succeeded in making her dispirited. She loved her work and managed to create a world for herself that was self-sufficient and rewarding.

After three weeks of rehearsals the first play opened: Bernard Shaw's *Major Barbara*. Penny, with earnest enthusiasm and not a great deal of skill in an ill-fitting costume, played Barbara, her first leading role. The local press applauded. "A promising start to the new season; a promising young actress", they appraised, but then they were renowned locally for their unswerving loyalty.

75

·· November approached. Christmas was drawing near, which meant pantomime time and for Penny, rehearsals for the chorus. She slogged and sweated in leotards and tights during demanding hours alongside a thumping tuneless piano in a dusty rehearsal room. The room lacked heating and ventilation. Mornings were freezing and later it was stifling. She and two other girls, one young and one not so young, all aspiring actresses, danced and sang for Giles, the well-meaning, zealous musical director. Every so often Penny, or one of the other girls, would be called to the main rehearsal room to exchange a few lines with the leading lady, soon to be Dick Whittington. Penny had been donated several of the more minor roles, all to be learnt in the quiet of her room after the show. In the evenings once the day's rehearsals were ended she hurried back to her digs to take a shower and a breather before returning once more to the theatre for the evening's performance.

"You always rush off home. Why not stay for a drink tonight after the show?"

Penny shoved her music-sheets into her shoulder-bag and smiled. "I'd rather not if you don't mind, Giles. I need to learn some lines."

"But you only have a dozen! And your singing is terrific."

"Another night," she hedged kindly. Dear Giles, lanky and concerned, with popping eyes and Adam's apple. A million miles from Harry.

Her routine had become set until February and there seemed little reason for it to alter, until one Friday evening in the first week of December. Detained at her dance rehearsals way beyond the allotted finishing time by Giles – who appeared to be concocting more and more excuses to keep her late, to lock her uncomfortably close alongside the piano – Penny came splashing through the rain and up the garden path before hurtling back to close the gate as instructed, realising that in her haste she had forgotten it. She hurried to the front porch, slipped her key into the lock, shook the rain out of her brolly, closing it securely (open brollys were forbidden inside the house for fear they 'fetched bad luck') and scrambled in her pocket in search of her pay-packet to give Mrs Hardcastle her expected rent.

She found the feared woman waiting for her in the hallway as she did every Friday (the-appalling-odour-of-fish night), but this week something was quite evidently amiss.

Neither said a word. Penny, not understanding, simply stared into the silence that hung like a lead balloon between them. The woman's expression was louring and grave. Her raw hands, pressed tightly against this week's pinny, were clasped in front of her as if to support her ample breasts. For one dreadful moment Penny feared there must be bad news. Something at home. Her mother or what? Her father had died when she was a child. She closed the door and waited heavily. Rain plopped from her hair and straddled her face. Finally, unable to stand the not knowing a moment longer she entreated, "What is it, Mrs Hardcastle, for heaven's sake, what's wrong?"

"I showed your brother up to your room," the woman announced with the gravity of a toastmaster, "but I told him quite plainly that my house guests are not allowed visitors, not even family. If you want to entertain you can do it all you please at the theatre. I make *no* exceptions, is that clear." She spoke her piece in one torrent, without pausing for breath, or to allow Penny time to express her amazement.

"My bro— ?" was all that she managed before the woman began again.

"I want no gossip in this street. He might be your kith and kin but the state of him. Look at the length of his hair! I tolerate no louts in this house, is that clear? Including brothers!"

Penny's confusion mercifully kept her silent. Mrs Hardcastle trained an unrelenting gaze upon her. "He's in your room this once . . . but never again."

She waited while Penny stepped past her, mortified,

creeping fearfully not wanting to tread on the woman's shadow lest it turn on her snarling, and yet anxious to run and discover. She began almost on tiptoe to mount the stairs. She had no idea who was waiting for her in the room above but in her craziest dream she was hoping beyond hope that . . .

"And Miss Morrison, you tell him from me . . . No paint on my carpets."

"What?" Penny was momentarily frozen to the spot and then she sang out her response, an aria of joy, while pounding towards the landing. "Thank you, Mrs Hardcastle, thank you. No paint on the carpets, no, certainly not!"

Inside her room she found him. Harry. She murmured his name. Harry, recumbent, languid across her bed, reading. He was dressed in a black shirt and jeans. Strange for her to see him thus. She had only known him in summer colours, tanned and stripped. The room reeked of grass. He was as arrogantly beautiful as she remembered him.

"Where did you find Cyclops?" he asked, smiling warmly, pointing a finger towards the floor beneath them. Penny giggled. "I hope you don't mind. She'd never have let me in if I hadn't said I was your brother."

She leant back against the door. Her heart was beating, hopelessly pounding like a kettledrum.

"If she smells that she'll call the cops." It was all she could think of to say.

"She won't," he rejoined, dragging extravagantly on the joint. "Nothing could overpower that appalling smell of fish!"

"How did you find me?" she asked, laughing, hardly daring to approach, noticing that the room had been untidied by his possessions, a suitcase, a suede coat, scattered across the floor.

"I've tracked you down. A woman-hunt!" he laughed. "Come here." He held an outstretched arm towards her. Tentatively, amazed, she picked her way across the shoe-box room, seeming so large now she thought she would never reach him, and perched beside him on the bed. His mouth lighted on her neck, a hand across her breast. "I've missed you," he declared confidentially. Penny's glance fell upon the clock. It was a quarter to seven.

"Oh God, I have to leave! I have a show. I have to get back to the theatre." She was on her feet, confused, unable to think.

"What time have you got to be there?"

"Now!"

"I'll drive you and stay to watch the play. May I?"

Finally, after days of endless sheeting, it had ceased to rain. A brief respite perhaps but welcome nevertheless. Tired after the show and blithely content to be in Harry's company Penny settled back and allowed herself to be driven. Idly she watched the late northern night unfold before her – the damp and deserted provincial streets, the spill of yellow street-lamps blurred by mist and the rain still dripping from the windscreen, the squelch of the tyres rolling against soaked macadam – her thoughts drifting softly within her.

"How did Mrs Hardcastle know you paint?" she quizzed suddenly.

"Mmm? I told her I'd like to paint her."

Penny laughed easily, uncertain whether he was teasing or not.

"You must understand, I had to charm her," he continued, "but she is wonderful. Like a great peasant Gertrude Stein. Rough cubist features. I don't meet many women like that."

She studied him, scanning every pore, relearning his profile, drinking in his features, wondering at him and about the women he did meet, reminded yet again of how little they knew of one another, of how sparingly they had spoken of themselves in Greece and how she would not let it happen that way this time. She would be insatiable, would discover everything there was to know about him. To begin with, what had brought him here?

79

Was it that same hopeless clamouring that had kept her sleepless and solitary? She longed to confess to him with what a wintry heart she had faced the dark prospect of never being close to him again, but all at once she was overwhelmed with such gratitude that he had finally found her, that he was here at last, that she simply shifted her gaze once more ahead of her, beyond the windscreen, to witness the car drawing up outside the Post House Hotel. She was content to be by his side and to demand nothing that night . . . except his body.

"I have to leave, have to return to London tomorrow," he told her on the Sunday evening as they lay flushed amidst crumpled sheets and newspapers.

She nodded and forced a smile. Each day she had been waiting for him to say this, preparing herself, arming herself against the words to come and now, uttered, felt hopelessly dismayed by them. She had a technical rehearsal the next day. It would be exhausting work and there would be late nights for the next couple of days. Better for her to be alone she kidded herself.

"Do you live in London or in Kent?" He looked astonished by her question.

"I saw the name tag on your case. P. Knowle, Canterbury."

"Ah, clever girl, well-spotted! My father's old case from his war-correspondent days. I'm rather fond of it. I live at home, in a manner of speaking. I've built myself a studio in the garden. I like to spend a couple of months in winter there. It's strange I have never got used to being out of England in December, and then early spring I go back to Greece or travel. You should come and spend Christmas with us." He touched her face, teasing at her hair.

"I have shows on Christmas Eve and Boxing Day. I shall have to stay here."

"Pity," he whispered, drawing her towards him. "Christmas with Mrs Hardcastle, that's too bad."

"She probably won't rent me the room after my nights

out this week. She'll call me an alleycat." Penny laughed, encouraged by his caresses, achingly aroused by him, taking hold of him, sucking him like a drug, breathing his sex, tasting it, its dampness sweet like almonds, wanting to give, to take, wanting pleasure, ahh Harry, longing to say the words 'I lov . . .' and not quite daring to speak them, desperate that they might never be together again.

"So sexy," he cried softly.

Just to keep him. To own him forever.

When Penny returned from the theatre the next evening Mrs Hardcastle handed her an envelope.

"Your brother," she had over-emphasised the word brother, "left this for you before he drove off this evening."

"Thank you." Penny took the letter and began ascending the stairs to read it in the privacy of her room.

"Miss Morrison."

"Yes?"

"You forgot to give me the rent money. It's Monday. You're four days late."

"I'm so sorry, Mrs Hardcastle," Penny cried, digging into her purse in search of the carefully retained bundle of notes. She leant across the banisters and handed them to the stout woman before clocking that she was almost smiling. Was she smiling? Was there a hint of a glimmer in her eye?

"He's not a bad young artist, your young man," she said bluntly.

Penny tried to conceal her astonishment and wondered what had prompted the remark.

"I'll show you the one he did of me." Before she could answer Penny watched the middle-aged woman disappear into her sitting-room – a room unknown to Penny where her landlady whiled away her solitary evenings watching the television set. Moments later she returned with a drawing, carrying it between her hands like some great harmless beast might fondle a bird. It was a sketch

81

of her signed with a flourish by Harry Knowle.

"Quite a good likeness I thought, don't you?"

Upstairs alone in her room Penny opened her note and read the few well scripted lines. He had written:

Christmas with Mrs Hardcastle. Well, perhaps I shan't leave you to face that alone.

See you soon, my bright Hesperides.

Yours,

Harry.

After such happiness those few months in the north fled by. Penny did manage to spend Christmas with Harry, obviously not at Mrs Hardcastle's although Harry had arrived from London with a gift for her. Penny no longer remembered exactly what the gift had been. Something porcelain, a dog she seemed to think, but even to this day she recalled just how thrilled the widowed landlady had been with it. There was such pride and such sadness on her great sallow face. It had been touching for the young couple brimming with their own happiness to watch the middle-aged woman unwrap it, picking at the tissue paper as though that were the gift itself.

"Poshly wrapped," she had said. "Soon see you got artistic inclinations, Mr Knowle."

She had offered them a glass of sherry and pointed them with great brute pride into her living-room, her sanctuary, the television room. It had been stiflingly hot and reeked of boiling Christmas pudding and gas. The television in the corner by the window had been decorated with silver tinsel. On top of it sat a dish, a glass swan, which had been filled with nuts. Next to it there had been a black and white photograph of Mrs Hardcastle's wedding. Penny had thought sadly that the television resembled an altar. They had drunk her health and eaten a Roses chocolate each before setting off on their own to spend a few days at the Post House Hotel.

After Christmas Harry had sat patiently through the pantomime and the next morning he had driven back to London, promising to visit Penny once more before the end of January, which he did, but after that weekend she didn't see him again until her return to London. He said he looked forward to her return, that he'd had a brilliant idea. He hadn't said what . . .

*   *   *

Penny shivered, poised in reflection and then slipped her coat more tightly about her shoulders. She was feeling vaguely nauseous.

"Cold?" asked Chris Grange. "We're pretty high, that's why. It gets cold at this altitude."

"It's getting dark, too." She glanced at her wrist. A pale line marked the spot where her watch usually sat. "Blast, I must have left it in the bedroom."

"Left what?"

"My watch. What time is it, do you know?"

"Four-thirty. I could do with some coffee, I know that. What time is supper scheduled?"

"When we arrive."

"I know that," he responded a mite too testily and then checked himself. "I just wondered what time we are due to arrive." He peered closely into her eyes as though searching for a speck of dust. A frown crumpled his commonplace good looks. "Are you all right, you look a bit pale? Seem upset?"

"I'm fine. I was just going through my lines," she hedged.

Leeds, northern England. January, 1973.

She very clearly remembered their weekend together in late January. It was the first anniversary of Bloody Sunday, the slaughters in Derry, Northern Ireland. There was a tribute to the families of the dead in one of the newspapers. Harry pointed it out to her. She paid little attention. Of course it was horrific, but as far as she was concerned it was simply another item of unpalatable news, fodder for the songs of John Lennon. She had little political conscience, was too ambitious, whereas Harry was incensed. He lay on the bed contesting the immorality of it, appalled by her indifference, citing incidents relayed to him by his father who had been a correspondent for several months in Belfast. Certainly she had been shocked, who wouldn't be, but not personally very concerned. That sort of thing never really touched her then. If Harry had not mentioned it she probably wouldn't have given it a second thought. If she had only understood . . .

*　　　*　　　*

Penny lifted a hand to her mouth, suppressing a cough, a wheezing for breath, and the hand fell limply back into her lap, seemingly wearied.

"It's very stuffy in here, might we stop the truck for a short while? I need some fresh air."

"But I thought you were feeling cold?" quizzed Chris, perplexed by this inexplicable turn in her behaviour but shifting forward, nevertheless, to grab the driver's attention.

Outside on the rutted mountain road all was misty, dark and still. No other vehicle from the convoy was in sight, neither ahead nor to the rear.

"I can't see any headlights. I think we must've lost the others," said Penny, grasping tightly at the partially open window. The driver stepped from the station truck to alongside her, eyes averted, paced out a few steps to the cliff's edge and unzipped his flies, preparing to relieve himself.

"Excuse me," said Chris, following suit.

"Jesus Christ, we're bloody high," he called back to her. She sensed that he was hiding a growing impatience, born of a confusion on his part. How could he comprehend or know what was happening? She must seem strangely nervy, remote, and at the same time capricious.

He couldn't know how this journey into her past might be affecting her. How she feared what lay ahead.

Penny closed her eyes momentarily, uprooting herself from her Leeds of two decades earlier.

6

Theirs was not the last jeep to arrive, several were still travelling. In spite of this the serving of the evening meal had commenced. Many of the crew members had been working for more than seven hours without a break – an hour beyond their union rule. Any further delay would be an infringement proving too costly for a film already several days behind schedule. It had therefore been decided to set set-meals aside and to serve the hot plate, lamb stew, without further delay. Local wines and beer were being served with the meal, a sign that no shooting would take place this evening. It was already almost eight o'clock. The length of time required for the journey as well as the set up had been underestimated.

The Greek caterers – an identically barrel-shaped husband and wife couple who had journeyed from Iráklion – had set up shop al fresco on a capacious terracotta-tiled terrace situated at ground level. Here, the crew enjoyed a spectacular view out across the southern orange grove plateaux. Beyond, the navy Mediterranean shone in the distance. Lit by starlight it seemed as though dark sweet wine and virgin's milk had coupled beneath the moon and bled their progeny across the water's surface to Africa.

The house – its outlook a millionaire's perspective – had been rented for the duration of the picture.

The heady altitude, a light brisk wind which was circulating the thyme-scented mountain air, the braziers glowing in the darkness and the clear cloudless, star-studded sky above them had each contributed to the party spirit stirring now amongst the motley working group. The night was alive with convivial chatter. Explosions of laughter soared high into the heavens like bracelets of far-reaching fireworks.

Penny and Chris had arrived ten minutes earlier and had quickly sussed the mood of the evening; of a tired yet benevolent crew ready to break loose for a few hours. Chris, cheered by the sight of it all, had disappeared to his room to dump his bag and take a shower, leaving Penny alone. She was in no shape for such merrymaking and had decided to grab herself a plate of something and creep off with it to her room. Strolling now towards the house – which was to act as mansion in the film, bedrooms for the cast, and dressing rooms (in lieu of caravans which could not have negotiated this climb) – she spotted Gaza. He was sitting alone at the mountain's edge on a bench which had been set there temporarily by the design department as dressing for the denouement: Harry's long-awaited return to Penny.

His silhouette was hunched. He was wrapped in a woollen rug, protection against the night air, poring over the pages of his script, utterly oblivious apparently to the camaraderie growing all about him. The light where he sat was insufficient for reading. He had reinforced it with a portable torch marginally more substantial in size than a fountain pen. Clutched between the fingers of his left hand resting on the bench was a plastic tumbler containing beer. This he was pushing to and fro and then round about in small neat circles. It was quite curious to witness, just as though he were summoning some external force with the use of a Ouija board. Penny watched him, this intense expression of his concentration, a solitary figure, isolated, lost in his own world, working in the midst of jollity. His brow was furrowed. He appeared baffled and overburdened. Occasionally he lifted his bent head, squinting, peering over the mountainside towards the coast. A man apart yet hungry for contact. Still the same Jimmy Gaza. She asked herself what he might be thinking of in those moments: his homeland, his childhood? He was Greek, he had been born in Athens and taken to America as a boy. Was he nostalgic now for those tender years? The years without guilt . . .

Shivering, she wrapped her coat more firmly about her and stepped on towards the house, intending to eat within, to keep warm. One of the young props boys had lit a fire for her in her bedroom and she was looking forward to curling up in front of it, but on an impulse she turned back, ditched her plate of stew onto a nearby trestle-table and weaved her way over to Gaza.

Whatever she thought of him as a human being, whatever had passed between them, she admired his commitment. He never gave up. One was drawn to him, his intense black aura. He was a fighter, living always for the picture he was currently shooting. He possessed no social life, no family. There was always only his work, and women, usually actresses. Didn't she know it.

Penny heard the faint tread of her heels clacking against the terracotta tiles. The wind, brisk but without force, gnawed into her cheeks. From somewhere a few yards behind her, muffled by bodies huddled together for warmth and companionship, there was the shattering of glass. A crystal explosion, sharp as a glinting knife in the black night, followed by a rise in the pitch of the light-hearted voices; giggles and comment.

It was possibly as much as three degrees colder here than below, alongside the littoral. Chris Grange had not been joking when he had remarked on the altitude they had reached.

"Watcha, Jimmy," she said, as casually as she could, drawing his attention by a gentle stroke on the back of his curved shoulders.

"This scene bothers me," he responded, bringing his world of concern with him. "It did when I first read the story and it still does in this fucking awful screenplay." Penny, caught out by the aggression in his words, drew alongside him, floundering uncomfortably. "Sit down," he ordered, beating on the bench with his tumbler-filled fist, spilling a small mouthful or so of beer. She hesitated, not knowing what to do. "Sit down," he repeated. She obeyed, meek as a kitten. Their eyes met for an instant before he turned to face the horizon.

"Don't make it too tough for me," she whispered, conscious of the team half a garden away.

"You know what's missing here?"

She shook her head, regretting having sought out his company. She had crossed over to him because she had thought she might find comfort from him. Stolen comfort. A reminder of something that had existed fleetingly.

"It's cute, Penny. You know what I mean?" Again she shook her head, not because she had not understood him but as a self-defence. "It lacks drama." Drama, he emphasised the word as though drawing blood from it, his very life-force. "This stuff is pollyanna!"

"Then why are you here?" she cried under her breath, careful not to draw attention to them both. Neither would relish the idea that the crew smelt tension between them. "What are you nagging me about changes for? If you hate it you shouldn't be here, you shouldn't have accepted it."

He turned his head to her, scrutinising her features, disbelieving her.

"Why are you here?" she begged, practically inaudible even to him.

His response was spoken flatly, without emotion, in contrast to her passion. "I told you a long time ago, I think you're a fine actress . . . you're no writer but that's beside the point . . . we can make this stuff work if you have the courage to change her. This young Penny kid, she's too damned nice. I want her jealous. I want to see her battling with herself not to knife Helen." He took a swig from his tumbler and looked at her, Penny seated and uncomfortable. He knew how to make her squirm, she had forgotten the power of this talent and once again she resented him.

"That's the script we've been employed to shoot," she replied curtly, "let's just make the picture." With that she stood and took a step away from him.

"You're leaving in a huff because you know I'm right. Don't be an ass, Penny. Stop running. Get some sleep and cream your skin, it looks like old potatoes. But think it through, I mean it."

She strode on without turning back to him. Several members of the crew called out a hasty goodnight to her. It was the tone in their voices that caused her to admit that she had been indiscreet. They sensed her anger, her panic. Crews always did. There was no fooling them.

Within the privacy of her unfamiliar room she took out her script and sat by the window reading by the glow from the fire and the light of the moon, but what need had she to read? She knew this story all too well. She calmed herself by watching the moon's reflection move gently across the distant sea. Remembering. A tear rose. With tired fingers she brushed it away.

And as she buried her head in her pages she realised that she had completely forgotten about Peter. She had promised to call him, but now it was too late. She had better work until she was worn enough to sleep . . .

London. Late February, 1973.

"It's not quite Mrs Hardcastle's style but I think you are going to love it!" sung Harry jubilantly, sprinting ahead, deftly ascending the creaking unlit staircase two by two. Two by two, until he reached the door, huzzaing and breathless. It was jammed. He was obliged to push his weight against it, heaving at it with his shoulder. "We'll have to fix this entrance, of course!" Once he had succeeded in unsticking it he began to wave his arms about, to bow and step aside for her, playing the role of medieval courtier.

Penny chortled, surprised by him, relishing the mystery and enjoying his boyish exuberance. But one step inside and she was instantly hushed, bowled over. "My God, Harry, it's vast!" Her well-articulated voice ricocheted across the cavernous space. "How did you find it? It's like a forgotten . . . otten . . . otten sound stage."

"It's a disused repository, I think. An old store-house for textiles."

She had been expecting something run down. He had promised her that during the drive out here, but not this. This was quite unlike anything she might have imagined.

"Isn't it terrific?"

Imposing in its theatricality, overfed with debris, it seemed as though she were standing in some great monster's belly surrounded by its innards. Every footstep, each breath disappeared into the vast emptiness and then boomeranged back to her.

Outside, beyond what remained of a precarious looking wooden balcony, the Thames rolled by, thick as swill.

Cobwebs hung from everywhere, the ceiling, the few rafters that were still in place, a legless wooden chair, planks leaning against a wall, wherever she turned her gaze; it was a stage set from Dracula. Rafters, damaged by dry-rot or woodworm, had keeled to the ground and lay like trees felled after a storm.

Stepping with care for fear the floorboards would subside beneath her, Penny picked her way to the wall of light and peered through the jagged triangles of broken windows. A wintry skyline. The entire area was virtually a deserted bombsite, no life surrounding them whatsoever.

"Oh God," she whispered, an unheard sigh, "it's like the end of the bloody world out there."

"I'm going to paint here, create a studio and later maybe exhibit. There's such an expanse of light." Harry spoke with an enthusiasm which she was unable to match.

She said nothing.

"Well, once we've slapped some paint on and tidied the place up a bit. I've had enough of Canterbury. There'll be plenty of room for all of us here." He wandered off in a direction towards a room he forecast would one day be the kitchen.

"I'm a terrific cook, Pen," he shouted from

somewhere out of sight.

"Great, I hate cooking." Audible only to herself . . .

*   *   *

Penny lifted her head and thought with a wry smile how minimally life had changed, since those years, degrees only. These days it was Peter who cooked. She glanced from the balcony window towards the horizon. The moon shone now over a distant promontory. One islet peeped like a mole from beneath the water. She remembered that tiny island. She used to gaze at it for hours on end, fantasising about it, from the beach in front of Harry's house. How she had loved him! Hidden somewhere along that coastline walked the ghosts of her past . . .

London. Late February, 1973.

The young Penny leant back against a strip of wall between two window-frames, rendered speechless by what felt like the sheer lunacy of such an enterprise. Quite clearly it had been abandoned for donkey's years, this warehouse in the East End docklands. And who had Harry meant by 'all of us'?

"Well, you haven't found anywhere better," he pressed, in vision once more, a note of impatience creeping into his voice. "I thought you'd be game. I love the place and I've taken it. If you fancy it then great! Let's get to work." Into the expanse his voice echoed, sonorous tones rolling around the stench of rotting floorboards.

She watched him scooting happily between one mouldy corner and another. It pleased her to picture him as a small boy in a backyard searching for disgusting slugs, but she could muster no joy. For some reason that she was unable to explain the place spooked her. Not ghosts but bad vibes. They cast a cloud about her, threatening her happiness.

"Well, what do you say?" he boomed, leaning, peering, far away across the room, then through a door to a small winding staircase which presumably led to an attic, the top floor of the warehouse. "We'll make the room above my studio." He could not read the despondency written in her heart. She didn't want to live here.

It was not because of Harry. Certainly not Harry. She loved him, of that she was certain, almost too much she sometimes feared. She wanted nothing in the world more than to be with him, she would do anything for him, even live here if she must, but something was troubling her, some premonition had lit upon her. It hung like a shadow about the dusty warehouse, lying in wait like some monster spider on one of the cobwebs.

"Hey Pen! Come and look at this! Blue tits nesting."

She strode towards him, staking out a path around dusty black telephones, curled and rotting yards of cord, telephone directories decades out of date, odd measures of disintegrating materials and green and red ledger books lying open and forgotten, their inky figures fading daily from the yellowed pages.

"Isn't it special here?" he enthused, swinging his long arms about her, gathering her towards him, hugging her like some Canadian lumberjack and kissing her full on the mouth. "We'll plaster the walls with naked drawings of you," he whispered provocatively. "And be immensely happy, you and I."

Swiftly and in response to his seduction she dismissed her nonsensical fears and slipped her fingers through his. "It'll be wonderful," she lied.

"That's my baby!" he whooped. "I love you!"

He took her to lunch to celebrate. They drank too much wine and went back to Penny's small room in Bayswater. She had been renting it since her return from the north two weeks earlier. There they smoked too much dope, made love and fell asleep until almost midnight and then went in search of take-away pizza from an all-nite joint she had discovered along Queensway.

Later as they lay side by side, replete in the darkness, they made plans for the studio. For Harry it was no longer a musty warehouse; miraculously he had already transformed it into his studio. He said, "I'll go back to Kent tomorrow," he embraced her softly, she was bewitched by his sexuality, lulled by him, "and I'll collect some of my gear. We can spend the weekend at the studio. Start to clean it up."

And so she had said nothing of her forebodings, wanting nothing more than to live with Harry.

He returned from Canterbury on the Saturday morning, his car laden with painting equipment, a record player, discs, his few clothes and a library of books.

With the aid of bottles of cheap wine, cheese, bread and ladles of steaming soup bought at a transport café about half a mile from the warehouse they braved the late February temperatures, scrubbing, gutting, disinfecting and scraping. And during the busy days that followed Penny submerged her first moments of uncertainty. It was as if with the cleaning away of the cobwebs all dark thoughts had disappeared. She was lighthearted once more.

On the second Sunday morning they awoke and found that it was raining, bucketing down. Nevertheless Harry was determined they should go to the studio. "We'll press on. It'll give us a chance to find all the leaks," he reasoned.

He deposited her at the corner and drove back to the transport café to buy coffee and bacon butties for their breakfast.

He must have been a boy scout, Penny bemoaned silently, regretting that she could not stay in bed and keep warm. She gathered her old mac up over her head and hastened along the cobbled towpath, negotiating a series of fast-gathering puddles, while alongside her the Thames gurgled and bubbled like a newly fed infant. As she approached she was surprised and mildly puzzled to discover that the door at street level, the great cumbersome door, was open. A hair's breadth only, but

94

it had been opened.

Someone must have been there, must have taken it off the latch, for she was certain that when she and Harry had eventually packed up the night before it had been she who had swung the door to, closing it with a settled thud. Bemused, she tilted her face up into the falling rain and peered towards the studio. All seemed still, but from the street she could not be sure. Cautiously she tiptoed inside. Berating her own impracticality, as she had not considered bringing a torch. She glanced about her into the darkened stair-well expecting to find a local tramp or drunk who might have passed the night there. Nothing.

"Anyone there?" she risked half-heartedly. A rasping cough scared her almost to death and then from above her a male's voice drawled, "Boy, am I glad to see you! I thought you guys'd never get here!" The voice was familiar, that scratchy timbre, but in her confusion she could not place it and the lack of light contributed to her inability to nail the identity, but as she stepped forward she recognised without a doubt the figure hunched against the stairs. It was Ches.

"I waited outside nearly an hour before I noticed that the entrance was unlocked," he chuckled. "Jesus, I got soaked!" Festooned about him almost as protection against the damp were his bed roll and two guitars.

"Hey Ches, where did you pitch from?" she exclaimed but in reality the discovery of him had caused a certain dampening of her spirits.

"Flew in from Californya this mornin'. Been home for a couple of weeks. Seein' my folks. Where's Harry? Promised me you guys 'ud be here first thing."

Harry had said nothing to her about Ches's imminent arrival and when the two young men greeted one another with loud whoopings and much enthusiasm, "Heyey, I found you!" and "Boy, we need your help, don't we Pen?" Penny merely smiled, affecting an enthusiasm, but in reality she was saddened.

She would have to share him now with someone else.

That night, after they had dropped Ches at a small hotel round the corner from her rented room in Bayswater, Penny sat listening to the rain plomp against the windscreen. "There'll be plenty of room for all of us," she repeated silently, despondently. Both were covered in plaster and stupefied by tiredness. Both longing to fall into her cramped single bed. It was already Monday, almost 2 a.m. They drove the last few hundred yards without speech, listening to Bob Dylan crooning on the late-night car radio . . . "All along the Watch Tower . . .

"so let us not talk falsely now . . . "

She guessed that Harry was unaware of the hurt and turmoil churning around within her and somehow that made it even worse. Was he insensitive to her emotional shifts, or did he just choose to ignore them?

"When did you know that Ches was coming over?" she asked.

"I called him as soon as I'd rented the place," he replied.

"Inviting him?"

"Sure." He turned to her, smiling, delighted that his friend was with them, assuming she must feel the same, ignorant of where her questions might be leading. And perhaps uncaring? Maybe there were others. Strangers, yet to appear. There was Sandy: mad stoned Sandy. Life in a commune, she abhorred the idea.

"Doesn't he work?"

"Sure. He's been working as a roadie for Country Joe. Finished a couple o' weeks ago and then headed west to see his family in California. That's where I caught up with him."

"So what will he do now, stay and live with us?" That was the question that she wanted to ask but somehow did not. Instead she said, "Will he go back and look for another group or will he stay in Europe?"

Harry swung the car into Kensington Square Gardens, crawling in search of a parking spot. "He'll probably go to Greece." He pulled into a space fronting

96

onto the gardens. They sat a moment without moving after Harry had switched off the engine, cutting short the music, listening to the rain. He bent towards her with glinting eyes lit by the neighbouring street-lamp. "Five minutes and we'll be cuddled up beside one another. Can't wait," he whispered, brushing her neck with his tongue.

Shadows of the winter branches in the gardens danced and embraced in the dripping darkness.

Almost as soon as they had locked the door they were lying together side by side like cutlery, wrapped in one another's arms, too whacked for sex. Sleepy, intimate and in love. She lay listening to his even breath creeping across the back of her shoulder, stroked his limp fingers curled around her breast, and pressed herself onto his small curled cock asleep against her buttocks. She loved him so much. She didn't want to share him with Ches and yet she feared that was what she was going to have to do. She counselled her sleepy thoughts against wanting too much of him, against being possessive.

During the working days that followed she grew isolated. The tomfoolery between the men made her jealous. She resented their friendship, it was longer standing than her own with Harry. But Ches proved himself an admirable workman and a warm-hearted guy. He helped Harry with the decorating and for that she was grateful. He cooked them mountains of glutinous brown rice on a travelling gas stove and showed himself to be an able carpenter. In spite of his physical disability he repaired the rafters virtually single-handed. Consequently within a few weeks the warehouse had been cleaned up and kitted out to a standard that was at least temporarily habitable although, Harry promised, a decent kitchen was yet to come.

"Wait 'til you've tasted my cooking," he warned with a twinkle. "You're in for a great surprise. Beats Mrs H's fish, that's for sure!"

They went shopping – always a trio – for mattresses and bedding; bought a dozen large cushions for lounging about on instead of chairs, a couple of kelim rugs (Harry already owned one from an earlier trip to Turkey), three heaters, a fridge and basic kitchen equipment. Curtains were voted unnecessary, there was no one to disturb their privacy. They had music, more albums, more home-made tapes and cassettes, than Penny had seen in her entire life, seemingly sufficient funds though Penny had occasionally wondered where it was all coming from, and adequate furniture. Their home was ready. The trio took up residence and all thoughts turned to the return to Greece. Penny said little. She had been talking to her agent about a role in a television series and was hoping that any day a call would come with an offer for the part. The dates would clash. It would mean that Harry and Ches would be away all summer and she would be alone in London. She decided that she would wait and see what happened before mentioning anything but the weeks went by and the call never came.

Within the apparent chaos around which their three lives were built – each one of them was without conventional employment – a Bohemian routine emerged.

Penny frequently wandered off to bed alone while Harry stayed painting. Sometimes when he fell into bed at her side she woke pleased to discover him there at last, already dawn. He had worked through the night.

Ches passed his days, and nights, rolling joints, playing music, writing lyrics and strumming along on his guitar to records of The Rolling Stones, Blind Faith, Country Joe and the Fish, Jimi Hendrix, The Band, and many others – many of the more obscure American groups. Penny had never come across them before but Ches played along with them all. Some of them he had worked with, had travelled across America with, and when he was stoned he would tell her stories that made her weep with laughter about his life on the road. Or speak of the pains and frustrations of America in the 60s; his stand against Vietnam – mercifully his lameness had prevented him being drafted but, like many others, he had friends who had lost their lives somewhere in Asia, or worse, disappeared without trace. Ches had marched in the south for civil rights, had got drunk with Dylan and had wept at the news of Martin Luther King's death. His father had been a screenwriter in Hollywood, hauled up before the House Un-American Activities Committee, blacklisted by McCarthy, driven out of the industry and starved when colleagues turned their back on him. Because of this Ches had been brought up in extreme poverty. He had left school at fourteen and gone to work. In those early tough days his family had needed his support.

Penny grew to accept Ches. Her heart forgave him for his intrusion. She learnt to appreciate him, to love his wry American humour, his strangely unconventional ways, and his loyalty to Harry and she could barely conceive now how she had felt such a force of jealousy towards him. One evening when he was strumming at his guitar – Harry had taken himself off to his attic – she laid aside her book, lured by his music. She watched him, studying him, curious about him and his lameness. She had never seen him with a woman, apart from Sandy, and so far as she knew they had not been lovers.

"Do you ever hear from Sandy?" she probed.

He simply shook his head. "She's a crazy kid."

"How did you meet her?"

"I knew her brother." There was a curtness in his response. He laid down his guitar, lit himself a cigarette and then wandered from the room.

She supposed him gay and then one morning she was alone with him in the kitchen. She was dressed only in pants and a T-shirt, making herbal tea. She felt his eyes on her and glimpsed him watching her. The expression was clear.

"Does Ches have a girlfriend in London?" she enquired of Harry when they were alone.

"He's not here all that much so I guess he does," he replied uninterestedly. And it was true he was away from the studio a great deal. Sometimes he didn't return for several days so Penny concluded finally that he was not so alone, he just preferred to keep his life private. But she did notice that when Ches was around there were always plenty of drugs about the place. That disquieted her. One night, unable to sleep, she mentioned it to Harry.

"Yeah, Ches's pretty burnt out," he answered. "But I'm gonna get him on the move again."

"How?"

"I'll find something."

"Where does he find the money from, to buy them?"

"Ask him."

Which, of course, she never did.

Harry's painting consumed a great deal of his concentration. Penny modelled regularly for him. She was grateful for the distraction. Within a short while, as he had promised, the walls were festooned with sketches and watercolours. Celebrations of her nakedness. But the weeks were rolling by and she was finding no work of her own. It felt doubly acute when she observed Harry's unrelenting commitment. As if their imminent departure spurred him on in some way. Unwilling to distract him she sat alone in the bedroom scribbling in a notebook. Rather than bottle up her disappointments, her creative barrenness, she attempted to write about them.

It was late April, a mild spring. Harry had suggested that they leave for Greece at the beginning of the third week of May. There were no objections amongst them and so it had been settled. They would drive down, all three of them, in Harry's car. It would be cramped but if they shared the driving and kept moving they could be at the ferry in Piraeus within five days, in Crete by the end of the week.

And then it happened! The call that Penny had been praying for. A job. More than a job, the plum role that she had been hoping for nearly two months earlier. Someone, another actress who had been originally cast, had dropped out and Penny was now being offered the role. Without hesitation she accepted, knowing that it precluded her spending the summer with Harry. She wanted to be with him but she needed to work. Her contract would commence on the fourth of May. The series, due to the other girl's illness, was already behind schedule. She had two weeks to break the news. She feared to do so. Her happiness at having found a job was dampened by the idea of disappointing Harry for the summer.

Inevitably each day that she postponed made the task more difficult. She told herself that she was being foolish, he would be delighted that she had found work. She must tell him, but still she hesitated. The costume designer phoned to take her shopping, hunting for her television wardrobe, and still she said nothing, even lied about where she was going. Her fear of losing or disappointing him ruled her waking days; even so she knew she must work.

One evening just as it was getting dark she returned to the warehouse – Penny always considered it the warehouse – and found him upstairs alone in his studio, his converted attic. The door was open. She tiptoed in and perched herself on a stool in the corner, without saying she was there, apprehensive about distracting him. She loved to sit and watch the shades take form. He was working on an oil-painting. It was an idea inspired by a watercolour he had completed a couple of months earlier – 'Penny Seated'. The watercolour had been set against the city skyline as seen from the studio. The painting was a closer study. Here, he was concentrating on Penny. Her limbs, her naked torso. Her head, face without detailed features, was tilted to one side, eyes closed or blinking. A scarf falling from her left leg.

He turned to her and winked. "Like it?"

"It's looking great," she encouraged. She was impressed by the growing stature of his work, the tirelessness with which he pushed forward, his confidence, his quest for self-expression. If he questioned himself she was unaware of it. He never spoke about his doubts, only about his ambitions. Rarely did he speak about himself at all. She envied him his clarity, his certainty and cursed her own diffidence.

"The BBC phoned."

A guilty flush crept across her cheeks.

"Phoned to give you your call. I've written it down. It's on the bed."

She said nothing. He knew. She watched him for a few moments longer, poised in front of his canvas, back to her, painting, assessing the impact of each considered stroke, cocooned in his world, then sheepishly she stole away, a culpable child, down the narrow wooden stairs to the note waiting on their bed. A foolscap sheet of paper which he had decorated with a china-blue watercolour, like a child's impression of puffy clouds, bore his message to her. In contrast the text had been written with green ink. Beneath the place and date of her first rehearsal were scribbled the sentences. "Great that you got the job. Silly that you said nothing. We could have celebrated."

"Ches, we're going to close off the attic, lock away the paintings and invite people over. To celebrate Penny's new role and to send us on our way," he announced a few days later.

The evening was a drawn-out crazy affair. Penny recognised only a handful of the hundreds who arrived and drifted about in an aimless sort of way.

Harry gloried in the triumph of his studio and the few paintings he had chosen to go on display. He played host with great relish, amusing and welcoming his bizarre collection of guests. He mingled, charmed (to Penny he confided, "You look ravishing"), socialised with everyone, shared their joints, served them drinks and delivered them to his groaning table of food, prepared, with Penny's assistance, by himself. He was permanently high, yet always in command, while Penny at his side was shy and diffident.

Amongst such a gathering she perceived herself the outsider and retired with her glass and a bottle of champagne to a cushion by the window from where she could more comfortably play the role of spectator; in her off-stage life she preferred such anonymity. The party had swung into full-tilt, her participation would not be missed. She was proud of Harry, also a tinge jealous of his surefootedness but always, above everything, she admired him and loved to observe him, but it had taken a social occasion such as this one for it to dawn upon her that she was not alone.

Everybody appeared to have been *bouleversé* by Harry. It was something that Penny had never twigged before. With a new urgency she watched as he strode here and there, master of his cavernous space, sporting a baggy black silk shirt, his Samson-long hair falling freely, flirting and bewitching without discrimination.

"There is something of the whore about him," she mouthed as though the idea fuelled her own love, her own lust.

Everybody was tactile with him, arms around his shoulders, breasts rubbing against his side, sidling illicitly close, chattering animatedly, craving his attention, lingering an extra stolen moment alongside his lean sensual frame. Yes, everyone wanted Harry and Harry thrived on their desire.

Penny's young cousin, Lizzie, came to flop at her side. Lizzie was seventeen, a delicate gauche creature with a bemused heart-shaped face and round green eyes. She was kooky, with strange out of place clothes, like a young secretary-bird with damaged wings. "Harry's so beautiful," Lizzie whispered shyly. She too, thought Penny.

"I know," she whispered proudly, also a little drunkenly, as though she were in some way responsible for his sexual allure.

As though he belonged to her.

There was a harem of women around him, flirting and giggling, skittish and lubricious. And then the next minute Nicholas Lockett, Harry's bespectacled gallery director, head lowered, brow frowning, intent on business or supposedly so, easing Harry towards the wall of paintings and taking every occasion to rest the palm of his hand on Harry's shoulder, coaxing him aside, away from his more frivolous chums, to have him to himself if only for a few short ecstatic seconds.

It was in that moment that Penny, for the first time, asked herself how she had held Harry's attention for so many months and then a cold dread crossed her heart. The certain knowledge that she must eventually lose him. It was simply a matter of time. This realisation sickened her until suddenly she caught his eye. Oblivious to her torment he raised his glass and grinned, winking at her, making saucy secret gestures with his tongue. Her heart soared. She loved him so, it suffused her entire being.

She was in love with Harry and in the midst of the noise, the smoke, the fug, the drugs and the party clatter she realised that she dreaded the prospect of life without him.

If she were sensible, and somewhere she had retained a modicum of sense, she could see that it couldn't last. She was too conventional for him, she worried too much, she wasn't too keen on this life style and apart from all this, there was her career. She talked about it infrequently but it mattered to her. She needed to achieve. And Harry, although he worked constantly, was easygoing. He was not a match for her earnestness. She should be the one to leave. "Go now before it's too late," she said aloud, and yet she knew she hadn't the heart for it.

No, she would stay with him. She would never let him go.

"He's mine," she said. The decision, the determined finality of it, both exhilarated and terrified her.

"Are you alright?" The tentative tinny voice of Lizzie sitting alongside her.

"Me? I'm fine. Just smoked too much dope, that's all.

I'm going to lie down."

Penny rose a little unsteadily, discovering that her head was swimming. She certainly had smoked too much dope, or drunk too much champagne, or both. The combination was lethal for her. Feeling giddy and woozy she pushed her way through numerous unknown bodies and party-frocks, determined to make the bedroom.

The room was like a shadily lit morgue with overcoats strewn across the bed, mounted in piles. She felt too wrecked to care and launched herself towards the mattress where she longed to rest for a few minutes to clear her head and then she blacked out.

It was Ches who woke her. "Harry's been looking everywhere for you," he said. Behind him was a dark-haired woman. She was leaning over his shoulder staring relentlessly like a hospital orderly. The two ill-defined faces bore quizzically down on her. "You doin' alright?" he checked.

"I smoked too much dope. It's the tobacco, it makes my head swim," she rejoined flippantly and lifted herself from the bed with effort. "What time is it?"

From a state of semi-consciousness she focused across the room. A trio of people were crouched on the floor, huddled close to one another, cross-legged, inhaling some lethal-smelling drug. A silent trio, staring blankly into space. Their bodies hunched and inanimate, like the pile of coats.

Music flooded into the room. Strange esoteric electronic sounds. "I'm going to find Harry." She rubbed her hands up and down the bodice of her dress in an attempt to iron out the shapeless creases caused by sleep and lurched from the room leaving Ches with his female companion. Pleased in some blurry way that he had after all found someone.

It was no idle whim that had led Harry to lock away the Turkish rugs, his paintings and the rest of their precious belongings as Penny realised when she crawled from beneath the duvet late the next morning. Stale tobacco, whisky, wine and God alone knew what other substances had stained and besmirched the studio walls and furnishings. Cigarette butts had been ground into the varnished floors. Even a spattering of bodies remained, long-haired nocturnal creatures, all contributing to the general untidiness of the place. "Ugh!" She skirted by them, curled and sleeping beneath cushions, dotted like dead men along her path to the kitchen.

Waiting for the water to heat she lolled for support against the refrigerator, nursing a very woolly, very thick head, listening through the walls to Ches coughing in his bed. It was a debilitating cough, scratching away at his strength, the like of which she had only heard amongst the miners in the pubs of northern England (Mrs Hardcastle's territory). Perhaps Mr Hardcastle had been such a man whose hacking cough had eventually destroyed him. Lost in such thoughts she hadn't noticed that someone was standing behind her.

"Hello."

Startled, Penny turned too quickly for such a hangover. "Oh," she wailed, "you gave me a fright."

Speaking with an accent and with irrepressible gaiety the stranger apologised. "We met last night, but you probably don't remember, I'm Helen," and without regard for the folk sleeping in the other rooms she doubled over with laughter, hooting like an over-excited owl, holding herself close against Penny's bare shoulderblade. "You were certainly out of it last night. Are you alright now?" she added with an overpowering unlikely sincerity.

Penny stared at her, tired and bemused.

She had dark hair, dark olive skin, and was wrapped in a shawl. This fell carelessly from her breasts to the curve of her perfectly formed buttocks. Peeping through the lower fringing were locks of chocolate-dark pubic hair. She looked tousled and unprepared, as one might after spending the night in an unfamiliar bed, and she smelt of a perfume that Penny recognised but

106

couldn't place. Some essential oil. Too musky for her own taste. Every last inch of varnished, bare-footed Helen conjured up images of arrogant sexual abandonment.

Penny withdrew to the stainless-steel sink to continue with the coffee which she was now feeling doubly in need of. Also to cut short the contact which she found overwhelming. "I'm better, thanks," she muttered briskly, sniffing Helen's perfume, reminded for some reason of Turkish delight. Eastern promise, she grinned silently. Fry's Turkish delight!

"Ches is still sleeping," Helen continued as if to explain her solitary presence and then, casually, she added, "Where's Harry?"

For no clear reason, and in doing it cracking her hip against the pine table, Penny swung her attention back from the preparation of coffee, as though something more crucial had been said. Either an inflection in Helen's accent or some instinct on Penny's part caused her to want to face the unknown woman directly, to take in her features and to learn something about her. "Harry's sleeping," she replied cagily. "I'm just making us some coffee."

"I'd love some herbal tea," Helen sung out and when Penny made no move to help her she stretched to the overhead cupboard in search of what she fancied. "I'll make it," she grinned complicitously. Penny smiled a tight-lipped smile (she's been here before) and moved away to the table in search of a tray for the cups that she had previously rescued and washed from the depressingly dense stack of crockery lying greasy in the sink. The sight of it made her feel considerably worse.

She stared out of the window and sighed, listening to the rain flowing into the drains, waiting for her coffee to percolate, regretting her thick head and conscious that she was feeling indisputably grizzly. Occasionally she glanced back towards Helen, more than a little curious about her. With her corny Turkish delight image she was not the girl Penny would have chosen for Ches.

Maybe she was just a one-night stand. She doesn't even shave beneath her arms, Penny judged ungenerously.

Helen ignored Penny's vibes and went industriously about her tea-making. Every few moments she ran her ringed fingers through her long dark hair in a pointless attempt to stop it falling into her face. Every gesture she made caused the bands of fine silver bracelets on both her arms to jangle against one another thus creating the illusion that she moved to a rippling of music. Penny was finding this intensely aggravating.

She sneaked glances at her. Helen was voluptuous, full and earthy, a vision of breasts and hair, and although Penny never as a rule found such women attractive she had to admit, albeit grudgingly, that Helen was bloody good-looking. And she knows it, she mused. She wondered about her accent which she was at a loss to place and settled on Italian. A southern Italian peasant, and then, given the rather outrageous drape of the fringed salmon-pink shawl, she decided upon Egyptian – Cleopatra gone missing from the local amateur dramatic society!

"How long have you known Harry?" Helen asked, breaking the silence. Funny, thought Penny. I was just considering the same question.

"A few months," she said aloud. Suddenly she was conscious that she was feeling not only hungover but also pretty blue. Her memories of the evening before were hazy but something was preying on her mind, some niggling doubt. Why did she lack Helen's inexorable confidence? Had something happened between her and Harry?

"Are you going back to Greece with him?"

Penny shook her head, "No, I have to work."

Harry was leaving in one more week. She was going to be without him for the entire summer. Was that why she was feeling depressed? Suddenly, unreasonably, she felt resentful towards Helen. She wanted to be alone with him. No more intruders. And she felt threatened by this ebullient woman. "Are you going?"

"Possibly. I have a house in the mountains there. It's very beautiful. Ask Harry, he knows it well. Ches says you're an actress. That's exciting! My mother was an actress, very famous in Greece. I'd like to be in movies too."

"Really?" The coffee was ready. Penny filled her two cups, rested the jug of milk in place and lifted the tray. "See you later," she said and slipped away conscious that she had been cold and unfriendly. She had just recognised Helen's perfume. It was patchouli oil. And the accent, how could she have missed it, was Greek.

It was still raining; an incessant rain. One that is known only in northern European climes – grey and sharp, a mean, pinched, cheerless sort of rain that falls from the sky without generosity as if its sole purpose is to dampen the already limp city spirit.

Penny brushed the Sunday papers to the floor and poured herself another cup of cold coffee while Harry, still sleeping, lay buried beneath the sheets at her side. She decided that she might as well take a bath and face the mountain of cleaning up. Someone had to do it and a little exertion might exorcise her weepy mood.

Alone in the living-room, save for the sleeping party-makers whom she regarded merely as untidy pieces of furniture, she swept and tidied with a furious resolution, determined to bury the testiness which had been building within her and the question which had been nagging at her the entire morning.

Grumpy strangers disturbed by the noise awoke and drifted away from around her. Helen floated to and fro offering to give a hand and then seduced by something more inviting disappeared again.

Harry eventually appeared, looking wrecked. "Too much champagne," he crooned, brushing her face lightly with a kiss and disappearing into the bathroom.

"Shall I make us some lunch or help you finish all this?"

"You make lunch," she replied, more tartly than she

109

might have wished.

He made the lunch which they took upstairs to the attic and ate together. Cheese omelettes and fries and a bottle of Burgundy.

"I want to finish this oil before I leave next week," he said. "Nicholas promised to exhibit everything in the autumn after I return."

"It's very good," she encouraged, without too much enthusiasm.

There was a sadness between them, growing from the knowledge of their imminent separation.

"Harry, last year when you went to Athens to buy watercolours . . . "

The vagueness of his expression told her that he was lost. He had forgotten, wasn't connecting.

"After we met you went to Athens, remember, to buy watercolours?" For a reason that Penny could not fathom, and from a place that she had not looked into, the question appeared. Suddenly it mattered to her, it mattered desperately to know where he had gone. Why, if he had later searched her out and found her, why had he not taken hold of her then? Why had he just disappeared?

"Why didn't you ask me to go with you?"

"That was last year. Does it matter now?" he asked, seeking through tired penetrating eyes to understand what was happening.

"Yes," she wept, staring into her cold mess of eggs and seeping ketchup. "Was there someone else?" she blurted out.

He stroked her wet face, reddened and made patchy by her tears.

"Was there, Harry?" she insisted. Knowing seemed to matter more than anything else in that moment, more than him, more than the constant gnawing fear of losing him.

"She was someone I knew before we met," he conceded, puzzled by the force of her concern.

"Was it Helen?"

110

Harry was startled by the question, by its ferocity.

"Does it really make any difference?" He rose and moved to the stool where she was perched, leaning forward, cradling her stomach as if in pain. Without waiting for her answer, understanding that for Penny it did make a difference, he stroked her hair and whispered, "Yes, Pen, it was Helen."

Penny exhaled, expelling breath as though releasing something long-held, an anxiety long choking her. Dark-eyed beautiful Helen, it would have to have been her. "Is she going back to Greece with you?"

"I don't know," he murmured. "Ask Ches."

7

Outside in the wintry darkness the mountain evening was winding down. Shouts of weary excess and jubilation shivered in the cool night air. The stragglers, the all-nighters, tarrying in the moonlight, were beginning to wend their ways to various corners of the house or grounds, ready to hit the hay. Penny was suddenly aware of voices calling from across the terrace, slurred goodnights. She rested the crumpled pages of her script onto her lap and relaxed her head back against the casement. She, as much as they, was conscious of the lateness of the hour. "Should've remembered to call Peter. Must get some sleep," she murmured, her lids droopy with drowsiness. She rose with a heavy almost half-hearted motion as if already believing that it would be a pointless exercise. The fire had died down to embers. Her limbs had gone dead, her buttocks were numb. Too long curled up immobile on the cramped wooden window-sill. She took a step or two towards the bathroom and the blood flowed back into her feet. They tingled and stung her.

A tapping at the door, at first unnoticed, interrupted her, intruding upon her private world thick with lingering memories. She glanced at her watch wondering who the hell it could be and a momentary rush of fear ran through her. Something had happened to Peter. Tossing her script onto the bed she drew her dressing-gown more firmly about her and made for the door, releasing it just a fraction.

"I was passing. Heard you moving. Thought you might be restless, might want to talk about the script." It was Jimmy Gaza. He looked dog-tired, dishevelled. Not for the first time in her life did she find him standing at her bedroom door. In former days it had threatened her and an age-old hostility rose up within her, an automatic safeguard, which she swiftly scuppered. Tonight he appeared a little pitiable.

"Were you sleeping?"

She shook her head. "No, I was thinking, reading the scenes that lead up to Nikos's death."

Whispered voices on the stairs caused them both to turn their heads.

"Let me in," he ordered sharply and, as if as a protection against gossip, judging uncomprehending eyes, she opened the door another foot, sufficiently wide for him to slip by her without brushing against her, closing it firmly after him. Moments later the voices had mounted to the corridor and passed by, making a business of talking quietly, giggling, preparing for a night of something unexpected. Gaza hovered in the centre of the room, at the foot of the bed, like an awkward butler. She smelt beer and cigarettes and late-in-the-evening odour.

"Sit down." Her words were spoken brusquely, almost an order. He was in because he had turned up and because she preferred the distraction of company to the interminably sleepless night ahead. He had unsettled her earlier but she was taking charge. She was feeling defensive in his company but she was determined to handle it.

"Why aren't you sleeping?" He sat himself on the bed and buried his head in his hands, rubbing at his face with his palms as though scrubbing himself with a flannel.

"I was going back over the story." She walked to the bedside, watched by him, and poured herself a glass of Perrier water. "You want some of this?"

He shook his head as if disgusted by such an idea. "Do you believe this stuff?"

"What?"

"All this. This kid and the painter."

Penny sighed and took a a sip of water. It revived her a fraction. "What are you trying to get at, Jimmy?"

He reached in his pocket for a pack of cigarettes and

slipped one between his lips, fumbling for matches. The bags beneath his small sharp eyes were accentuated by the darkness in the room. She thought he looked more than a hundred years old.

"You gotta light?"

"You know damned well I don't smoke and what's more I don't like you smoking in my room."

"Doesn't mean you don't have matches. Have you?"

She glared down at him. He had leant forward, resting his elbows on his knees, head down as though unaware of her presence, as though she didn't exist. She knew this. He'd face her when he was ready, not a moment before. "In the bathroom," she responded testily.

"We oughta go back over the whole damned thing and see what's missing," he called. She could hear him inhaling on the cigarette while at the same time running water into the sink, to splash on his face no doubt.

Don't shout, she thought, unless you want the whole bloody crew to start gossiping. "If you think so," was all she said.

He reappeared at the door and faced her. The glow of the lit cigarette burnt brightly in the darkness, half illuminating his craggy pitted features.

"What made you write this?"

"I thought it might make a good story, that's all."

"Who's the guy?"

"Someone I met on a beach."

He glared at her with an intensity, a certainty that unnerved her. "It feels pretty ugly what you're carrying, huh?"

"You're tired and you've had too much beer. You're getting out of your depth, Jimmy."

"Don't give me that shit, Penny! I know you too damned well. You despise me and you think that makes you feel good. It makes you self-righteous, that's what it makes you. You've been lying to yourself for years! You can't do that in this job. Not if what you want is good work. I don't give two hoots about you being a good

114

person but I'll give a whole lot to see you front up. Face it, Penny. Use it. You think I don't wake up every day haunted by stuff in my life? Believe me, I do. So, let's look at what we've really got here."

Crete. Late summer, 1973.

Penny's charter flight landed her back in Crete. Harry was not there to greet her because she had not informed him of her imminent arrival. Why? Because she wanted it to be a surprise.

Directly she had been cleared through passport control she hired herself a truck and headed along the winding, skerried mountainous roads, travelling ceaselessly back to the village as though nothing else in the world mattered, driving south. Back to Harry.

She arrived after nightfall. Wearied by the concentration and the travelling she drew the jeep to a halt in the square and gazed stupidly at the bus terminus where one solitary vehicle had been left stationed in preparation for its next day's journey back to Iráklion. She sat a moment in stillness, imbibing the warm night, enveloped in the darkness, listening to the waves licking against the deserted shore. To and fro they rolled, tempering the palpitations of her restless heart. She was both elated and speedy with nervous anticipation.

She stepped from the jeep and stretched, reaching heavenwards with every young muscle, inhaling the heavy perfumes, treasures from the towering pines and the fire-red geraniums, awakening her nubile body. She was hungry for Harry, for his embraces, and she allowed her sexual desire to flood in upon her.

Nothing had altered in the year that she had been away. Another white cube house or two may have been erected, there were perhaps a few less hippies strumming guitars or wandering aimlessly beneath the stream of moonlight but little else. It was reassuring.

She carted her suitcase in the falling darkness towards Harry's rented home, listening for music or other signs of his presence, but she heard only the lazy guggling of rockpools and the crunch of roped soles. Her own espadrilles treading against the irregular path. Every footstep was bringing her closer to him.

Her step faltered between his and the neighbouring house as she trod the familiar rutted walkway. She had caught sight of a play of shadows cast on the sand directly in front of her ... a corner of the house, branches of the tamarisk tree, the head of a figure moving into view, and then ... her pulse beat rapidly in her stomach ... the lengthened shadow of the figure itself hovered and then came to a standstill. She knew without hesitation by the form, by the length of the falling hair, that the silhouette belonged to Harry. Her mouth became parched, her heart beat heavily beneath her breast. Fourteen weeks they had been separated. She had counted every day, battling so vigorously with herself, with her stupid volatile emotions, trying not to miss him or to drive herself crazy wondering if he were with Helen. Her constant yearning for him had worn into her and she was wary now of a rush of pent-up sentiment. She longed to simply let go of her suitcase and run to him, a scene she had seen in so many films, but instead, needing to be certain, she merely quickened her pace, stepped onto the sand, which spilled into her shoes, and waited in the falling darkness for him to discover her.

Pressed against the trunk of the tamarisk tree, feeling its bark against the small of her back, she drank in the moment, the stillness of the night. The sight of him restored her equilibrium.

He stood, profile to her, leaning into the open doorway, holding a glass of red wine in his hand, silently observing the water lapping metres in front of him. He was not expecting her. Clearly he had not heard her footsteps, and, most importantly, he appeared to be alone.

"Harry," she muttered softly. Too softly. He did not hear.

Smiling, she deposited her suitcase in the sand and stood framed within the feathery shadow of the tamarisk. From wherever, some place inland, an owl hooted. In the village someone's child began to bawl. Elsewhere a bouzouki scratched out a native tune. Harry took a leisurely swig from his glass, his other hand high above his head rested against the door frame.

She watched him in silence — her breath light and quick against her flushed face — almost as a voyeur might watch, taking pleasure in the proximity of his body and its language, waiting to speak again, tantalisingly, until eventually, with a dry disbelieving mouth, she articulated his name.

He turned his head swiftly but doubted the soft note of her voice, yet still his blue eyes searched for her. "Pen, is that you?"

She moved a foot from beneath the shadow of the tree and stood, nodding, smiling at him.

"What are you doing here?" he enquired, puzzled.

"Aren't you pleased to see me?"

For an endless moment she stood in terror, her wide hazel eyes searching his for some understanding, until he jettisoned his glass and its contents onto the sand at his feet. She heard the lip of the glass land and sink into the yielding sand and waited while he stepped towards her, gathering her into his arms.

Motionless they stood, inhaling one another's proximity beneath a parasol of stars. Wine leaking from his discarded glass stole silently between the particles of sand as waves washed against the shore. Sketched in the distance behind them other young couples were strolling, bare- or sandal-footed, hand in hand to supper.

Penny felt the strength of his breast against her cheek and was restored. Doubt slid away from her. Long months of empty hankering dissolved. He drew her inside the untidy house and led her up the stairway to the room where they had first met, where they had first loved, and where they were now reunited and there they stayed locked in one another's embraces until early morning . . . It was only then that she recollected leaving her suitcase beneath the tamarisk tree and, when she went in search of it, to her amazement and delight she found that it was still there. Later, she and Harry sat in the sun and ate yoghurt together.

He seemed pensive, affectionate yet preoccupied and prickly.

He explained that he was hard at work on an oil-painting which he was anxious to finish before the weekend.

"Where's Ches?"

"Went off to the mountains to visit Helen."

It was the first mention of her name since Penny's return.

"Is that close by?" She detested the question; clear that she was testing him, that she mistrusted him.

"You'd need a car. It's a bit of a distance. Inland, along the south-west stretch of the island."

How many times might he have made that journey during these fourteen weeks? She refrained from asking and Harry, being Harry, proffered no answer. Instead he disappeared inside to work, out of the sun. Rather than simply idle away her day on the beach and because she was hellishly restless she decided to rent a bicycle from Spiros. Spiros owned the beach taverna which she and Harry had frequented the previous season. She found him sweeping around the tables looking sullen.

"How's your crazy young son, Demetrius?" she enquired light-heartedly. "Did he make it to Athens, after all?" But Spiros was unwilling to discuss anything apart from the hiring of the bike.

His reticence confused Penny, she had known him so warm, so extrovert, so jealously proud of his solitary offspring, but she dismissed it as a mood and set off into the baking day, deciding to use her spare time profitably, to do a little sightseeing. She would start with a visit to Phaistos, simply because it was the closest. Off she rolled for the day, singing into the wind, singing to keep her spirits up, to ward off the doubts looming. In spite of a stabbing misgiving she willed herself to be happy, content at least to be back in Crete.

Phaistos drew her away from her anxiety. Its cinema-scopic splendour overwhelmed her, exciting her imagination. She wandered about the ruins dreaming herself into long-since vanished times while a welcome breeze whispered through her loose summer clothing. At midday, to avoid the scorching heat and the noisy queues, the bus-loads of tourists, she considered return-ing to the house to share a sandwich with Harry. But some insecurity changed her mind and she cycled the length of a dusty rutted lane, flying past olive terraces, easy pedalling downhill, to a small taverna whose sign she had spotted on her approach. It was spacious and welcoming, yet almost deserted, unfrequented because it lay about four kilometres inland.

Towards evening, fatigued and sticky from dust and heat she returned to find Harry, relaxed now, sitting in the shade drinking ouzo with a dark-haired stranger who rose to greet her. "It's good to see you again. Wel-come back to Crete." The greeting had been formal, it lacked the warmth of any smile.

"Thank you." She was searching keenly, sifting through her memory trying to place him. It took a moment but eventually she recognised him, Nikos the heroic Athenian painter. She had met him briefly the summer before. He had grown older, seeming far more now than his less than forty years. His face had hollowed out, he was scraggy and unshaven and he had removed his splendid moustache. Gone was the proud musketeer. In his place stood a man with weary features filled with a tempered dismay. She detected great sadness. It was a shock to behold such a transformation.

"I was saying to Nikos that my painting is finished, or will be tonight," said Harry. "I thought we might drive to the mountains tomorrow. Join Ches and Helen for the weekend. We can take your jeep. My car is a bit tight for three."

Penny glanced at Nikos, not understanding. "How's your family?" she ventured.

"Visiting my mother on the mainland." His response was chilly, defensive. It puzzled her.

"I did some shopping. Bought some salad, some fetta and stuff while you were sightseeing. I've asked Nikos if he'd like to eat with us," Harry told her. Nikos had graciously accepted their invitation.

"Has something happened?" she asked once the meal had been prepared and they had, all three, settled at Harry's handmade table alongside the Mediterranean.

"I have a brother in Athens," Nikos explained softly. "A rather well-known young doctor. He's been arrested and thrown into prison. But worse, they've locked him up at a place called Asfáleia. It's renowned for its inhuman treatment of the prisoners."

"One hell of a place."

"Why?"

"Crimes against the State, what they refer to as Un-American Activities. Car bombings, stuff like that. America supports our Colonels."

"Is that why your family have returned to the mainland?"

He nodded and tossed a chewed olive stone into the sand.

"But won't it be dangerous for them there?" she asked.

"They have gone to stay with my mother. She's a widow. My brother lived with her until his arrest so now she's alone. All this has been a terrible blow to her. She's an old lady, she needs support, companionship, at this time. Melina, you remember my wife, she offered to go because I could not. I dare not leave here. It would be too dangerous for me."

"What about your children?"

"She's taken them with her. She thought it would be better for my mother to have her grandchildren around her. Give her something to occupy her."

It seemed curious to Penny that Nikos should put his

family at risk like that. She wondered why he could not have gone himself.

After supper all three of them walked the length of the bay, strolling in the fresh night air, and they sat for a while in the sand. A light breeze drifted in from Africa. Penny listened silently as the two men talked and drank another bottle.

Nikos, drunk, maudlin and lost in his past, spoke of his father.

"He died in the great winter famine in '42. Greece was occupied and there were severe food shortages. The rations were being stolen before they reached the people. Thousands starved to death. My father was amongst them. I was less than seven years old and my brother not even two. My mother brought us up alone. She was twenty-six and a widow . . ." He pummelled at the sand with the dead wine bottle. "Alone. Now Greece is oppressed again. My brother, like my father, is fighting back. My mother lost her husband. She fears now that she will lose her second son. I cannot stand by and do nothing!" he raged, tossing the bottle irreverently into the sea. It plopped in the darkness, salty sprays rose a short way into the night. Penny glanced towards Harry who was sitting some distance from her, seemingly unaware of her. She wondered if it was painful for him to see his friend so miserable, so lamentably wretched. She had no way of knowing.

She felt content to be back in the village but the atmosphere had visibly changed. Was Harry slipping away from her? Even Spiros, welcoming, ebullient Spiros, from whom she had hired her bicycle that morning, had behaved cautiously, if not suspiciously, towards her. It seemed that the political problems from the mainland were finally catching up with the people here.

Nikos worn out by his own anger and enfeebled by alcohol wept like a broken man. He buried his stubbled face in the curve of his elbow. Penny sat at his side lightly caressing his arched back.

"Go back to the house, Penny. I'm going to walk him

back to his place," Harry suggested. "I'll see you back there in a while."

"But why?"

"He won't make it alone. He's drunk too much," he whispered to her.

"But why can't I help you?" she rejoined, injured by Harry's abrupt dismissal of her.

"Just let me handle it will you, Pen." And she knew better than to argue with his determination.

Penny lay awake that night feeling crushed, cut to the quick because Harry was not dealing more openly with her, and she felt a dreadful disquiet for the future welfare of Nikos and his family. It crossed her mind that Nikos might probably be in some kind of personal trouble. Some problem which he and Harry had chosen not to disclose to her. His eyes were those of a tormented man, a hunted, despairing one. A man in mortal danger. They betrayed a truth which neither he nor Harry would share. The fear expressed was too exaggerated even for a brother.

Penny longed to confront Harry, to encourage him to confide in her, to woo him back to her, but by the time they went to sleep it was late. After Harry's return they had made love, at her instigation, but it had turned out to be a somewhat disconnected encounter during which few words had been spoken. Nothing had been mentioned of their months apart. There had been no time. She lay sleepless at his side now, aware that there had been a change in him, shrinking from what might have brought about this change. He seemed remote, more sombre than she had known him in the past. His enthusiasm had disappeared, so too his humour and love.

She cursed bitterly their plan to spend the weekend at Helen's. It did not bode well.

They set off the next morning before dawn in Penny's hired truck, driving west along the coast with the sun rising steadily onto their backs. In spite of complaints of a headache and a hangover Nikos was in good spirits, if a trifle over-hearty, reiterating continually the wisdom of travelling before the sun got too high. Penny wondered why he had arrived at the house weighed down by two bulging bags; one a Gladstone bag cut and sewn from a local cured leather, the other an earth-brown shoulder-bag, slung over him like some hefty great root bulb. She was curious to know why he should be travelling so uneconomically and presumed that he must be armed with various painting materials so that he might take advantage of the spectacular mountain views that both he and Harry had promised her.

He installed himself in the truck next to Harry, who was driving, and she settled herself in the back, moderately comfortably and only momentarily disgruntled because Harry had not even thought to offer her the seat alongside him. The two men conversed in Greek, rarely bothering to address her, though with the rattling of the engine she could not have heard them even if they had. Their conversation was heated and intense. Many cigarettes were lit and after several desperate drags were tossed from out of the open sides of the truck onto the narrowing bitumen road. She idly speculated about what they might be discussing but eventually she settled back to enjoy the monumental nature. She was wrestling with her ever-increasing jealousy towards Helen. She blamed her for what she perceived as the dampening in Harry's ardour. How much had he been seeing of her and how was she going to stand it when they were all three together?

They stopped en route for a swim and a picnic on the beach, enjoying sandwiches and fruit which Penny had hastily thrown together before their departure. She spoke and ate little during the sojourn. Harry didn't appear to notice. Nikos on the other hand showed himself more sensitive. He found an amber pendant attached to a gold chain. It was knotted and sand encrusted, buried beneath drift-weed. He returned to the salt water, washed it clean and then offered it to Penny as she came dripping from the sea.

"To complement your eyes," he said as she, with his

123

help, clipped the gold chain around her neck.

After breakfast they took a route which led them inland towards the upper mouth of the stupendous Samaria Gorge. The road wound, as though travelling up river, through lush tableland where the warm air was perfumed with citrus fruit and the light became soft, subdued, dreamlike. Pruned, neatly toiled orange groves surrounded them on every side. It seemed suddenly magical, almost out of human time, and an idyllic prelude to their approaching weekend. She felt seduced by the loveliness. It offered a portent of blessed days, better tidings than she had been figuring.

As they climbed higher into the mountains the road disappeared. It had disintegrated into a dirt track. The air grew crisper, not cooler, simply less dense. The vegetation became more arid, there were fewer flowers, fewer colours, little more than irregular clumps of perfumed shrubs scattered about the hillsides, parched by the dry cloddy soil. They spotted an occasional herder, solitary souls living isolated in their *mitatos* (stone huts) watching over their goats and sheep. It was high summer. The goats were close by, clambering here and there. In winter they would be driven back down the mountain to graze within sight of the villages.

Quite suddenly the sniffle of breeze that had been protecting them disappeared and the heat became intolerable, just as though they had driven into a bread oven. It accentuated the appalling stench of petrol fumes which had begun rising from the jeep and gnawing into their burnt senses. Penny began feeling nauseous. Even the men had grown silent. Nature was mistress now. They were irrelevant alongside her awesome majesty. Just as the citrus groves had lured and lulled them with their gentle femininity, now this with its arch regality could terrorise and crush them.

And then a little after ten o'clock – almost five hours after their departure – as the jeep struggled mule-like to drag its unwilling load up the winding granite hillside, Harry pointed out their destination.

"See there," he said, "where the nature is more varied, more cultivated, that's Helen's place."

It loomed like a fairy tale out of the now lunar mountainside. Surrounding them now as they approached, almost as far as the eye could see, terrace upon terrace of crudely irrigated olive trees. Circling the base of each trunk were lengths of black nylon netting, laid in preparation for the upcoming harvest or more likely left over from the last, for this was not the season when families gathered together on the terraces with sticks to beat the olives from the trees.

They passed through a village, the last before their destination. In reality it was no more than a hamlet with its modest clump of ill-assorted houses built in higgledy-piggledy rows clinging precariously to the mountainside. One might believe that any movement would send the village circling into space, lost forever in the universe. The streets were quite deserted but the *kafenéion*, the local coffee shop was not. Obviously this was the meeting place.

"Let's get a drink," Nikos suggested testily. "I need cigarettes and aspirin. This bloody heat is stewing me."

"*Yássou! Yássou!*" An elderly woman dressed entirely in black cried out to them. Greeting them warmly she dragged out chairs for them, pointing and guiding them towards an uneven table sheltered beneath lush vine-leaves. Harry shook her hand; she was smiling like a grey-haired girl thrilled to bits to see him. He ordered two beers from her as he and Penny settled themselves in the staked-out shade, grateful for an opportunity to be out of the heat. Nikos had already disappeared inside, striding towards the bar. His need was apparent.

"She seems to know you very well, that old woman?"

"Sometimes I bicycle from the house and stop for a beer. Strength for the climb back up again."

So it would seem, she deduced, that Helen's home has been welcoming him.

"The change in Nikos is quite shocking." Penny refused to reflect on the idea of Harry and Helen

125

together. Thankfully, at that instant their two beers arrived.

"And some water. *Neró, parakaló.*"

The old woman nodded cheerfully and disappeared inside, in search of Penny's water while Harry supped at his drink. Penny glanced about her. A sweet smell of fig leaves encompassed them, cradling them seductively from the heat. An aged mustachioed man riding a grey mule, his short-haired mongrel following a few weary lengths behind him, clopped through the village at a snail's pace. Past the coffee shop he went, waving economically to recognised companions.

"Whereabouts are we exactly? It seems so foreign, so unlike anywhere else I've visited."

Above her in the blinding blue sky an eagle pitched in search of its prey. Harry didn't respond. He was preoccupied, lost elsewhere, studying the faces of the drinkers in this outdoor café.

"Once upon a time all these men were partisan soldiers, defiant brothers, now they are unlikely olive farmers, all ageing Cretans."

Their weather-beaten brown skins were as creased as old potatoes. The couple of dozen men were sitting in groups of twos and threes, hiding themselves from the mid-morning sun. Some were drinking coffee and *ráki*, others were locked in weighty dispute over unknown matters, a few were playing cards or backgammon, while one or two simply sat, side by side, silently agitating at their worry beads. In spite of the heat they were dressed in jackboots, elegant pantaloons, and wore black beaded kerchiefs wrapped about their skulls like curtain fringing. Harry nodded a greeting.

"*Yássou,*" several returned delightedly. Their watery eyes burned with the pride of a life courageously lived.

"You know why I love this island?" said Harry. "Because here men like Nikos might have a chance to survive the dictatorship. Look at these old guys sitting here. Every single one of them, without exception, would line up and fight for their freedom again if they had to, in spite of their age, with that same fury that strengthened them against Metaxas before the war. Their sons and wives too. These people spit on the Colonels. They despise them. The only reason they do nothing is because Athens has not touched them here, not yet. Greek politics is not necessarily Cretan politics. But they would risk their lives again for their liberty, if they had to. You just have to ask them."

"I think you're being romantic," she laughed, edging him away from what appeared to be an ill humour.

"And what do we do? Sod all. At best we write protest songs and smoke joints."

"What's wrong with that?"

"Don't be naïve, Pen. Even Ches, lame as he is, marched for civil rights in the south in the sixties. He left school and went out to work at fourteen because his father had been blacklisted by McCarthy in Hollywood. I can't sit back and do nothing."

Penny watched an anger rising within him. She had never seen him like this before. She turned in search of Nikos. He was drinking at the bar, slaking an unquenchable thirst, a bottle of Metaxa his companion.

"I hope to God Nikos is going to be safe up here. Come on, let's get going," said Harry, rising. "I promised Helen we'd be there for breakfast." He deposited a handful of coins on the table in front of him and strode on ahead without even a cursory glance back towards her.

8

"You're late!" cried Helen, waving and cooing with much urgent enthusiasm. Dressed in a bikini and open shirt, she was straddled across a scooter which she used, apparently, for getting about the grounds. "Ches and I have been waiting since dawn. We're ravenous!" And the scooter roared off in a cloud of dust, billowing cotton and long dark hair. It led the jeep-weary trio from the wrought-iron gates where Helen had been waiting for them towards the house. This proved to be as dramatic as the setting in which it had been built. Bananas and lissom palms flanked the climbing driveway. The air was clear and smelt sweet and birds busied themselves in the unexpected forest of green.

Nikos let out an appreciative whistle while Penny's heart sank slowly. I might have guessed, was what she was thinking.

The exterior of the mansion, for that was what it was, had been whitewashed and constructed around a central courtyard in traditional southern Mediterranean style. Every aspect, save for the south which overlooked the valleys and distant ocean, was sheltered by fragrant aspens and towering cypress trees. As they drew to a halt Penny spotted someone waving from the flat roof. It was Ches, silhouetted against the sunlight. He was standing beneath a great vine which had been trained across the roof and was supported by lengths of trellised cane, thus forming itself into an immense, natural, elongated parasol. From it hung bunches of rich ripe grapes ready for the eating.

They descended from the jeep.

Helen, chattering in Greek, warmly embraced both Harry and Nikos. "Grab your stuff," she added in English before giving Penny a perfunctory kiss on her right cheek. "Come on, I'll show you around."

She headed off towards the inner courtyard with the two men escorting her. The conversation had reverted back to Greek. Penny's presence had been forgotten or worse, dismissed.

Multicoloured exotic birds cawed and screeched, scudding about the place like witches on broomsticks. Fresh spring water ran through the central courtyard. Tumbling from the rock from which the house had been constructed it flowed through the court and by its natural music cooled the inhabitants.

Penny learned later that Helen was the daughter of a wealthy Greek industrialist who, after an acrimonious divorce from Helen's mother in 1970, had settled an estate on his only daughter, a portion of which Helen had spent on the building of this fantastic summer house.

In Eastern fashion, shoes were removed and left at the door. The quartet entered, barefooted, into an opulence which almost surpassed the beauty of its natural setting. Sweeping expanses of white marble floors were punctuated by pillars and archways inlaid with jet and mother-of-pearl. There were no doors. A labyrinth of open-plan living areas, leading one to another. These rooms were multi-layered with a step here, a corner there. A generous supply of embroidered cushions in varying shades of terracotta and kelims had been scattered about the place. Unfamiliar Eastern music was playing. Wherever the new arrivals and their hostess wandered piercing scratchy notes accompanied them. To Penny's ill-attuned ear the scrannelled melodies set her teeth on edge. Memories of fingernails on blackboards. She was overwhelmed by the affluence and wished that she hadn't come but resisted the notion that her return to Greece had been a mistake.

"I think I'll go and find Ches," she announced pointedly, drawing their attention towards her, feeling nettled by her inability to speak the language. Helen was flirting outrageously with Harry, she had slipped her left arm through his while with her right hand she was gesticulating, apparently pointing out directions to the various bedrooms.

"He's on the roof," replied Harry, smiling at something one of his companions must have said.

Helen being witty, no doubt, thought Penny, responding, "I know," curtly, intending her vexation to be noted, but he was paying no attention.

"Shall I come with you?" whispered Nikos.

Penny shook her head. She wandered off in what seemed an inner direction in search of stairs.

Persian and Siamese cats roamed about the place with self-conceit. She counted five. Two had sprawled themselves across the furnishings, another was coiled alongside a pot bearing an African oil-palm, the others were on the move. She had never before witnessed such vain wealth. It had an unsettling effect upon her which was somehow intensified by the cats. Their limpid Oriental eyes seemed to bear down upon her. She found them nothing short of malevolent.

"You haven't found Ches? He's sitting outside on the roof-terrace, reading. Let's all join him." Helen's voice from behind her. The commanded party moved forward, led as always by Helen – who had discarded her shirt, leaving her with the bikini – through French windows into a blanket of heat. From there they ascended a whitewashed stone staircase, which had been carved into one of the exterior walls of the house, to a terrace one level below the roof. This overlooked a sweep of verdant valleys that led rippling without breath to the distant emerald Mediterranean.

Ches was lounging in the shade of a sprawling, fruiting fig tree. The ripe fruit exuded a heady perfume.

"Lunch first, business later!" Helen clapped her hands, her bracelets jangled. Moments later, wine, glasses and water arrived, carried on an ornate silver tray by a strikingly handsome young Oriental boy. Penny smiled seductively at him. If Harry was going to play around with Helen she would have her revenge.

The boy, astounded, disappeared hurriedly.

Helen poured wine while her guests imbibed the beauty of the landscape which surrounded them. From the courtyard below, shattering the tranquillity, a macaw screeched ferociously, screeching and screeching without respite. Across the backdrop of mountains it sounded, down into the valleys, echoing like a razor-sharp death-cry. Penny felt sweat break out on her neck. She shifted in her chair and sipped rapidly at her drink. Without shade the heat would have been insidious. It beat into her like a tribal drum warning of some upcoming disaster.

An overwhelming desire to flee suffused her. Anywhere, just to get away from the place. She found it oppressive. It was not simply the heat. A portent of something unknown settled within her, as though an act irreversibly evil were about to be committed. She longed to flee to the coast, to the African winds, to be alone somewhere with Harry, anywhere other than here. And yet she was curious about all that she was witnessing, drawn in against her volition.

"Thank you," she murmured, her voice came uneasily. Helen had placed dark voluptuous olives onto the table in front of her.

Conversation returned to English.

"Nikos, your wife telephoned." The tone of Helen's voice was disarmingly seductive. She smiled towards Penny as if in some way this called upon her as accomplice.

"You should have told me sooner. What did she say?" Nikos's bleary ochre eyes expressed his concern.

Helen, serious now, glanced furtively in Penny's direction before replying. She spoke in Greek. Nikos took a long drag on his cigarette, stubbed at it anxiously and left the table after refilling his glass to take it with him. He hurried from the terrace back down the stairs as Helen called after him, "Yours is the room straight ahead of you," adding coquettishly, out of earshot, "Next to mine."

Two servants appeared, soft footing to and fro like shy girls, bearing dishes laden with hors d'oeuvres, several varieties of olives, fig-leaves stuffed with rice, taramasalata, an assortment which the two men placed on the table in front of the seated group, before melting once more out of sight.

When they had disappeared Helen turned to Harry and said, "Melina asked me if I thought Nikos would be safe here. You know I could only say, let us hope so. She is very frightened for him and for the children. Did anyone see you arriving?"

Harry, guarded as ever, shook his head. He was sitting to Penny's left drinking in the atmosphere, listening to Helen without regarding her. He drew out a tobacco tin and rolled a cigarette. Nobody touched the food. "You should have been more encouraging. Otherwise we'll never persuade her to join him here."

"She probably shouldn't have gone back to the mainland at all," Ches added eventually.

"What is she so afraid of?" Penny asked. "His brother was arrested because he is in opposition to the government. And has expressed it openly, violently. Why should that affect his brother's children? Unless Nikos is in trouble himself." Almost before Penny had finished speaking Nikos stepped back onto the terrace. He looked distressed and worn out.

"Melina says that the police came knocking at my mother's door early this morning. They were asking for me. They have been harassing the children, asking them of my whereabouts."

"They'll never find you here," assured Helen. Her manner had assumed a more confident, comforting air.

"Nikos, for God's sake talk to Melina. Tell her to come back immediately. Bring the children here. Your mother, too. No one will trace you here, and Helen doesn't mind." Helen smiled, affirming Harry's words. "I'll meet them off the plane in Iráklion and drive them straight back here myself. It's safer than returning to the village. You never know who's informing – "

"Harry's right," Helen interrupted. "The less people know what's happening the better for you."

"Phone her back now and tell her to make the arrangements. If she's afraid, if she prefers, I'll meet her in Athens. Tell her. But she mustn't phone here again. It's too dangerous."

Penny listened to Harry's words, to his instructions to Nikos, with an incredulous ear. Nikos was not convinced. He sat and lit a cigarette and poured himself another wine. "She's concerned for my mother. She's an old lady. Too old for such travel."

"Nikos," persuaded Helen, "I can fly to Athens with Harry. I'll drive out alone to Vouliagameni, we'll collect the children, Melina and your mother and take them back to Athens. We can spend the night at my apartment and then Harry can bring us all safely back here. Phone Melina, Nikos. Nothing will harm your mother. Anyway it's not her they are searching for."

Nikos glanced at his watch, nodding an agitated submission. "They've taken the children to the beach for lunch. I'll call later."

"Good. Let's eat." Helen offered a dish first to Nikos and then to Ches who simply shook his head.

It occurred to Penny, who was speechless, that Helen was now quite openly flirting with Nikos who seemed, in spite of his family concerns, not blind to her charms. At the same time Helen and Harry interacted as though they were a couple of long standing. Penny was jealous and confused. Certainly Helen was strikingly beautiful, even more so than she had first seemed on that rainy May Sunday in London. She observed her ceaselessly throughout the lunch. Why did Helen toy with Ches, which she did? Surely not to remain close to Harry because if that were so, judging by the ease and unspoken knowledge and affection between them, Helen was expending unnecessary energy. A blind fool could see that Harry cared for Helen. Except me, I must have missed it, thought Penny miserably.

She glanced from one to the other of them. Both were

133

handsome and gifted. The idea of it caught in the pit of her stomach. Had he spent many of these past fourteen weeks wrapped in her embraces? Yielding to her decadence. For that was what this place represented to Penny. Decadence dressed up in all its seductive finery like some palatial whorehouse along the glorious path to Hades. She was out of place here, shy and ill at ease, saying little and yet, Penny asked herself silently, how far would she go to be with Harry?

"I was looking for you earlier. Where have you been?" Harry asked as Penny pushed open their bedroom door.

"I took the jeep down to the village."

"Why?"

"You and Helen disappeared."

"We were in the garden, sorting out arrangements with Nikos. What made you go back to the village? You know it's a risk."

Penny felt his eyes boring into her back as she crossed the room and ditched her bag onto a dressing table stool. "I needed Tampax," she lied.

"Helen would have given you some." His disbelief threatened her.

Without thinking or anticipating she rounded on him as he lay naked and outstretched on their bed. "I just wanted to get away for a bit! Is that alright or do I need Helen's permission to go out?"

"What's the matter?" he asked calmly, suppressing his shock at her unheralded violence, surveying her face, usually so open, for clues. She seemed suddenly like a deprived adolescent, hungry for affection. She was blotched and sunburnt from too long in the wind and a private shedding of tears.

"Where did you and Helen disappear to after lunch?"

His eyes expressed his surprise.

"Tell me, Harry!" she screamed. This outburst of jealousy perplexed him. Here was a Penny he had never met before.

"I told you we were in the garden. Afterwards we

134

went to Nikos's room to ring Melina. She's finally agreed to come back and bring her mother-in-law. So I'll fly up to Athens early next week, Monday or Tuesday, and shepherd them here with the children. Do you want to tell me what's the matter with you?"

"I would have thought it was obvious," she snapped.

It was late in the afternoon. Harry had been napping. He was clearly unprepared for such a scene and chose to remain silent for the moment, time for him to consider. Penny tossed her book, *As I Walked Out One Midsummer Morning*, onto the floor. She had taken it with her, something to stare at over a cup of coffee, whilst she sat alone and miserable in the village café. As she watched Harry, she was seething.

He rose from the bed and crossed the room to the main window, opened the shutters and welcomed in a flood of burning afternoon light. He glanced towards Penny. She had plumped herself onto the stool where she had previously flung her bag. She clung to it now, resting it in her lap like some discomforted commuter on a crowded London tube.

"What am I supposed to do while you're in Athens?"

"You can stay here and wait for me, laze by the pool, enjoy your holiday, return to the coast, whichever you prefer. I don't understand what you are making such a big deal about."

"I don't understand why you're doing this?" she returned abrasively, asking herself why he had not suggested that she go with him and fearing her own answer.

"Doing what?"

"Why are you going up to the mainland? Why can't Helen go?"

"She is going. We are going together."

The confirmation of this fact came as a blow more dreadful than her fear. Her voice was strangled, suppressing the anger and hurt born of her jealousy towards Helen. She knew she was making herself look ridiculous, she wanted to avoid appearing petty-minded or selfish at any cost, yet she felt betrayed by him and just as importantly, concerned for his safety. "You'll get arrested and never get out of the country," she said weakly.

"Why on earth should I?"

"Aiding and abetting members of the resistance. It's not your battle."

"It is my battle. Nikos is a painter. He's not allowed to work. If it were the other way around I would expect him to do the same for me."

"I want to come with you."

"I'd rather you didn't."

"Well, I bloody well don't want to stay here on my own!" It was feeble reasoning and she knew it.

"You won't be alone. Nikos will be here, so will Ches. You can go back to the village, if you prefer. I'll meet you there next weekend."

"Why can't I come with you?"

"Because it's dangerous." Impatience was creeping into his otherwise well-controlled replies.

"So why is Helen going with you?"

"Because she's Greek. Because she was brought up here, because she speaks the language better than I and because she knows and cares about these people. They are our friends, they need our help and she has an apartment where we can stay in Athens."

"Our friends! Exactly."

"What do you mean 'exactly'? Penny, why are you carrying on like this?"

"Like what?"

"You are being difficult and resistant and behaving like a jealous child."

"Because I don't know what's going on!" she wailed, sensing the treacherous tears begin to mount, causing her to feel like a fool. "You've never mentioned any of this before! Harry, it's dangerous. You said so yourself. I'm afraid for you and I don't trust Helen. I don't even like her."

"Come here," he said, approaching her from the

window, stroking the nape of her bowed neck, taking her in his arms and lifting her from the stool. Side by side, she still clutching her bag for no apparent reason and he, naked and holding her tightly, crossed the room to the bed. "Come and make love to me." She fell helplessly onto the mattress at his side. Having him, she reasoned, would make it easier to bear her jealousy. She could not break, or even fathom, the bond which continued to live between him and Helen and she could not share his concern. It was not her concern. Why would he risk his liberty? She was merely an onlooker in this political wrangle but as long as he loved her, and she believed in that moment that he did, she could bear anything.

Late that evening after more than a thimbleful of the local wine and several inhalations of pungent hookah hemp by the side of the floodlit pool Penny had loosened up. She felt no pain, had touched the lotus and was more than a little mellow. Even Harry's behaviour was altered, he had become positively uxorious towards her although he remained adamant about his plans to go alone with Helen to Athens. Helen's capricious attentions were, this evening, once more directed towards Nikos who, though drinking little, was in much merrier spirits and received them uncomplainingly. All in all they appeared a carefree band, liberated from the political doldrums that had seemingly enveloped them since Penny's arrival, two days previously. That time was so distant to her now! Under these circumstances she had almost dismissed, albeit temporarily, her jealousy and concerns and had forgotten entirely her afternoon flight to the village.

Ches, always the solitary minstrel, crooned and strummed on his guitar and they swam, all five, naked in the pool, frolicking and fooling until they tired themselves out, reeling from a surfeit of delightful delirium.

"Let's go," Harry whispered to her and dripping wet they climbed the marble staircase to their suite above the valleys and there they lay, unclothed, uncovered and silent. The night air was balmy. It carried with it an intoxicating scent of mountain pines and herbs which caressed their dazed senses while they made love in a hushed silence just as though words or sounds might threaten them or endanger the spell which had been woven about them. And finally, they slept.

"Someone's shouting, listen!"

At some point later in the night Penny was woken by a disturbance in the gardens beneath the window. She turned to Harry and shook him by the shoulder. "Someone's shouting. Can you hear?"

A man's voice, thick as grit.

Its menace disturbed the macaws in the courtyard. They began to flap and scream maniacally, to set up a blood-curdling skelloching. It rose to within earshot as though from the bowels of the earth. A bird's screech, piercing and female, like a banshee wailing from the subterranean depths, calling of an impending death. Warning of disaster . . . Warning of death . . .

And then there was the monstrous beating at the door.

"Jesus!" Harry breathed. "What in God's name is happening?"

Penny lay for a moment or two listening to the horrifying shouting, her eyes screwed shut, too afraid to open them. It was why she had not noticed that Harry was no longer at her side. Rolling onto her left flank, needing the reassurance of his touch, she stretched out her hand searching for him but found only the empty sheet, still crumpled and warm. Terrified, she opened her eyes and glanced about her, listening for sounds of him.

"Harry?" she whispered. There was no reply. In the darkness nothing except shadows moved. The room, save for a mild wind lightly nudging against the shutters, was in stillness. It was in monstrous contrast to the noise below. Screeching of wheels, beating on doors and

138

cries of "*Astinomía!*" She was too petrified to move . . .

* * *

Penny turned now to Gaza, outstretched on her bed, eyes half closed yet ever wakeful, searching for the clue, the flaw in her story.

"During the years that followed that terrible night, whenever I thought back trying to recall what time we had been disturbed I was never able to calculate it. Or why I had not understood the beating at the door, the realisation of what was happening. Harry, quick as lightning, had got it, but then perhaps he had been waiting for it. The appalling screeching of the birds was all that I ever recalled. Their fearful cries have never left me and in some strange way it was as though, that night, time stood still . . .

Gaza glanced towards the clock ticking conspicuously by the bedside. It was twenty-eight minutes past two. He was checking, noting it, not because he was restless, far from that, but because he wanted to mark the light outside in the sky. Silver against navy, a penetrating starlight with an almost ghostly hue to it. He was able to perceive it clearly through the window beside which Penny stood in shadow, hugging tightly at her own small frame as though stifling abdominal pain. This was the light in which they would shoot the scene. Their work had been in progress now for almost two hours. It occurred to him that this was the first time that he had seen her mature face in such a light. Crow's-feet notwithstanding, and they could easily be concealed, she was a beautiful woman. Must be almost forty, he gauged, or thereabouts. We should tell this story, he reflected, with the advantage of distance. A woman coming face to face with her own past, a woman whose true self has been strangled by guilt.

"*Astinomía,*" she whispered in the darkness. "I had not understood, comprehended then the meaning, the terrifying reality of that word."

"You hadn't come across the word before? After how many months in Greece? *Astinomía*," repeated Gaza. "They were shouting, 'Police'!"

9

Crete. Late summer, 1973.

The entire house was pulsating with the tread of marching footsteps. Foreign voices barking. Incomprehensible sentences. Aggressive orders.

"*Astinomía! Astinomía!*"

That one word Penny had finally understood. It was being repeated frequently. She picked it out from amongst the babble. "*Astinomía!*" Echoing around the open cavernous spaces. It was being pummelled into her. A burn on the spirit. "*Astinomía!*" A mark she was to carry forever, for slowly it was dawning on her just what had brought these men here.

And as if to further rattle and confuse her Harry had disappeared, fled it seemed. She steeled herself to go in search of him but the thought of it was petrifying to her. What if she could not find him? If instead she came face to face with an intruder, one of the aggressors?

Rising briskly but stealthily she stole from the bed, a pointless precaution for she could not possibly have been heard above the din. Without daring to switch on a light she grappled like a blind thing for some article of clothing to cover her trembling nudity. Eventually, because in her terror she could not settle on anything, she stumbled to the bathroom, whispered his name, "Harry? Harry?", confirmed positively that he was not there and grabbed a towel.

Outside their room she paused in the darkness to momentarily catch her breath, to take stock, as though praying for some divine guidance. The marble floor beneath her sticky bare feet felt cool and benevolent. Her shivering body under the towel was damp from dread and warm perspiration.

What if the others had all been arrested and she had been abandoned? Alone in this malevolent place. She listened again for sounds of someone. It was dead silent.

The echoes, the marching and the screeching of the macaws had ceased. It was unnerving. The silence hung heavily in the oppressive air . . . and then she understood why it made her uneasy . . . it was like the stillness that heralds the approach of a cyclone. When that silence descends the birds and the wildlife freeze. They listen, they wait, and then beat a hasty retreat, batting like hell to escape in time.

It was strangely discomforting because it had only just occurred to her. The crashing, the banging, the shoutings must have ceased some time before, while she was searching for something to wear, but the palpitating, the knocking of her heart had numbed and deafened her to that shift between sound and silence. Both were disquieting but the silence was infinitely more menacing.

She lifted her warm foot from the floor and ran the sole of it up and down her shin, dreading her own movement. Every step she took would be leading her towards something hideous. She approached a terraced walkway. It led her away from their room, her security. Beneath it lay a small courtyard, still and empty, where not even a wretched limpid-eyed cat stirred. The pounding of footsteps must have been an exit then rather than, as she had originally imagined, men breaking in.

She was debating which direction to follow next when something on the ceiling to the left of her along a short passageway caught her attention. It was the elongated shadow of a moving body, swaying like a great bat threatening an attack. Swiftly, instinctively, she pressed her body hard against the white stone wall, seeking to be absorbed, to be rendered invisible, and she waited, counting time. If she were in danger who was there left to help her? Why were there no sounds from the others? No one approached. Into the night's eerie stillness came a muted thud followed by a swift rearrangement in the shadow-play on the ceiling. No longer a bat the adumbration moved sharply from side to side; a great cat whose prey was being ripped to shreds. Penny, a diminished figure before this, watched in horror. Then a whimpering, barely audible, broke out. Gingerly she crept forward a few more paces and then paused once more to listen, steeling herself not to call out, a signal of her cowardice, a cry to Harry for help.

Beyond the open terraces an owl hooted and somewhere within the surrounding mountain summits a small bird or mammal let out its final cry trapped between the jaws of its swooping predator. Within the heart of the house muffled voices began to speak. Short sharp bullet-brisk sentences in Greek, threatening tones, incomprehensible syllables. Penny's fingers rose unconsciously to her throat and pulled at the amber stone, skidding it along its chain, twitching and twisting it. She took a deep breath and tiptoed towards the open archway above which the shadow danced, braving the threat of violent strangers but it was her companions that she saw there, allies, not the strangers she had been so dreading.

The open entrance revealed a king-size bed situated against the walls of the left-hand corner of the room. Its bed linen was all dishevelled, hanging like fallen petals from the centre of a flower, as though there had been a fight or a bout of energetic love-making. On the bed squatted Helen with Harry sitting at her side. Her body was pressed up against his and she was clinging to his shoulder, monkey fashion. His left arm was gripped firmly about her buttocks drawing her even more tightly to his flesh. Both were naked. He, save for a lightweight sarong which hung loosely from his hips. Penny stared miserably at them, shrinking from the truth; the mess of the bed, their proximity, their intimacy, at Helen's naked voluptuousness, her large breasts, the rotundity of her stomach, her dark pubic hair illuminated by a slim shaft of moonlight shining through the casement. It required only a split second to take in this tableau as she rounded the corner, before she opened her mouth to speak, before anyone had time to notice her. They were not aware of her arrival, or even aware of one another. Their attention was locked into something terrifying across the room.

Before Penny's eyes had adjusted to the dim light, before she had had a chance to register the horror of what was happening, from the same direction as their gaze, came a low-based moan. Two burly men were leaning forwards, menacingly, in an unlit corner near the window. Beneath them, dangling from their grasp like a lifeless puppet was a figure on the floor, unrecognisable, hidden by the darkness. He was on all fours, cowering, a trapped beast, his naked penis drooping beneath him, his forearms resting against the marble tiles, grovelling in pain. A revolver was pressed against the crown of his head. Blood stained his weeping face. It was Nikos.

A deathly cold realisation crossed Penny's trembling heart. The police had got hold of Nikos.

One of the two men barked something at him in Greek. Nikos shook his head. In response to this refusal the same man huffed, made a clipped grunting noise then gathered up his strength. Swelling his chest to almost cartoon-like proportions he booted Nikos in the balls while his companion thudded him with the butt of the revolver. Nikos let out a monstrous groan and crumpled to the ground, splayed in agony.

"Stop that!" Penny's shriek, her shrill penetrating call had broken the spell. By accident she had drawn all attention towards her, momentarily, and Nikos, the whites of his crazed eyes blazing in the darkness, grabbed his chance, his only chance. Hurling himself across the room towards her, out of balance, flying past her, bumping against her shoulder, he sped towards the terrace walkway. From where he had fled a gun was fired splitting open the whitewashed plaster behind Penny, missing her by a hair's breadth. She screamed out, her knees buckling with fear. Out of sight along the corridor Nikos had leapt in swashbuckling style from the terrace walkway down into the courtyard below. The two men visible now as heavily armed, uniformed police took to their heels in pursuit of their erstwhile captive, brutally shoving her out of the way, leaping towards the stairwell, shouting to Nikos, ordering him to stop. Penny was thrust to the ground. Her forehead cracked against the wooden base of the bed.

Harry took chase, sprinting fast, leaving the two women alone in the room.

"Are you alright?" Helen leapt briskly from the mattress, heaved Penny from the floor and slumped her back up against the foot of the bed. The blow had rendered her insensible.

"Ches!" shouted Helen.

Moments later an inner door opened and Ches appeared, dressed in a sarong. He made his way to the rug and crouched awkwardly, kneeling on a scattering of cushions alongside Penny. "I've checked everywhere, the place is clean," he reassured. "What's happened?"

"Help me." Between them, he and Helen took hold of her, each an arm, dragging her to her feet. Outside a door slammed, an engine ignited and then died, not engaging. It started up again, and so on. Ches took one look at Penny and disappeared, limping as fast as he was able, leaving Penny in the arms of Helen. "Bring some water!"

He returned with water and a phial which he handed to her. "Drink this," he whispered, pouring the unknown liquid into the glass. It was impossible to make out exactly what it was in the darkness, but too stunned to think or argue she imbibed the mixture.

"Put the light on, Ches, and help me get her onto the bed."

"I must help Harry."

"Help me with *her* first. Do you think I should try and put a call through to Melina?" Helen's hands were clumsy and trembling, her naked body blotched with concern.

Whatever Penny had just swallowed made her instantly woozy. Her limbs grew weightless. She began to moan. The pain in her head was splitting it apart and yet, quite suddenly, she was feeling terrific, harmlessly out of control.

Ches stroked at her wild hair, brisk preoccupied gestures. His voice was anxious. "No, don't phone. Not yet. Wait and see what happens. He might get away. Shit, I hope he fucking does! Come on, honey, lie down."

"I just heard a car."

Penny's mind was rambling, concussed and doped. "Is there still something going on between you and Harry?" she mumbled.

"I gotta go and check on Harry, man. She'll be alright here with you. Give her a few minutes. That stuff'll kill the pain."

Helen was perched beside Penny on the large unmade bed listening to Ches. A sheet, the only remaining bed-dressing was coiled extraneously about her feet. Her eyes were trained upon Penny. Her penetrating gaze reminded Penny of the cats' eyes that had so disquieted her earlier in the day. Green eyes, she had green eyes.

"Are you jealous?" Helen teased with a smile, attempting to lighten Penny's shock.

"Of what?"

"Of Harry . . . and I?"

"Should I be?"

"That's a good answer." Helen laughed audaciously. "Indeed why should you be?" and she rose from the bed.

"Cut it out," Ches snapped, disappearing. "Stay with her. I'm going to help Harry. Shit, the fucking cops busting in here! How the hell did they find us?"

"I'm coming with you."

"No, stay here! Take care of her."

*   *   *

"I was naïve, and very stoned on something, heroin,

146

morphine, I never discovered what he had given me. Helen terrified me with her aggressive self-assurance or so I perceived it at the time. I judged her evil. I would have just turned and fled had I been able and had not a shot rung out from beneath us. It was followed by a discordant screaming which chilled us both. 'Nikos! Oh my God!' Helen wailed. Our personal jealousies were forgotten in that instant. 'Stay here,' she said. 'No, I want to come,' I moaned, trailed the sheet from the bed about me and latched onto her wrist refusing to let go. Helen took me by the arm and unwillingly led the way. I trusted she knew where we were going, from where the cry had been discharged.

"It was already too late. Nikos, in spite of being wounded had taken it into his crazy head to try and get away. It was with my jeep that he eventually escaped. In desperation he had tried the police car but had failed to start it. I had left the keys in the hired one, the one in which I had driven to the village earlier that day. In fact the day before. By now it must have been close to dawn although still dark. Nikos had been waiting, craftily, until the two cops were confused. They had heard him run or so they thought. In fact it had been Harry. Ches had gone after him and both had set themselves up as decoys . . . "

Penny paused in reflection, remembering that night. The light from the window behind her cropped head haloed her. Gaza noted that, now, too, it must be almost dawn. He took a swift slug, slaking his thirst, from Penny's glass of Perrier (stale now) on the bedside table alongside him. He had understood, knew what had to be done with the script, but intended to allow her to finish her story.

Crete. Late summer, 1973.

"They're not here," Helen cursed, and swung round the pillar against which she had been leaning. "Harry!" she bawled once more. Her voice echoed through the empty chambers. There was no response, only the screech of the birds outside in the courtyard and then, from a distance, the unmistakable roar of engines on the move. "Jesus! Come on, we'd better go after them."

Penny, confused now by what exactly was or had been going on, stumbled mindlessly after her companion, out into the fresh night air, while Helen continued to yell out the names of the two men. The birds were behaving hysterically. Like bellows furiously at work they flapped their wide wings and mimicked with high pitched shrieks Helen's cries. In the distance several more gun shots rang out. Everywhere beyond the villa tyre marks had been spun into the dust but there were no signs of human life about the place.

"Fuck, they must've gone off with my car!" Without another word Helen sprinted through the courtyard, towards the garage in front of which Penny's jeep had been parked. The garage doors were open. Both cars were gone.

There was nothing left to do but wait. "Nikos must have made a getaway in one car and the boys taken chase in the other."

The waiting seemed interminable. Penny paced, the dull pain in her head receding, sanity returning. Helen was smoking pungent cigarettes. She was dressed now in a baggy coarse-cotton shirt. Her gold flat flipflops crunched on the road. They accentuated her slender legs, her broad swinging hips. The two young women spoke sparingly. At one moment to Penny's surprise Helen took hold of Penny's hand and grasped it firmly with both hands, holding it against her full bosom. The cloth of her shirt was warm, Penny felt the intensity of body heat. "I'm praying for him," Helen said simply.

Fresh mountain water gurgled about them. It flowed fast as if echoing their agitation. Both women watched and listened. Anxiously awaiting the longed for return of the engines as the plum dawn rose around them painting the sky and mountains in livid crimson hues. Early light crept through mists and silhouettes, day coming to life from a Japanese ink-drawing of hills, with the ocean in the distance ahead of them. Inhalations of sharp, clean air, undulating valleys, bruised rich colours, jagged strokes, blood-red geraniums falling from pots like wounded men.

Finally, more than an hour later, it was Helen's jeep they spotted chugging up the hill. No sign of Penny's truck on the road beyond. Harry, from behind the driving wheel, and Ches (whose leg seemed to have worsened with the strain), stepped from either side of the vehicle.

"Where the hell is he?" demanded Helen, unable to keep the strident note, the panic, out of her voice.

"Driven over the side of the mountain," Harry replied as he approached.

Penny felt her skin go cold. She shivered and wrapped her arms about herself. "Oh dear God, don't let that be possible," she murmured out of earshot.

A strange warm sensation crept like an insect across the back of her neck as she listened numbly while Harry related the news. His voice was tired, flat. Suddenly the water falling from the mountain sounded torrential, intolerably loud.

"He was driving too fast, couldn't brake and skidded off the road on a bend," he explained. "We stopped and then continued on past the next couple of villages searching out a track to get to him but it was impossible. He's plummeted miles. We couldn't even see clearly where he's landed. There were flames, way down. Probably him."

"The cops are trying to get down to him," said Ches, ashen, disappearing into the house.

"He won't have survived. Were your papers in the glove compartment, Pen?"

Penny nodded. "Driving licence, yes."

"Because the cops'll be back."

The suite of offices bearing the name of the Police Commissioner proved to be nothing more impressive than a series of sparsely furnished cubicles leading to a single room with two chairs, one placed either side of a desk. The room had been slapped with a coat of white paint years ago. It lacked any decoration save for a black and white portrait photograph of Papadopoulous hanging on the wall behind the Commissioner's chair.

Penny had been waiting in it for what seemed an eternity. She glanced at her watch for the umpteenth time ruminating upon whether or not they were planning to charge her, and if so for what and if not why were they still holding her? One way or another she had to get her passport back and get out of this place. She began worrying about what might have happened to Ches. Was he still there? She hadn't seen him since the two of them had been dragged from the house earlier that morning and had been escorted to this small-town police-station. Both had been been locked up in the cells below, separately, and that had been the last that she had seen of him. For the best part of the day she had been stuck there.

"Am I being charged?" she had requested of a rather spunky young police cadet who had simply smiled, shrugged and returned with a plate of fairly greasy moussaka which she had been unable to touch. She had been feeling sick and bad-tempered, caused by lack of sleep and a vague headache, a hangover from the fall and the drugs. The cell had been airless, stifling, with circling mosquitoes and an unrelenting stench of urine seeping in from the all-purpose lavatories situated further along the corridor. Finally, an hour or so earlier she had been released, led up a flight of stone stairs, brought to this office and told to wait for the Police Commissioner who would be arriving from Iráklion shortly.

Eventually the door was pushed open and a short stocky fellow in marine-blue trousers and a white shirt strutted in. His manner meant business. Penny took an immediate dislike to him. No hope of charming this guy, she thought miserably. Suddenly, and for the first time, it seemed a very distinct possibility that she might never get out of this place. Resting against his ribcage were two beige files which he carried as an army sergeant might sport a staff. His black-haired head was greased. He held it studiously aloft to avoid the risk of premature eye contact.

"Penny Morrison?" he quizzed authoritatively.

She nodded, studying him as he crossed the room. He was venal looking, vulture's eyes in a bloated grasping face. He had a small pencil-thin moustache, almost a caricature of a fascist police-officer.

"Oh Jesus, I'm going to get booked," Penny thought. "I don't know what for but I can just feel it."

She smiled a weak half-hearted smile, appraising the situation, wondering if there was any point in trying to win him over. She had to get out of here.

She noticed that he walked bizarrely. His legs were too short and his belly too thick. It unbalanced his movements so that Penny was instantly reminded of a hard-boiled egg. This image of him caused her to giggle privately and released her mounting apprehension. He arrived at his desk and still he hadn't looked her in the face. The shirt he had chosen was too small for him and, as with many overweight people, succeeded only in accentuating his shape. It stretched tightly across his stomach creating unsightly folds. The sleeves had been rolled up to just beyond his elbows giving the impression of a man who might work with his hands, perhaps a car mechanic. Great, a fascist car mechanic! Not an impressive figure, she concluded.

He introduced himself as the Acting Police Commissioner for the island of *Kríti*, explaining with pride that the Commissioner himself had been promoted and sent to the mainland. He then plumped himself into the oversized chair beneath the Colonel's photograph, regarded Penny for the first time and placed the two beige files onto the desk in front of him. With minute precision, and a meticulous and vigilant eye, he positioned them alongside one another and then retrained his gaze

151

onto Penny.

"Miss Morrison," he began, "I suppose you are aware that you are in serious trouble?"

There was no doubting from his tone that he quite clearly knew the answer to his own question.

"I don't see why," she retorted, playing a little the role of vulnerable, confused female.

For a moment he said nothing, simply glared at her, pouted his lips in thought and then peered inside one of the two beige folders. A British passport could be glimpsed, no doubt her own. She considered grabbing it and making a bolt for it, then checked herself. That would be sheer madness.

"Tell me what happened, your side of things," he said, without looking up from the file but with a little less aggression in his manner.

She had twice previously explained the circumstances of how and why her car had been taken. Once to the two duty officers who had arrested her and once more at the station desk when a statement had been taken from her. Now she was uncertain whether Greek inefficiency meant that he had not been told the details of these previous interviews or that he simply wanted her to go through the whole damn thing again, for his sake. She took a deep patient breath and began once more.

"My jeep, the one I'd hired, was taken by – " she paused considering the repercussions of the next word and then sped on "– an acquaintance." He said nothing. Clearly he wanted it all. His eagle's eyes gave little away. She did notice though that those same eyes were roaming about her body.

"It was early in the morning. Two of your men had broken into the house . . . " Nothing. His fingers were intertwined and resting on the beige file unopened now on the desk in front of him.

"They were looking for drugs. What about your boyfriend?"

"My boyfriend?" She was confused by his change of tack and with a monumental effort restrained the note of desperation creeping into her voice.

"Mr Chester Cunningham."

Penny paused. She shook her head. "I'm sorry, you're misinformed. He is not my boyfriend."

"Who gave you the drugs?"

"What drugs?"

"You were reported to have been in a state of," he glanced at the sheet of paper in front of him, "'intoxication believed to have been caused by illegal substances'."

This was almost certainly going to become awkward.

"A medication."

"Explain yourself."

"I was hurt. Mr Cunningham gave me something to ease the pain. One of your two men had knocked me out, concussed me." And then reconsidering her position she added more emphatically, "Not an accident. I was quite definitely pushed."

"How were you involved with the dissident Nikos Koumoulides?"

"I hardly knew him."

"But you were found at the little party where the accident happened?"

"From where Nikos left, yes."

"He was your lover?"

Penny sighed. "He was not my lover, no, he's . . . "

"You are living on the beach? Making free love and taking drugs with the hippies?"

Salacious old bastard. His thick lips curled like rubber as he rolled the words around in his mouth moistening them with saliva.

"No one is living on the beach. We have rented a house here in a village by the sea."

"We? At what address is that?" he persisted.

"Harry Knowle . . . "

"Ah, I understand now. You are staying with the artist Mr Knowle and his wife."

"No . . . you don't . . . " Penny was about to claim that she was Harry's wife and then some instinct warned her off. A memory of Harry and Helen on the bed protecting one another, Helen's familiarity with him, their plans to help Nikos, Nikos across the room snivelling with pain, some curious fear of her own humiliation, her growing uncertainty about Harry, a desperate need to get out of here with as little involvement as possible, whatever, the clammy doubts rose within her and stopped her tongue. Her eyes sought his, this small man whom she could envisage beating octopuses to death on the rocks along the beach. With vulnerable, alarmed eyes she pleaded with him not to confirm for her something about which she preferred to remain ignorant.

"Yes, that's the address," she conceded feebly. He had marked the change in her tone, had chanced upon her vulnerability.

He stood up, almost no taller standing than he had been seated, paced out his steps around the desk and rested himself on the corner alongside her, facing her. She resented his cocky strut and the air of triumph which imbued his every gesture. He had scored one over her, he knew why but he was not giving it away.

"You know, Miss Morrison, that possession of cannabis, possession of all illegal drugs are prisonable offences on these islands? Both you and Mister Cunningham are suspected of having been under the influence of drugs. You will both be sent to Athens for trial."

"You can't prove that! Your men came back and turned the house upside down. They found nothing!"

"I shall be obliged to put you both under arrest."

"But on what charge?" she protested.

"Proving yourself innocent will be a long process unless . . ."

"Unless?" she was hooked. She wanted no fuss. A clean exit.

"I haven't looked at the file. I do not know exactly the circumstances of the case. Would you stand witness to your friend's honour?" He slid his fallen arse from the table and walked around her, hovering about her shoulders like some gross insect.

"If I'm able, of course."

She felt his thick stomach pressing against her upper spine and imperceptibly she realigned her body in the chair.

"And for yourself? In spite of such parties you seem a decent young woman. I hear that you have, shall we say, behaved decently. Would you say that you have behaved well?"

Before she could speak, before she could assess what it was he was trying to draw out of her, Penny felt the touch of his fat workaday fingers on the downy hair of her neck. A cold sweat broke out beneath her curls. Her back went rigid. She felt her heart and her breathing quicken their pace. A nausea welled within her, disgust and anger, a longing to lash out at him, to rip his lascivious face with her fingers and a confusion for the sake of herself and Ches. She remained passive, inwardly tight, as the palm of his thick hand slid towards her throat and beneath her light summer shirt down onto her left breast.

Like an animal who has successfully stalked its prey Penny froze, considering her moment.

"I think you'd better give me our passports and let us out of here," she said in a measured tone. His second arm wrapped itself about her and the anger burst from her. Like a rocket she slapped her elbow into his stomach, winding him and rose spinning to her feet.

"Give me our passports!" she ordered emphatically, struggling to restrain her fury. "Nikos's death was no accident! You know that as well as I, and your two officers brutally assaulted him, hurting me in the process." She held her hand outstretched towards him, imperiously demanding the requested passports, standing her ground as she watched the mask of self-assurance momentarily fall away from his face. "Give me the papers."

No matter what she might be guilty of, he had overstepped the mark and they both knew it.

And then without another word he returned to his

155

desk, strutting once again – like some second-rate actor who knows only too well with what a lukewarm reception his show has been received, overplaying all the more, forced to rekindle a glimmer of his former self-ordained authority – to the Commissioner's chair where he regained his stage, the two beige files in his hand.

"Yes, I see here that all charges against you both have been dropped. You are free to leave." He pronounced the written decision with a sharp edge of triumph, tossing the previously meticulously placed files carelessly back onto the desk. An American passport slipped from between the beige cardboard covers and rested on several unanswered question sheets printed in Greek. He searched for the other, hers, amongst the papers. Without regarding Penny he picked up the two passports.

"Sign here," he commanded, a last stand.

With barely a glance downwards Penny scribbled her name alongside his fat dirt-stained fingers. Their eyes met and she read his smirking humiliation as he handed the passports across the table to her. Swiftly she accepted them and without another word or look to him she withdrew from his office. Free to leave. And leave she must . . .

*   *   *

"I fled back to the village, to Harry's house. He and Helen had flown to the mainland to Melina. I packed up my things and before I left – it was Tuesday afternoon – I took my rented bicycle back to Spiros.

"'You look very sad, Penny,' he said to me. 'You going home?'

"I nodded, trying not to weep, not to make a fool of myself. He was after all Harry's friend.

"'Problems with Harry?'

"'Something like that, Spiros. How much do I owe you for the bike?'

"He shook his head and put his arm on my shoulder. 'Nothing. You don't owe me nothing. Come inside, I give you a drink. Cheer you up.' And I went inside, and I allowed him to make love to me. He was alone and I was broken, my shame could get no worse. He told me that his son had gone off to Athens to join the resistance, that Harry and Nikos had encouraged him. And then I took a taxi to the airport. I had no jeep. It had gone over the side of the mountain, with Nikos inside it. And somewhere, must have been during a scuffle, I had lost his amber locket.

"Life looked pretty black. I was leaving, leaving my beloved Greece, leaving Harry forever. I hadn't even written a note. If I had it would have read, 'You bastard, you only had to tell me. I might have understood!'"

10

"Okay, now in your story Penny, the young actress, intends to fly home to London, takes a taxi to the airport but in the very last moments she loses her nerve. She is unable to leave so she changes her plans and returns to the mountains, to Helen's, where she finds the enigmatic Harry. He is alone. We discover him drinking, waiting for her, missing her, hoping that she will come back. We have the scene where they are reconciled. He tells her he loves her, that Helen meant nothing to him, that if he's hurt her, he is sorry. The story ends happily. It stinks."

"Why?"

"Why! Give me a break! Because it's romantic hogwash. Pinchbeck emotions. Mills and Boon. I don't believe a word of it." Jimmy Gaza paused, rolled himself off the bed, rose and stretched. His shirt was hanging loose about him, floppy as pyjamas. He unscrewed the cap from the Perrier and stared at the label on the bottle as though it said something alien and unpleasant. "Jesus, I hate this stuff," he moaned half-heartedly.

"It's good for you."

"That's why I hate it." Even so he quaffed the liquid, wiping his mouth with his creased shirt sleeve.

Outside the first glow of light was appearing, ascending beyond the window. In the distance a cock was crowing. They had talked away the night.

"It's not even Hollywood, it's sub-Hollywood!"

"You look as if you could do with some breakfast." She smiled. The antagonism that she had felt towards him had inexplicably disappeared, lost somewhere within the fragments of her story. As though in the telling she was discovering a way to trust him.

"Yeah, breakfast would be terrific," he drawled. "But

first . . . " he began as he stepped towards her looking, if possible, more dishevelled than the previous night yet somehow, paradoxically, more energised. She studied the stubble that was shadowing his face, somehow rejuvenating it, and she saw a warmth, a burning excitement in those tired but sharp bright eyes.

" . . . you know what we are going to do?"

She shook her head, stepped away from the window, yawned loudly and threw herself like a rag into an armchair. "Tell me."

"We're going to change the order of shooting. I'll let Frank know. He can announce it to the crew when we go down for breakfast. We are going to start with the big car stunt, the death of Nikos. The stuntmen arrived late last night. I'll work with them this afternoon and we'll shoot it after dark."

Penny looked puzzled. She was not following him, was not clear where he was leading her or why he should be feeling so pleased with himself, but whatever it was an instinct told her not to trust it.

"You don't get it?"

She shrugged. "Why are you changing the order?"

"Because we're going to need a bit of time. We're not going to make the picture as you have written it. We are going to write another scene."

"What other scene?" She could not hide the mounting terror in her voice.

"The scene you never wrote in the story. The scene at the café."

"What scene at the café? There is no scene in a café," she snapped.

Gaza moved towards her and grabbed her by the wrist, heaving her from the chair. His eyes were burning and she remembered why she had hated him, the loathing came flooding back to her. "And we're going to change the scene at the police-station with the Acting Police Commissioner. The reason for your release. You didn't get outa there because that guy made a pass at you, did you?"

159

"Let go of me, Jimmy! You're hurting my wrist."

"Did you?" he shouted, spit spraying against her complexion.

They were face to face, confronting one another in the harsh reality of morning light. A new day dawning. The tears mounting in her tired eyes told him better than any words that he had guessed the truth.

"You betrayed them, huh, Penny and then because you couldn't live with what you'd done you begged for Ches's freedom. That's the way it went, isn't it? He touched you in return for Ches's freedom. One lousy fuck and you hoped to be absolved."

She pulled her wrists, tugging them away from him but his grip was too firm for her.

"Remember what you called me, when some friend of yours died, huh? Stinking fucking traitor. Beating at me with your fists, hot tears, remember that? You're no different, eh. It was you who called in the police, isn't that so? That afternoon in the café. You sold your friends down the river and you expect me to believe you didn't understand the meaning of *Astinomía*?"

"No!"

"You wanted to spite Helen, right, and what you did was you killed Nikos. Mebbe indirectly but you killed him."

She began to whimper feebly, shaking her head, attempting a denial that her tiredness would not assist her to deliver.

"If you want to get it outa your system, if you want to exorcise it, Penny, tell it like it really happened. Face it. Face up to what you did."

Sobs hiccupped out of her, choking her. It was exhaustion. Years of self-loathing. She was hot and clammy with shame yet shivering, trembling from a lack of sleep, a lie unfolding. "I haven't got the strength."

"Yes, you have. Trust me."

Her eyes held his. Trust you, they questioned. Trust you.

"Let's get some breakfast. You need to eat." Tenderly

160

he ran his hand across her cheek, taking hold of her, holding onto her. She felt the heat of his breath. It reminded her. She nodded submissively. And when she was quiet, "Go wash your face. Do something with yourself. I don't want my crew to see you like this. They'll think I've been bullying you." He smiled, he was almost human.

"You have," she teased weakly, a defence, and padded through to the bathroom to dab cotton-wool pads soaked with astringent on the puffy flesh surrounding her eyes. As she reached the door, he spoke her name. "Penny." She halted, ready to listen but unable to turn.

"I want to know that you're with me," he said, "that we're making the same picture." She took a step further, her head was bent. "It'll be a good film, an honest one. Or do you want the pollyanna version?"

Glancing back at him, he thinking how sensual she looked, how vulnerable and broken, she muttered flatly, "Whatever you think."

She peered in the mirror and stared at herself. Fragments of another woman were emerging there. Disappointed eyes. A woman less conventionally beautiful than the woman she had always presented, older, stripped bare, bruised, but here was someone that she could address, perhaps could even learn to live with.

It was a fact. She had killed Nikos or, at least, she had been responsible for his death. Albeit indirectly. A betrayer of friendship, as she had so hard-heartedly judged Jimmy to have been, or simply a stupid unthinking girl possessed by jealousy? Whichever, it had cost her dearly.

Perhaps now was the time to face up to it, to tell the truth, to redeem herself through the process of work. Was that possible? Even learn to forgive herself, to offload the burden of that dead life.

The door opened a fraction. Gaza leaned in. "You gonna stand and admire yourself all morning or are we going to get ourselves some breakfast?"

*

161

Breakfast was just about finishing when they arrived downstairs, though with no crew call until later in the day people were still sitting together sipping coffee, lounging about and lighting up 'just one more fag' before they dragged themselves off to their various duties. A mass hangover floated gently in the air and with it a sense of camaraderie.

This grand salon in the rented house looked like it had been abandoned. Carpets had been rolled against the walls, furniture stacked to one side and cloaked in dust-sheets, paintings covered with bubbly plastic and reels of sellotape. Everything removable, filchable or damageable had been protected against the arrival of a film crew and against all possible or unforeseeable accidents.

The expansive space was now furnished with trestle-topped tables and light wood benches, kitted out as a makeshift dining-room. Such dressing appeared most bizarre in this setting of classical murals and crystal-chandeliered ceilings which echoed now, not with the strains of sedate music, but with the unexpected clatter of knives and forks, scraping plates, voices shouting, humming, chattering, and bench legs being grated against marble floor-slabs.

Penny glanced around the unfamiliar room. She had been too exhausted the night before to explore.

"Design did a great job, eh, finding this place? It's a terrific location, more conventional I guess than the architecture of your Helen's mansion but that'll be adjusted. Few rugs and cats about the place!"

"It'll serve the film admirably."

"Come and meet the stunt guys," Gaza suggested, when they had both helped themselves to plates of warm greasy food to be washed down with mugs of hot instant coffee. It would probably taste disgusting but it would be comforting. From a lack of sleep and an idea that she had somehow been through a crisis she was feeling light-headed and feeble, standing, vaguely lost, in search of a place to park her plate. She glanced helplessly in every direction.

A paranoia suffused her – that the whole room could read the truth, that somehow it was written across her harassed features. She felt an overwhelming desire to simply drop the plate and run for her life.

Gaza, without glancing towards her but ever sensitive to her innermost thoughts, took her by the arm and guided her towards a table at the far end of the room where three Greek males sat huddled in less rowdy conversation, occasionally casting glances towards their more extrovert companions, the pack of film technicians. These were the stunt men. Gaza introduced them: two youngish boys, both giving the impression of being rather cocky and self-assured – she could not catch their names above the din – were to play the two invading police officers, and a bearded fellow, robust and curiously florid for one of so dark a complexion.

He was named Theo.

"Theo's gonna perform the stunts," explained Gaza.

Penny nodded admiringly. Some of these stunts she knew were highly dangerous, action shots, running, jumping, escaping and driving scenes, all of that was reasonable, but the car over the side of the mountain bursting into flames ... It would take some skill. It would be crucial, knowing the exact moment to jump from the plummeting car.

For the acting scenes and the close-ups of Nikos Gaza had cast a rather well-esteemed actor from the Greek National Theatre in Athens, Giorgios Archimede. He was expected to fly in at some stage during the next two or three days but had not as yet arrived.

It was still very early, barely eight o'clock.

"May we join you?" said Gaza, expressing a degree of humility that Penny on a less vulnerable day would have criticised, judging it phoney. The men were more than happy to shove their crude plates and cups along the table and budge up on the benches thereby making room for director and actress to sit down. Penny was seated next to Theo who nudged himself closer by the breath, or was it simply a question of his bulk?

"I gotta surprise for you guys," began Gaza, slicing into sausages, spreading egg yolk here and there and generally coming to life in spite of an entirely sleepless night.

Work, thought Penny, was as always his motor. He was alive with an idea. Shots to be executed, danger ahead, charged by the prospect of a new scene that for him would change the balance of the film. People hated him but they loved to work for him. He was an inspiration. Brutally confronting yet brilliant. Compelling, charismatic. And she, like everyone, felt no different.

She found herself wondering again why he had accepted this film. He had reason to humiliate her, to pay her back. When he had first read it and agreed upon it had he been intending to confront her with its lack of honesty, or had she given herself away?

Others who came across her story, would they ask themselves about its truth?

Gaza had switched to Greek. Penny stretched to another table in search of salt and pepper. She smiled and winked a slightly forced good morning to Chris Grange whom she spotted lolling against a rather glamorous, nubile boy from the wardrobe department two tables to her left. She was suddenly aware of the trembling of her hands, her vulnerability, of being close to the edge. As she accepted the small glass cruet pots from an unknown woman sitting alone at the other table she almost allowed one to fall. The woman, wearing a smock and chunky silver jewellery, her silver-grey hair dragged from her face and coiled into a bun, must have read it because her severe features broke into a smile. She looked like a refugee from the Left Bank during the wars, smoking a cheroot and drinking a cognac. Penny was feeling fragile. The other woman knew it. Discreetly she signalled to her bottle offering Penny a shot. Penny acknowledged her kindness but shook her head. As soon as she could she would telephone Peter, find some courage.

A swift glance about her showed that people looked the better for a night of partying. Less vital perhaps than on previous days, but clearly bonds had been formed between the various nationalities, shynesses, tensions, had been broken down. There was a sense of a teamship amongst the seventy or so folk breakfasting around her.

A rapping of fork against wood on a table close by her brought silence to the room. Frank, the first assistant, was about to make an announcement.

"Okay guys. We've got some changes to the schedule – " The crew sat reasonably attentive, although not all, and listened to the change of plan " – so that means costume and make-up at four o'clock. Car-chase rehearsals straight up after breakfast. We've got a challenging day ahead, so let's get to it."

The speech had inspired an exodus albeit in dribbles and small groups. A few seemed annoyed or perplexed by the change, others were wanting to know why. No explanation was forthcoming. No one besides Jimmy Gaza and herself knew about the as yet unwritten scene, or God forbid, anything else that he might have in store for her. Penny, unable to touch the bulk of her plate, but heartened by the prospect of a shower and a phone call to Peter, rose and left the dining-room. As she did so Theo screwed his burly face into a wink. Penny smiled, more from confusion than anything else.

A few moments later she felt a hand grip her by the wrist. She was caught: one foot on the first tread of the stairs, someone unknown behind her. She turned to face him, her back to the open doorway, from where she had just retreated.

"Tonight," Theo whispered, almost conspiratorially, but with a male arrogance that both astounded and amused, "when I have driven the jeep over the side of the mountain and jumped unnoticed from a vehicle alive with flames I shall drink your health and, if you will allow me, I will make ancient Greek love to you."

"Don't be ridiculous, Theo," she said as lightly as her

own heaviness would allow.

"You think me ridiculous?" he jested, but she saw the thickset child in him bury his hurt pride. "But tonight you will be astounded. I dedicate this stunt to you, beautiful English woman. The death of the Athenian revolutionary, dedicated to you."

"No!" she cried and grabbed her hand from his with a firmness that surprised him. "No, don't do that. I don't want you to do that."

"Then what would please you, tell me, anything I will do it for you."

"Do what you like," she said, more curtly now and with a fear that almost buckled her. "But don't dedicate that stunt to me."

With that she pushed past him, leaving him rebuffed, his Falstaffian frame still and puzzled. Without turning back she hurried up the stairway and ran the length of the corridor to her room as though in flight. But she knew it was not from Theo. He did not trouble her. But the stunt, the death of Nikos, dedicated to her; there was something very black in such an idea.

After a shower she attempted to call Peter. There was no reply at the farmhouse. She thought it curious, it was still so early, but reasoned that if he were working in the fields with the labourers he would have set off soon after dawn. She lay down on the bed not so much to sleep, although the idea of sleep was a seduction to her, more to consider the past. The truth that Jimmy Gaza had drawn from within the story she had told.

London. September, 1973.

After traipsing despondently around the outer suburbs of London with various ragged or pencil-marked editions of the *Evening Standard* under her arm and fists full of loose change for the telephone in her purse, Penny settled on a top-floor flat in Kentish Town. The neighbourhood was seedy, the apartment grotty but it was spacious and unfurnished.

166

She had resolved on a new beginning and was setting about it with brittle freneticism.

She dwelt on Nikos's death and the events that had followed the accident as rarely as possible, stifling the distressing images but, try as she might, they resurfaced constantly, if not during her waking hours then at night in her dreams. Violent nightmares haunted her, distorting her perception of reality. She found that she was no longer able to move about the city alone after dark. She grew fearful of any stranger walking behind her – she was dreaming regularly of small creatures being clubbed to death – and worried constantly that anyone trailing her was bent on retribution.

Even after several weeks back in England she had still not returned to the studio to collect her belongings. She was not strong enough to face it and yet she knew it had to be done before Harry's return, or was she secretly hoping to turn up and find him there. As far as she knew Harry, Ches and Helen were still in Crete and, unless their plans had changed, they were due back early October. She endeavoured not to think of him but knew that once her flat was painted she would need her few sticks of furniture, her winter clothes, her books. The very idea of her possessions muddled in with his made her morose, her records alongside his, her underwear packed untidily in the same drawer as his, sketches he had given her left lying on their bed. She would have to sort through the lot. Every article carried a memory. She knelt on her uncarpeted floor with a paint-brush in her hand, an electric kettle at her side, weeping, wiping her paint-stained face in a worn-out T-shirt and deploring the real bloody mess she was making of her life.

She began to lose her resolve, kidding herself that if she were with Harry he would help her find the strength to face the nightmares, to overcome the constant reminders of Nikos's death. Constantly, almost without realising it, she would lift the telephone receiver to confirm that the line was operating. Why didn't Harry ring?

He had found her once before, he could do so again if he wanted to. Or had he discovered the truth?

Sauntering along the King's Road one Saturday afternoon she bumped into an old mate from drama school, Bill, who was also currently unemployed. He invited her for a capuccino and told her that he was going crazy searching for a room. Penny offered him the small second bedroom in return for a share of the rent and help with the decorating. She cherished his company, confiding only that she was recovering from a broken love affair. He led her through endless junk shops rummaging for sticks of old furniture, cooked her steaming great bowls of brown rice and then sat up half the night with her gossiping. It brought her respite from her nightmares.

Neither had any work or any money, yet Penny was beginning to feel more optimistic. She received a letter from her agent informing her that the television series she had filmed earlier in the summer, the one that had kept her from going to Greece with Harry, was due to be screened on Sunday evenings commencing the first week of November and that the BBC were considering a second series. She had bought herself a second-hand VW Beetle earlier in the year and decided that now was the time to return to the studio to gather up her belongings and deposit her keys. Bill agreed to accompany her.

It was a Tuesday, mild and sunny, a rusty autumn afternoon. They mounted the stairs, she and Bill, and after ringing the bell and receiving no response they let themselves in. The door was jammed, reminding her of her very first inspection of it. This time it had been wedged with mail which had been accumulating, uncollected on the carpet. She stepped uninterestedly over the letters. The space felt cold and unwelcoming, causing her to shiver. She was reminded again of that first visit here and how she had felt afraid, felt the place had been warning her, a warning that she had never heeded.

It smelt damp and forgotten and as deserted as she

had anticipated. She felt both a sense of relief and disappointment. Bill knelt by the door scooping up the letters, bills and circulars. During the preceding year he had been engaged by a repertory theatre in Glasgow and was visiting the place for the first time. Its capacious size impressed him.

"Here, some of this mail is for you. I'll leave the rest on this table," he called over to her. He approached alongside her and stuffed the envelopes into her shoulder-bag. "Hey, somebody here paints very well!" Penny said nothing. She was rediscovering the numerous watercolours and oils that decorated the walls. Almost without exception they were studies of her own body.

"They're good aren't they?" she mused.

"Sure are!"

"We'll plaster the walls with naked drawings of you," Harry had said to her, only a few months previously. "And be immensely happy, you and I." She felt his presence everywhere and knew how much, in spite of everything, she still loved him. But what was it that Ches had said to her in Crete before she left Helen's? "He just doesn't want to get his cardigan caught, Pen. Not a second time. Leave him be, he'll be back."

"But he is married to Helen, isn't he, Ches?"

"You better ask him that. How the hell should I know!"

"I'll just gather my stuff together," she said now to Bill. "You stay and look at the paintings. If I need any help, I'll shout." Leaving Bill to browse amongst the drawings and artwork she disappeared into what had been their bedroom. Its emptiness, its disused musty smell confronted and disturbed her. Hastily she began throwing her clothes and few possessions into the assortment of carrier-bags that she had brought with her. Forgotten and crumpled, lying beneath the bed which she had slept alone in throughout the summer, she came across a note from him. "Silly that you said nothing. We could have celebrated." She smiled

169

recollecting the occasion. She too had hidden truths and left things unsaid. Not the same, though.

"Let's go out to the movies," she suggested when all her farrago was crammed into the various bags and Bill had helped her lug everything down the stairs and into the boot of the Beetle. She drew the stable door closed with a resounding thud, and mourned fleetingly the keys which she had tossed onto the double bed, the double bed they had bought together.

She had left no note nor a forwarding address. What right had she to expect him to contact her?

During the drive back to Kentish Town she glanced through her mail: a bill or two, notification of a change of accountant's address and one other letter, airmail, that caught her attention, hand addressed, Harry's writing, a Greek stamp, posted in Athens, weeks earlier, just days before she had left for the island. She opened it feverishly and sat silent, stunned by its contents. Folding up the flimsy blue sheet of lined stationery and placing it in her wallet she felt an overwhelming need to bury the past, to immerse herself in the world of work.

"You okay?"

"Yeah, fine," she lied, "I just need a job." If only she could turn back the clock, if only she had not fallen prey to her own jealousy.

Later that evening, when they returned to Kentish Town after a film and a vegetarian meal at Manna in Primrose Hill, she found a script waiting for her in the letter-box. Attached was a handwritten note from her agent.

They would like to see you for the part of Rose tomorrow afternoon. Read it tonight and let me know what you think. I'll be at the office in the morning as of nine-thirty. God bless, Ben.

It was a new German play which had never before been produced outside Berlin, to be performed at the Hampstead Theatre Club, one of London's most

170

established fringe theatres. The role, which was a moderately challenging one, included several scenes in which she would be obliged to appear nude. Penny finished reading the play, flicked through her own scenes once more and switched out the bedside light, deciding that, should it be offered to her, she would accept the part in spite of the nudity. The salary she knew would be a pittance but better to work she thought, lying alone in the darkness, than to sit at home thinking of the past, waiting for the telephone to ring.

Her thoughts turned to the airmail letter that had been posted to the empty studio – too late.

Pen,
    I think it's better if you don't come here now. Will explain everything when I return.
    I love you. Please don't doubt it.
    H.

She thought of Harry and his present whereabouts. She thought miserably of Helen and of all that she had discovered about the two of them. Prompted by the woman in the mountain café and the Acting Police Commissioner's remarks (that odious little man) she had pressed Ches, during their journey from the prison back to Helen's house, for an explanation.

"Listen Pen, this ain't my shit to be discussin' with you!"

"Ches, I just want to know what's really going on."

"Ask Harry. He'll tell you."

But she hadn't been able to ask Harry because once back in the mountains she and Ches had discovered an empty house and a note from Helen explaining that she and Harry had left for the mainland to find Melina and the children. "We must do all that we can. She will need our strength and protection now," it had read. The note was addressed to both Ches and herself.

"You'd better tell me what's going on, Ches. Why were the police brutalising Nikos?"

And so, reluctantly, he had begun the story. Two years earlier when Harry and Helen had first married in Athens she had introduced him to a circle of people, many of whom were artists or intellectuals, members of an underground organisation in opposition to the junta. Amongst them were Nikos and his brother. They had begged Harry to help them, to raise public funds for them outside Greece, without disclosing their identities. Harry refused, arguing that he was a painter and not involved in politics.

"You are nothing if you are not given the freedom to express it. First and foremost there is the truth; it belongs to us all and differentiates between none. Don't turn away from your duty, Harry. We are an oppressed people and we are calling for your support," Nikos had retorted angrily. And so, occasionally, on return trips to England, Harry had reluctantly agreed to carry letters but had offered little further assistance. Slowly though, during these two years, he had grown more demonstrably sympathetic towards the group.

"And Harry and Helen?"

The marriage had lasted a matter of months only.

"Are they divorced?"

Ches shook his head. They had never divorced. Legally they were still man and wife. Ches's words had wounded Penny profoundly but, strangely, had not surprised her. In her bones she had known on that wet London Sunday that Helen's role in Harry's life was not to be underestimated. She might have resigned herself to Helen's presence had it not been for the unpalatable fact that Harry had obviously never sufficiently trusted her to confide the simple truth to her. This realisation staggered her and she could neither understand nor forgive him, unless there was some explanation she still did not know.

She had mounted the stairs to the room in Helen's house that had been theirs for a matter of hours. The bed still unmade, yesterday's clothes still strewn about the floor. As far as she knew Harry had not even bothered to contact the prison, to confirm that she was safe. He was concerned for Melina's safety, but what about hers? She asked herself why that might be. Driven by her own shame and guilt she had decided at once to quit the island.

Afterwards, sitting alone in the plane to London she had considered the implications of what she had done. She had behaved selfishly, thoughtlessly dwelling only on her own pain, her unreasonable and probably unfounded jealousy. It had been that which had driven her. But no matter how she coloured the events, diluting them to alleviate the guilt, nothing altered the appalling fact that a man had died. And that she had been the catalyst.

During those last hours in Crete she had viewed her position and had concluded that her only action was to leave him, whatever he might say if he had known. And yet leaving him she had lost a part of herself, the part of her that had contained him. To discover that she was so vulnerable, so empty without him was painful and demoralising; with him had gone her strength, her peace.

She rolled onto her side now in her Kentish Town bed, cursing Harry and the very day that she had met him. She curled her legs up against her stomach and wept herself to sleep. "I will get that part tomorrow," she promised herself, "I'll bury myself in work."

On the whole the play was favourably reviewed. Penny received one or two good notices, which bolstered her confidence, and one other – a rather cutting allusion to the way in which she 'sported her body'. It spoke not at all about her performance. Needless to say it was written by one of the tabloids and she dismissed it as meaningless and spiteful. For the rest her role was ignored, it not being integral to the plot. Each night the auditorium was packed with out-of-work fellow actors. Almost every one of them had worked with someone in the cast, were looking for work, or were friends of friends or friends of the director. It was Penny's first role in London and she wondered wryly whether all actors performed solely for the pleasure of their fellow actors or whether sometimes the general public wandered in to see the show. Most members of the cast seemed to be married or settled with young children; this accentuated her loneliness.

Three or four days after the play had opened the director invited Penny to dinner. Glad of the company and a chance to know him better, she had accepted. She knew he was taking over another theatre and hoped that he might offer her another role; but it was not a role he had in mind.

They began to meet after the show two or three evenings a week. It was a casual affair which she fell into simply because yes seemed less complicated than no. He was attractive and shared her love for the work – that was about it. They never made their affair known. They never went anywhere together, except to her place. There they would share a bottle of wine, sometimes a bite to eat, discuss the evening's performance and then make their way up the stairs to her bed. Early the next morning, after one cup of tea, he would 'dash'. He had begun work on another play, his mind was elsewhere. She wondered despondently why she had not been offered a role.

"Because you're having an affair with him," suggested Bill. "He doesn't want to complicate his day." She pondered about this during her walks to and from the Heath. The idea that it might be so hurt her. Yet she accepted that Bill was probably accurate. Better to have me tucked away, unpack me when he needs me. She resigned herself to the idea, for, she too, needed him – a diversion from her longing for Harry and the guilt about what she had done.

The director had been married but was now separated, or so he had told her. She discovered later, when his wife turned up in the bar after the show, that in fact they were still together. He had lied; she promptly stopped seeing him. Just like Harry, she thought bitterly, and then reminded herself that in fact Harry had never mentioned the subject. She had simply assumed he was single. She was still thinking of him, comparing everyone else to him, constantly remembering, constantly hurting. One part of her struggled to forget him, the other yearned for him to telephone. If he tracked me from Greece to Mrs Hardcastle's in Leeds, she reasoned silently, why couldn't he find me in London? If he really wanted to. Perhaps he's not back yet, but she knew that he had returned.

Strangely, she felt his presence. It was drawing closer.

The following Friday evening after the show Penny headed out of the auditorium. She was tired, dishevelled and in need of a drink. Carting shopping bags down the stairway towards the small foyer bar she spotted him. He was there, really there, leaning against the bar, a lager in his hand. Her eyes swiftly scanned the place in search of the other familiar, unwanted faces. He was alone. No Helen, nor Ches, just Harry. He was smiling, focusing on her, seemingly pleased to see her. Her heart had begun beating at the very sight of him. As she approached, without waiting to enquire what she might like to drink because he already knew, he turned to the barmaid and ordered her a dry white wine. She propped her shopping against the bar, trembling, swimming in the smell of him, his height towering over her, his body next to hers. Neither spoke before the drink had been dispensed, Harry had paid and he had turned to her, facing her directly.

"Good to see you," he said, handing her the wine glass.

"Thanks." She took a swift sip, much in need of it. "Did you see the show?" she asked as casually as she could.

He nodded. "Think I bought the last ticket," he smiled. "A smash hit. Is it going to the West End?"

She shook her head, feeling shy with him, tongue-tied, lips like chewing gum, almost as though they were strangers.

"Probably give them a heart attack in Shaftesbury Avenue," he teased. "All that sex and nudity."

After their drink he offered her a lift home. "I have my car," she replied.

"Then I'll walk you to your car."

She had no reason to refuse him. In any case she didn't want to.

Outside in the crisp late autumn night he carried her shopping. A year ago this weekend, she thought, he had turned up in Leeds. It all seemed history now. Her scrubbed face stung from the stage make-up and her heart beat overpoweringly fast, being so close to him and yet feeling so far from him, so punctured by him.

If only I hadn't run away, she pined. "How's Ches?" Inherent in the question was also, how's Helen? What has happened between you? Stifled rage and a sense of betrayal.

"Ches has gone back to the States for a while. He's had an offer to tour with Dylan and he wanted to stop off in San Diego. Spend a little time with Sandy's family. You remember Sandy?"

"Sure."

"Some guy found her in a *pension* in Paris, on the Left Bank. She'd OD'd on heroin."

"Oh my God." She was genuinely shocked.

"A waste of a life. Ches says that she began to get crazy after she heard that her brother, Tom, had been killed in Vietnam. Never got over it. Tom was Ches's oldest friend."

Penny's Beetle was parked a leisurely distance from the theatre, along a leafy Belsize Park avenue. They strolled amidst the late-night, street-lit shadows, listening to the soles of their shoes sounding against the paving-stones.

"I was disappointed not to find you at the studio when I got back," Harry ventured, lightly brushing his fingers against her hair. "You disappeared from Crete so abruptly. I hadn't expected you to vanish entirely. There

176

was no reason to. Was there?"

She said nothing, remembering the afternoon when she and Bill had gathered together her pieces and how she had wished it could have been another way. "I was pretty shocked about you and Helen. You never said anything."

"Yes, I did. Where are you living now?"

"Not about being married to her! I'm in Kentish Town. Quite close to here. It's pretty ghastly but cheap, and my flat's alright."

"By yourself?"

She shook her head. "A friend from drama school shares with me. Helps pay the bills." She was aware that she was falling over her words, breathlessly apologising for everything. It accentuated her sense of loss of him. The distance between them.

"I never lied to you. It just didn't seem important to me that we'd actually married. It was only for five minutes anyway! And I suppose I thought it would come to light in its own time. This it?" As they approached the car, she nodded, searching in her shoulder-bag for the keys and worrying that she'd left them on her dressing-table in the theatre.

"Have you eaten?"

The keys were in her purse. "Bill, my flatmate, usually prepares something, thanks." Instantly she regretted her words, could have bitten her own tongue.

"Would there be enough for three?" he pressed. "Or is Bill . . . ?"

"There's enough for three," she replied.

Penny unlocked the scruffy door to her fourth-floor flat. As always it had to be kicked. "It's an inelegant entry," she explained half-heartedly. The pair stepped into the dark deserted flat.

She was edgy. "Oh God, sorry about the mess." She switched on a lamp and cast a glance about her as Harry prowled the place like some restless cat in search of a spot. A hastily scribbled note from Bill was lying on the floor next to the telephone, with several biros and Bill's open diary which Penny closed discreetly. The note read:

Pen,
    Gone to Charlie's for the weekend. Back late Sunday. Sorry about the mess and the no shopping.

"I think we might be a bit pushed to find something to eat here," she smiled. Harry shrugged easily and paced towards her. Fearing her own weakness and her need for him she hurried to the kitchen in search of supper.

They dined on baked beans on toast and a bottle of unchilled Muscadet floating with ice cubes.

Later, listening to an old Stones' album, *Beggar's Banquet*, both lounged comfortably on the carpet, at ease once more in one another's company. Finally. It had taken half a bottle of wine before Penny had begun to relax, to be caught up in his spell once more and bask in the pleasure of it. Her anger towards Harry had temporarily dissipated, buried beneath longing, and she found it impossible to rationalise why she had been so strongly resisting him.

He stayed the night. Penny had promised herself, or almost promised herself, that she wouldn't let things drift back, but she loved him and, what the hell, he had taken the trouble to find her, yet again. They made love and they slept, they made love and they slept, they woke and they made love and they lay dozing into the dawn.

"It's been such a drag to be on my own," she whispered into his warm, damp salt-sweet flesh. She hoped he might admit to the same but instead he stroked the profile of her face with his strong hand and pulled her back on top of him.

Below, along the busy street, articulated lorries puffed and trailed through overcrowded traffic lanes. Penny lay drowsing, hearing nothing, lost in her own satiated delight.

She opened her eyes and was dazzled by a shaft of early November sunlight. It shone lemon through the attic dormer-window to where she lay regarding Harry's suntanned back. She felt such heady joy at being close to him once more. Without wishing to wake him she laid her fingers against his flesh, reassuring herself that he was no apparition, and she slid herself towards him, softly kissing his back before slipping from the bed, downstairs to the kitchen to prepare coffee for them both. No milk! No matter, it seemed like those early days when they had first been together. Alone. Before Ches had turned up from the States and before Helen had walked into her life. Just the two of them.

She was preparing a tray to take back upstairs when Harry appeared at the kitchen door wearing her silk kimono. His Christmas present to her in Leeds.

"Hi. Where's the bathroom?"

Both hands full, she nodded to a door across the hall. "Breakfast's ready when you are."

"I brought a painting to the theatre for you. It's still in the boot of my car," he yelled above the steam and running taps.

"Really?"

"When I've had my breakfast will you run me back up to Hampstead? I can give it to you then."

"Sure." A twinge of disappointment descended that he should leave so soon.

They sat together with black coffee, eating soft-boiled eggs and toast. She sensed him preoccupied, doodling on the telephone pad, making an effort to appear otherwise.

The drive to Haverstock Hill amongst the Saturday morning shoppers — beneath brooding clouds and un-forecast rain — seemed tense, or at the least, unrelaxed. At some point outside the bedroom, in the real world, though exactly when she could not tell, they had become strangers again. Like the weather, an unpredictable change. Now they had become, not lovers, but two people who had passed a night together, wading in uncertain waters. He had moved away from her, she could feel it in his silence, had distanced himself. "Where are we now?" she asked herself.

And suddenly, out of the blue, into that very silence which in a perverse way had also encompassed them, bonding them together, Harry said, "Helen's having a baby."

It pierced her, stinging like a razor wound. She changed down into second gear, sucking in her breath, verbally cursing the car ahead of them. She had swung off the main road a few minutes earlier, accidentally placing them now in a side-street bottle-neck. "Fuck this traffic!" and then with an icy calm, "Is it yours?"

He nodded, resting the flat of his hand against her fingers. "She wants to have it."

"Of course she does." There was bitterness, an overwhelming desire to be violent, to rage at him, at the slow-moving traffic. She wanted to kill him. "So why the hell did you come looking for me?"

"I wanted to tell you, wanted you to know."

"Jesus! And why did you have to make love to me? Dig open my feelings again!"

He looked out of his window. A mother wheeled a small boy past in a push-chair. Harry sighed, checkmated.

"Is that why you brought me a painting? Is that my consolation prize?" Penny spat out the words, haranguing him with fury. It was not what she had wanted to say. She had never wanted things to grow ugly between them. If only he could understand how let down she felt. The lump in her throat grew heavy and seemed to sting her.

"Pen, listen, you don't understand."

"Why did you have to bloody well turn up again?" There was a strident weariness in her voice. She reflected on all the work ahead, the clearing and packing away of him yet again. She had been surviving, reaching out, seeking to find a way to exist without him, to insulate herself against the pain – the gap that had been left by his absence. Her work, her new flat had been untrammelled by him. They had been without memories of him and now he had thoughtlessly walked into that world and touched it, leaving his cavalier prints about the place and she would have to begin again, spend time erasing him.

"You left without letting me know where you were. I don't know why. I saw a review in the paper. Calling or coming along seemed the natural thing to do . . . and there's something I need to ask . . . " he whispered dully.

"I don't think you have any idea how selfish you are," she said, pulling the car into the kerb, barely listening. The engine idled softly like some mildly disgruntled pet as they sat beside one another, staring into the starkly cluttered Belsize Park morning. Neither attempted to move, until finally she said, "You can walk from here, it's not far, half a mile or so."

"What about the painting?"

"I don't want it, thanks."

"Listen, Pen, Helen and I had split up more than a year ago. As far as I was concerned . . . "

"She's pregnant, Harry. She's having your baby. You're married to her. I don't want to see you again."

"I want to ask you a question," he said with a resolution that dismantled her. "Helen says it was you who tipped off the police that night. That's not true, is it?"

A cold dread crossed her heart. If things had been different she might have admitted the truth to him, attempted to explain what had led her to such a thing. If there had been a slip of a chance for them to be together again, for him to learn to forgive her, but this way what was the point?

"Go away, Harry."

He took her by the chin, forcing her to turn towards him. "Tell me, Penny, that it's not true."

"Of course it's not," she lied, knowing that her jealousy, her betrayal born of that jealousy, had driven them irrevocably apart.

181

11

It rained the entire weekend, miserable drips seeping and settling everywhere, dampening Penny's flat spirits. Discarded egg-shells, coffee-stained mugs, Harry's perfume on the linen, fleeting images of him, fragments of their few hours together invaded her new territory. She was going to have to begin again. She tortured herself for sending him away and she tortured herself for still needing him, for loving him in spite of everything. She performed poorly and she slept fitfully.

On the Monday morning she woke early, listened to the fall of the rain scuttling from the roof, feeling jaded but with a renewed resolve. She walked to the news-agent's and bought a paper and later, after several cups of strong coffee, she telephoned her agent and told him that when the run of the play was over she wanted a job that took her away from London. Perhaps a touring company or another stint with a repertory theatre. Anything to distance herself from him. This time she would make sure he did not find her and if he did, she would refuse to see him.

Penny's play finished in early December. Finding herself unemployed created insecurity. She feared work would never be offered again. The television series that she had filmed during the summer was being transmitted and was making little impact. Consequently the BBC decided against picking up the option, leaving Penny with no prospects.

The days had to be filled. All too readily her thoughts drifted to Harry, and to Helen who was one more month pregnant. The idea of Helen's gravid stomach began to dog her. Helen's voluptuous figure filling out relentlessly, flushed with health, proud and unabashed, it rankled, it gnawed. Her loneliness festered like a scab.

No further work came along in those weeks prior to Christmas and she heard nothing more from Harry. She was becoming crazy for him to make contact, believing that if she could just speak to him again she would tell him the truth, and somehow make him understand what really happened and he would forgive her. She considered phoning him. But what if Helen should answer? Would she simply replace the receiver like a thief or a mistress? Would Helen know that she and Harry had spent a night together?

Her friendship with the director, such as it had been, had entirely petered out. He had moved on to yet another production, another young actress and there was, of course, his wife. Bill, loyal friend and cinema companion, still unemployed, had found himself a distraction, a Chinese boyfriend, and was spending more and more time away from the flat at Charlie's. Penny was alone for great chunks of the days.

She spent the hours brooding — strolling across wintery Hampstead Heath, staring at the robins, in a duffel coat and jeans or sitting alone in the flat curled up in front of the gas fire, scribbling in her diary, writing self-indulgent poetry or reading second-hand paperbacks that she had purchased for a few pence at a shop in Flask Walk, and she waited for the telephone to ring.

She had no spare cash to enable her to go out, to help her to forget her dismal circumstances, no money to buy presents or decorations to indulge in the distraction of Christmas — her sole income was a weekly dole cheque. The very idea of a festive season made her want to weep. She thought back to the year before, to Leeds, to her cosy little gas-reeking room at Mrs Hardcastle's, which over the space of time had become imbued with a rosy romanticism, and to the joy on Mrs H's face when Harry had offered her his gift. She posted the ex-landlady a Christmas card notifying her of her change of address. Perversely, when the woman responded a few days later sending 'seasonal greetings to the both of you' it allowed her to feel closer to Harry.

And then the week before Christmas a handwritten card arrived. The envelope had not been addressed by Harry so she did not immediately guess where it had come from. It was an invitation to a New Year's Eve Party at the studio, Ches's handwriting. A cruel irony. When Harry and she had been together it had been Ches who had invited Helen. Penny knew that it would be foolish to accept and yet she knew that she would be unable to resist . . .

* * *

"God alone knows what I might have been hoping for."

Suffolk. Christmas, 1973.

The day preceding Christmas Eve Penny watered the ferns and the rubber plant, emptied the fridge, locked up the flat and set off for Suffolk in her Beetle to spend Christmas with her mother in Sibton. Bill had taken the train along the south coast to Bognor Regis the day before, to his family. She travelled in the early morning to avoid the predicted heavy exodus of traffic. The light was clear, and the stark brown earth was as crisp and white as icing sugar from the overnight frost. It felt gratifying to be heading out of the city and a sense of her former optimism crept back as she began to look forward to the few days ahead of her.

"You look plain wore out, m'gel. Big black bags under your oies," her mother greeted her, once the tea had been made and they had settled comfortably either side of the blazing log fire.

"Not been sleeping well. Nothing to worry about, Mum."

"Few proper dinners, that's what you need."

It felt cheering to be home, to be cosseted and considered.

On Christmas morning she and her mother set off for Mass. It was the first time for several months that Penny

184

had been inside a church, not since her return from Greece. Her all too imaginatively drawn mental picture of Nikos's charred and broken body, the burden of her guilt, had turned her away from God, a shame that she was powerless to allay. It was as a gesture to her staunchly Catholic mother, as well as an inability to admit to herself that she had lost her faith, that she agreed to attend.

The two women walked the three and a half miles alongside one another, gloved hands placed firmly in mackintosh pockets to protect fast numbing fingers against the cold. They crossed fields, strode past leafless or berried hedgerows, closed gates and stepped over stiles in their sturdy walking shoes and their church-going Sunday best. The muddy, sorrel-brown lanes had been hardened by the frost, making the tractor tracks as tough underfoot as walking barefoot on shingly sand.

Christmas morning: the remote humming of an occasional engine, robins chirping in the skeletal trees, grazing stock oblivious to the Christian feast, not a shepherd dog in sight and ahead of them drawing closer church bells pealing.

Few words passed between the two women but Penny sensed her mother's curiosity, it burned into her. She had observed also the sidelong questioning glances. Too proud to ask. "You'll tell me. In your own good time. You always 'ave," would be her refrain if Penny were to confront her. It brought a sadness to Penny's young eyes as she thought of how it would be if the older woman knew. Instead she listened to the comforting tread of their feet crunching on the dried earth.

"What are you staring at, Mum?" she asked eventually.

"Me? Nuthin'. I ain't lookin' at nuthin'. Just wonderin', that's all."

About my London life, no doubt, the unexpected recent move and the boyfriend who, during this visit, I have not spoken of. Not once. Nor will I now. Not until I'm ready, she thought, walking at her mother's side and

185

she rested her arm about the older woman's waist. She was as proud and as staunch as ever, her solitary mum, and Penny loved her for it. "It's good to be back, to be with you for Christmas." She grinned.

"I'm glad to hear it," the older woman responded, registering a minimum of emotion on her face.

After church, while Mrs Morrison basted the turkey and pottered in their low-ceilinged kitchen, Penny took the dog for a walk.

"Sure you don't want me to help, Mum?" she asked whilst burrowing in the darkened cupboards for a pair of wellingtons her size.

"No, you go on out with Spot. I prefer to do it myself. You know that. Any'ow, the li'le bugger's gettin' on moi nerves. Overexcited 'e is, 'cause he smells the turkey."

Penny took the car, thinking she'd drive to Aldeburgh and wander along the beach, but changed her mind along the way and went to Snape instead, to the Maltings. There, the familiar slab of land planed out before her towards a hazy soft-hued horizon while her breath rose up crisply in front of her into the raw winter noon.

She stood to gaze, to breathe in the familiar landscape, while the mongrel cantered on ahead of her, wagging his unlikely tail. Spot, the dog, and the flatness of the quaggy terrain with its lack of topographical complexity soothed her broken spirit. Here there were no skyscrapers bearing down upon her, oppressing her already distracted thoughts. And the sky, an uncluttered expanse of grey liquid, released her spirits like a kite circling in the wind. She loved Christmases here when the days were clear like this and the colours of the light were hazy, diluted almost as if by heat. Spot panted on ahead of her. His clouds of contented breath the same colour and texture as the distant horizon. Not a soul in sight. How could there be today? The women were perspiring in their overheated kitchens preparing Christmas meals, while the men sat supping with their cronies in the local pubs. There was an order here. Simplistic perhaps but, nevertheless, it served and thus, survived. London was a great distance away. So was Harry and the traumatising memory of Nikos's death.

Until she returned to the cottage.

"Your young fella' telephoned. Said to wish you a happy Christmas," her mother informed her the moment she unlatched the kitchen door. She stooped to tug at her muddied wellies. Fresh air had pinked her features. Her eyes burned as she listened to the faint hint of accusation in her mother's voice. "Could've brought 'im 'ere, you know, if you'd wanted. Unless you're ashamed."

"Oh, Mum." Exasperation cloaked her unwanted joy.

"I told 'im so 'an all. I said whenever 'e wants 'e's welcome 'ere. I'd be glad to be introduced."

"You had no right to do that! Why don't you mind your own business!" Her tone was razor-sharp.

It struck like flint, halting her mother in the business of potato-peeling. The older woman, wounded, glared at her only daughter. Her eyes blurred by restrained tears, she searched for the reason for such an unexpected outburst and in that second she realised that she had been barking up the wrong tree. She had put two and two together and reached her own conclusions but she saw now that they were way off-beam. Maternal instinct had let her down.

"I'm sorry if I've said the wrong thing, gel. I thought . . . "

"Please don't Mum, I shouldn't have shouted."

Penny understood all the questioning glances and what her mother had concluded was the cause of her silence, and the sheer inappropriateness of the idea softened her anger and shamed her. "Here, why don't you let me do the tatties?" she tendered and, before her mother could react or refuse, she crossed the steamy kitchen in her socked feet and reached for the knife. Mrs Morrison gave it up meekly but she stood her ground. Penny took up the work.

"I didn't invite him, Mum, because we've split up."

"What on earth for? I thought you was so keen."

"Just weren't suited, I suppose," she lied. Her gaze was averted, while her back hid her from the steely eyes of a canny mother.

"Well, 'e's obviously not so set on the idea. Said 'e might stop by."

"What?" She spun round.

"I said not today, o' course. An' you'd be glad to see 'im, too. I can tell."

Harry arrived towards tea-time on Boxing Day while Penny was tidying up the garden. She had been assigning herself physically demanding tasks ever since her mother had warned her about his possible arrival. Lost behind a box hedge – clad in a pair of her deceased father's discarded corduroy trousers found whilst clearing out an upstairs cupboard earlier in the day – she knelt, dead-heading the lower half of a climbing rose. She heard the Morgan draw up, had been expecting and dreading its arrival since lunch-time, but restrained herself from leaping to her feet, assuring herself that it was safer and more dignified to remain hidden behind the hedge. In any case, she argued, it might not be him. A foolish bluff. There was no doubt in her mind about who had arrived.

Her mother trotted down the cobbled path to welcome him as he called out a greeting.

"Mrs Morrison? I'm Harry Knowle. Happy Christmas." His tone was ebullient, ringing into the crisp, dusky, russet-sweet light.

Briefly, Penny, from her unobserved post behind the hedge, was reminded of how much Harry enjoyed Christmas. Her mother's response was softer, and consequently inaudible – no more than an insect's hum winging its way across the plants.

"Where's your lovely daughter?"

Never less than charming, she thought scathingly. He'd woo the wings off a bat!

Moments later she spotted black skin cowboy boots rounding the hedge and he was beside her. She sat back

188

onto the almost frozen grass placing her gardening gloves and sécateurs at her side. He lowered himself onto his haunches and handed her a gold foil-wrapped gift.

"Your Christmas present," he said.

"You're good at that, aren't you?"

"What?"

"Nothing."

She let it slip into her lap, discovering its weight. Something heavy in a rectangular box. But she made no attempt to unwrap it.

"What are you doing here?" she said abrasively.

"Silly question." He glanced about him and then upwards towards the cloudless sky. "It's a great spot you've got here." And he held out a firm hand to help her up. "Come on. Your mother's making tea."

"I suppose you brought her a present too."

"Of course," he replied with furrowed features. "Why do you ask?"

Penny shook her head and they strolled in single file back along the stoned walkway – breathing in the wood smoke that seasoned the late-afternoon air – heading towards the main stretch of garden. Then side by side they walked across the front lawn, past the original front-door – locked for donkey's years, the bolts rusted from the perennial damp and now overgrown with unpruned honeysuckle – directly to the kitchen door. Spot, who had been dozing on the carpet in front of the fire and the silent flickering television screen, was awakened by the sudden surge of activity, and came sniffing about them, perked up at the thought of company.

"Yours?" Harry asked, bending to ruffle the little fellow's crown fur.

"Mum bought him after dad died. He's getting on a bit now," Penny explained. Spot barked, a gruff recognition that he was being paid attention to more than anything threatening.

"That's right, you told me he died, your father."

"Yes, he died."

189

"Shall I serve tea by the fire?" Mrs Morrison sung out from the kitchen.

"I'd better go and help her," Penny responded. She rose, leaving Harry crouching beside the dog. She glanced back towards him, caught him looking at her and they smiled at one another. It felt strangely bonding to entertain him here, in this private world, which she so rarely shared with friends from London. She loved him so.

Later they drove to the village pub, just the two of them. A calm had resurfaced, the intoxicating calm of simply being close to him. Penny had dropped her guard and with it the smarting of the wound; all of that had settled somewhere temporarily out of reach. She felt reassured, believing that when she told him the truth, which she fully intended to do, he would understand. She was seduced once more. His warm skin, his pensiveness, his beauty.

"She's very generous, your mother."

"Yes, I worry about her, being so much on her own."

"She must look forward to your company. It was kind of her to invite me."

"I think she thought I was having your baby," she laughed but in an instant remembered Helen. The guilelessness of her foolish admission stung her. I could bite my tongue, she thought sadly, and fell silent. They drove the last few hundred yards without conversation.

"Here," she pointed as they arrived outside the Rising Sun Inn. She wondered if Harry was also thinking of Helen.

Inside, bunched up beside one another in an over-crowded lounge, she sipped at a saccharine-sweet Dubonnet and lemonade. The village pubs hadn't cot-toned on to wine yet. Those with off-licences sold Blue Nun by the bottle but that was the extent of their range. Her slip of the tongue, the nearness of him, the smoke, the noise and the overwhelming heat made her head swim. Harry smiled tenderly and laid his palm against her flushed cheek.

"Where's Helen?" Penny asked crisply. It seemed her only defence.

"I owe you an explanation — "

"Not necessarily," she interrupted. She was tense and curt, almost afraid to hear what he had to say.

"Yes. About Nikos, about why Helen and I disappeared to Athens."

Penny plumped her glass back onto the table. It landed clumsily. Nikos, she thought. It was she who owed the explanation.

"I can't forget him. His posture that night — crawling like a beaten animal — his terror, it dogs me constantly." He spoke almost inaudibly. "Sometimes at night I still hear him yowling."

Penny's manner changed, as had her features. She looked like a wizened child, despairing, knowing it was time to confess to him the truth. "It was me," she wanted to say, but the words would not come.

"Do you think of him, remember him?" he asked.

"Always," she responded, with a bitterness that he would not understand and clearly mistook.

Harry took a lengthy swig from his pint of bitter and replaced it onto the table, inches from her own glass. He sat silently, weighing his words with deliberate care. "Forgive me, Penny, I never meant to involve you." His words caused her heart to contract. If only he knew, she sighed. "At the outset I sympathised with Nikos and his friends, but I wanted nothing to do with them . . . When I saw that it was too late, that I couldn't turn my back, I scribbled a note telling you not to come. It must have gone astray."

"It was waiting for me when I returned," she said flatly.

Across the lounge a door opened and someone entered. The movement distracted Penny's attention, as did the familiar face, now ancient and feeble. In her mind's eye she visualised the airmail letter, vaguely wondering if it would have made a difference, if she had received it in time . . .

"I was confused, hellishly jealous," she wanted to tell him. "I didn't know what was going on. I drove to the mountain village to get away from Helen's, to breathe freely for a while. I never intended to betray you. I meant no one any harm. That night, it never occurred to me . . . like you I thought we were being raided. And then, not hearing from you, locked up for hours at the police-station . . . even that arsehole of a police officer knew about you and Helen . . . I felt so angry, so ridiculous and so soiled . . . "

           *   *   *

That's a lie, thought the mature Penny rising from the unfamiliar bed, distracted by the sound of engines revving up on the mountainside. Someone was shouting instructions to the stunt men into a loudspeaker. She crossed to the window but could see nothing of what was happening outside. Her view overlooked the sweep of verdant valleys that led to the sea.

The rehearsal was taking place somewhere alongside the house.

I did intend to betray them, she thought, gazing blindly at the scenic landscape. Perhaps not as I set off in the jeep but most assuredly the moment I started talking, confiding, in the café.

Questions asked, a growing idea that I held the means to put paid to Helen in some way. I did not think it through. Not death, no certainly not that. But if someone had asked me during that day if I wanted Helen dead, what would I have responded?

I would have done anything to keep Harry for myself . . . Perhaps I should have said nothing and kept my paltry guilt hidden. What use was my confession?

A knock broke her concentration. Without her response the door was opened. Gaza stepped in a foot or two. He had showered and shaved. "Ready?" he asked. He was carrying his script and sheets of blank paper.

12

Suffolk. Christmas, 1973.

Old man Packer, with checkcloth cap in hand and check woollen scarf wrapped tightly around his throat, latched the public house door behind him and led his black and white mongrel dog into the midst of the smoky ambience. Balancing uncertainly on fragile limbs he hesitated while his watery eyes peeled the hearty throng in search of a familiar face.

"Over 'ere, Joe lad!" someone cried out, their voice thick with the local Suffolk accent which seems to turn every statement into querying surprise. The old pensioner started, raised his walking-stick in recognition and shuffled through the tightly packed tables to join his toothless companion, his mutt padding faithfully at his heels.

"I certainly had never intended to involve you," Harry repeated. Penny, listening, pictured a younger Packer as he manoeuvred his way to the available seat. She saw that his old dog was almost blind now. When she was a child and her dad was still alive, they used to saunter up the lane together to Joe Packer's cottage to buy vegetables freshly gathered from the garden for their supper. This scenario with its bittersweet memories momentarily eased her, distracting her from Harry, his marriage, the fruitlessness of Nikos's death and from her need to comprehend why things had turned out like this.

"How much did you know about what's going on in Greece? We never really talked about it, did we?"

"Apparently not."

"For example, the Government there?"

"Look, I don't need a lecture on politics! I can understand now about Nikos but I don't see what this has to do with you and Helen and why you had to deceive me," she snapped, immediately regretting her anger. "Sorry."

She felt trapped by pent up emotions, contradictions, which she was struggling to suppress – a need to beg him, or life, or fate, or whatever the hell it was, to turn back the clock, to wipe out these last few months – and the knowledge that she could hold off no longer. She had to tell him the truth but her courage was seeping away, her certainty that he would understand and forgive her was waning in the fug.

Life had seemed so simple all those years ago in the shadow of Joe's pink Suffolk cottage. She heard once again the endless yapping of his puppy dog and remembered carrying the brown paper-bags bulging with leeks and potatoes pressed tight against her flat undeveloped bosom, her father tall and protective at her side.

If she had never returned to Greece perhaps none of it would ever have happened and she would have remained ignorant of their marriage. She longed now for that ignorance and felt a hurt swell up within her and bind her throat. She was forced to keep her eyes averted. How could he have been married to someone else and say nothing to her? Her own naïvety rankled her. She blamed herself, not him, for being raw and foolish. She had believed so implicitly in their union and she had trusted him, utterly trusted him.

All around them sat small groups of East Anglian farm labourers, lolling within stretched legs' length of a blazing log fire. Their faces were weathered, ripened by alcohol and by the glow of the flames. Voices raised, chattering, laughing, arguing freely. They were drinking ale and celebrating Christmas just as they had celebrated every other Christmas before. The conviviality surrounding her counterpointed her own misery. So little had changed in this rural backwater of England. There was an innocence here. She had lost hers on that mountainside in Crete. Nothing could ever be the same again.

There were a few faces that still seemed familiar to Penny. Fred, an impoverished local farmer, once upon a time a good friend to her now deceased father. He had grown wizened too since last she had seen him. Tom Petty, a blacksmith from one of the neighbouring villages, who, she had worried in the years gone by, had been a little sweet on her widowed mother. She had liked him right enough, used to call him Uncle Tom, but not once her dad had died and she had feared that he might install himself as her new father. It seemed so mean-spirited now; to have denied her mother that chance of a second handful of happiness. He raised his glass to her as he always had in earlier days, to make her laugh. She buried her pain and lifted her glass. "Merry Christmas," she mouthed. And Arnold, once upon a time a frequent visitor to her home, lawn-mower salesman, ironmonger, jack of all trades, a decent enough sort of fellow. He caught her eye and bowed his flushed face and she returned the shy uncertain greeting. Few of these fellows would ever have much to show for their labours, almost without exception their homes were cottages, or farmhouses on the estates of wealthier men, but tonight they seemed unconcerned by the hardships of their feudal-based existences and the precariousness of the land which, one way or another, most of them lived by.

Harry seemed unaware of, removed from, the surroundings. He was fiddling with a beer mat, scribbling and doodling on it, first one side and, when there was no space left, the other. Occasionally he lifted his eyes to glance at Penny.

"This your local then?"

She nodded. "My dad used to drink here when I was a kid. In the summer I used to accompany him. He used to buy me a lemonade and a bag of crisps and sit me in the garden. I used to wait hours for him."

It was a modest bar, this snug. A multicoloured paper-chain hung in sweeping loops about the walls, partially covering faded photographs of various Aldeburgh lifeboat crews. Women were welcomed here; it carried no stigma to be seen supping in this snug. There were several females present now, backs to the wall, huddled in their winter overcoats, gossiping with their husbands and neighbours, their workaday hands wrapped around half-pints of stout, their only bit of finery a worn thin band of gold.

In the public bar across the way it was noisier, filled with thick-set young men telling jokes about sex, or playing darts. These were the local lads, labourers, factory-workers or employees from the local nuclear power station – Sizewell. Heavily made-up girls wearing tight sweaters and out-dated mini skirts swanked at their sides. These were a 'certain type of girl' who smoked cigarettes, drank spirits and chewed gum. Unmarried girls were silently frowned upon, covertly talked about, if they were seen frequenting bars. All part of the local mores with which Penny had been brought up. London had changed all that, and student life. It had introduced her to her first taste of hashish and her first sexual encounter but nothing had prepared her for Harry and Greece. Harry's betrayal of her with Helen, and more importantly her response to that, had damaged her, a wound compacted in tissue which would repair but would never entirely heal. Or so she felt now. She almost envied the frowned-upon girls in the public bar their carefree laughter and their apparent hardiness.

"Can I get you another drink?"

She glanced at the empty glass, traces of the burgundy liquid had stained the base, her lip-gloss had imprinted itself on one side of the rim. She shook her head. "No thanks, it's pretty disgusting." She laughed soullessly and pulled a face. They smiled at one another, momentarily bridging the yawning gap that lay between them. Harry pulled a Marlborough from his pack lying on the table and lit it, exhaling before speaking.

"Have I told you about Helen's mum?"

Penny, surprised by the shift of thought, frowned and shook her head.

"She was a beauty, Lila. She's dead now." He dragged on his cigarette, lost in his pictures of Lila, and then broke into a smile. "I was in love with her, from afar. Secretly and hopelessly in love with my mother-in-law!" he laughed and Penny saw that he was teasing, but only partially so. "She was an actress, rather a famous film star in Greece. Married to some rich cat, in textiles or something. He adored her. It was a perfect marriage because Lila needed to be adored. Even by me!" he laughed again, giving way to a boyishness, a frivolity that Penny had rarely seen in him. "But their marriage broke up. Lila had many friends, most of them in the film industry; composers, screenwriters, directors, all well-esteemed, creative people, many of whom were communists. In 1967, when the dictatorship moved in, or soon after, they were rounded up, hunted down and imprisoned. Some of them are still in prison. Lila was bitterly opposed to Papadopoulos, loathed him. Her sympathies were with the people, unlike her husband who was a friend of Colonel George. She began supporting the communists, giving them large sums of money. Her husband found out. He was furious with her, forbade her to mix with these people and then when she refused he beat her. It didn't stop her. He threatened to disinherit her or hand her over to the police. Finally, she left him. He kept everything. She was penniless, she'd given everything to her friends, to the cause. In 1971 she died of cancer, alone and out of work. She was heart-broken, so many of her comrades, respected artists, were in prison or in exile." Harry fell silent, lifted his glass. It was empty.

"I'll get us another drink," Penny whispered. When she returned he continued.

"I think the loss of her mother sent Helen a little crazy. We had only been married a short while. I guess I didn't understand what was happening. She was, still is, voracious, red-blooded. It's part of what I loved about her, still do, and part of what, finally I couldn't cope with. Things began to go wrong pretty quickly between

197

us. We started fighting. I was working. She was frustrated, overwrought, began accusing me of not spending enough time with her. She wanted me in a way that I couldn't deal with so eventually . . . I just took off to the beach, to my retreat, my house in the village. I was pretty miserable about it all, just got stoned with my friends and buried myself in my painting. And then I met you . . . "

"Why didn't you say anything at the time?"

"I wasn't ready to talk about it and . . . it didn't seem any of your business . . . "

"Not my business! You let me fall in love with you knowing all the time there was Helen." Penny was suddenly conscious of the rising level of her voice. Old man Petty threw her a glance, shot a look to Harry and raised his glass once more, this time with a flushed mischievous wink. Penny smiled half-heartedly and inched towards Harry.

"All you had to say was that you'd been married." She was irritated by his doodling, wanted to yell at him to stop.

His words were faint, his eyes concentrating on his hand scratching out soft looping shapes with a pencil. "Listen, we met on a beach," he defended, "I thought it was a passing affair, a fuck . . . "

"Then why did you turn up in Leeds?"

"I continued thinking about you and decided to find you." He lifted his head and grinned. "And I couldn't've missed out on Mrs Hardcastle, could I?"

Penny did not bite. She was in no mood for his humour. "And what about Helen? Where was she?"

"In Athens. I saw her a couple o' times. Told her it was over . . . but you know it's not easy living in a country that's governed by a dictatorship. It changes people. Her mother had died, her father had no time for her. Our marriage might have been finished but we still continued to care for one another. We were pals, and she has friends in trouble. She came looking for me in Crete, said that even if I turned my back on her I could no longer deny them. It was time to help. I agreed to do what I could on the condition, no violence. We started to work a bit together. She was all screwed up, craved affection. Said she still wanted me, us. She was in bed with Nikos the night he was killed and now Melina and the children are living at her house in the mountains. For her there's no dichotomy in that."

"Where was I in all this?"

He sighed, scratched at the beer mat with his nail. "I was committed to you."

Penny felt her heart lurch at his use of the past tense. "So why did you disappear to Athens with her? She could have gone alone. You could have waited to find out if I was alright."

"We were thinking of Melina's children and Nikos's brother — " He broke his sentence, stopped doodling and dropped the pencil onto the table, dragging at his cigarette. "You remember he was a doctor?" She nodded. "He died in prison. The official cause of death was suicide by hanging but Mrs Koumoulides does not accept it. Now she fears for her grandchildren. She has asked Helen and I to help get them out of Greece, to bring them to London."

"And what have you said?"

"We'll do what we can. They can stay at the studio with us until we find them somewhere to live."

"I see." *We'll* do what we can. Everything you say, Penny was thinking, all you talk about is you and Helen. What about me? Why have you come here? Why are we sitting here talking? "And the baby?" she mumbled. The words all but stuck in her throat.

"Helen wants to have it and I can't stop her. It will give her something to concentrate on." He seemed uncomfortable with the words that he was speaking. "I have to help her out, Pen. I can't just turn my back on her. She needs me."

Penny felt asphyxiated, drowning in the knowledge that this was really the end. She longed to roar out loud, to let out some terrible cry of pain. Months of anxiety, months of willing him to return – begging an invisible clock to turn back time, to allow their lives to be as they once had been – all these flooded in upon her, suffocating her.

"Tell me when it happened, when she got pregnant." The demand whipped out of her, sharp as a razor slash. If she could only find some way to hurt him, some way to hate him, to be revenged for loving him so much and trusting him so completely.

"What difference does it make?"

"It matters to me!" she sobbed, burying her face in her glass. "Was it while we were still together, while I was working in London?" He said nothing, clearly unable to handle her show of emotion because it chilled him to see how he had hurt her. "Harry, I need to know," she pressed. The extent of your betrayal, she thought, how little you valued me, us.

"In Athens," he whispered. His mouth was dry, his cigarette clinging to his tongue.

"When you went back for Melina and the children?"

Harry nodded.

"At her apartment?"

He nodded again.

"Never before, while I was here, working?"

He shook his head and she realised that she had misjudged him, mistrusted his loyalty.

"She slept with Nikos and then she slept with you. Suppose it's not yours. Suppose it's his! What then?" He reached for his packet, took out another cigarette and lit it. "Why, Harry? When you said you loved me."

"I did love you."

"No!" Anger burst within her like a flood.

"Listen, Helen was my wife. She said she needed me . . . and it didn't feel like it would make any difference to us."

"How can you say that?" she accused furiously.

"Stop it, Pen, please."

"I want to tell you something," she whispered, an insane intensity drying the words in her throat. "Helen was right. It was me who tipped off the police. I went to the village, back to the café. I wanted to get away from you, wanted to sort out what was going on up there, at that monstrous house with the cats' eyes. The woman who had served us our beers, she recognised me. She noticed that I was upset, she brought me water. I was weeping, trembling, a hurt bottled within me. She was gracious. '*Yássou*,' I said. She smiled, sat down at my side, stroked my face. I broke down. Her kindness, her compassion, overwhelmed me. I began to pour out to her what was in my heart. Of course we couldn't understand one another. There seemed no harm in telling her, unburdening everything. She told me you were married. I don't know how I understood, sign language, fingers pointing to fingers. I thought I would die. The pain of such a discovery . . . She asked me about Nikos. Was he wanted by the police? Why? Someone had been asking about him. I told her I couldn't say. She asked me if there were drugs at the house. I tried to deny it. She whispered that Helen was frowned upon . . . I went further. I confirmed that she was evil . . . Even that night when the raid began, it never occurred to me. Only later, at the police-station, when they let me go. I was free to leave, they said, because I had helped them with their enquiries . . . "

Without thinking – all thought had been obliterated in a rush of blind emotion – Harry shoved his arm across the table slinging their empty glasses to the floor. "You treacherous little cow."

Fingers of beer splashed against her tights as the dregs of his drink hit the vinyl floor. The smashing of glass broke through the fuggy, crowded environment. All eyes turned towards them. Embarrassed locals viewed them uncomfortably. Such expressions of emotion were unheard of here. Tom Petty buried his head, rummaging all of a sudden to refill his pipe.

Mascara had smeared itself across Penny's cheeks, stinging her eyes, distorting her vision, and she wished that of all places in the world it hadn't happened here. It added to her humiliation. Harry had bitten into this world too, this last bastion of her innocence. She shoved the table which stood between them out of her way and beat a hasty retreat from the pub . . .

*   *   *

"I was almost twenty-two years old. The hurt weighed intolerably, tearing me apart, as though I might never live through it. Like a raging crazed beast that has been shot but not killed I was intent on destruction. The following afternoon I drove back to London, recklessly. All I wanted was to die, to kill myself, to put a stop somehow to the pain . . . I knew the flat would be empty, that Bill would still be away . . . "

London. Christmas, 1973.

Bill unlocked the door of the flat and called out Penny's name but there was no response. Presuming that he was alone – that she was out, maybe at the movies – and that the flat was empty, he headed directly to his own room to dump his heavy suitcase, intending, afterwards, to make for the kitchen to stick in the fridge all the Christmas leftovers that his mother had insisted he cart back with him.

At first he feared burglars but as he took in the scene, made a swift mental check, he realised that nothing had been stolen. It was curious, his camera, his records, his books, all still there, yet everything in the room had been turned upside down, drawers, cupboards left unclosed.

He thought he could hear the indistinct murmurings of conversation followed by several chords of string music coming from the next room, the living-room. It was the television playing at low volume. "Penny!" She must be home and hadn't heard him come in. He called out her name once more. There was no response. He was really nettled that she had been through his things and worse, had left them even untidier than they had been before. Slamming the door to his room he stepped across the hallway to the living-room. The door was closed. He shoved at it carelessly, hell-bent on venting his displeasure. "Penny!"

She was slumped in front of a magazine on the floor wearing a dressing-gown, looking uncharacteristically haggard and unkempt. It was two o'clock in the afternoon. She appeared to be sleeping, but something about her appearance troubled him. He forgot his previous ill-temper.

"Hey, Pen," he ventured. Her face was resting against the open pages of the glossy magazine. All he could see of her was her outstretched legs and back.

"How was Christmas?" he probed, fearing to step foot into the room. Ginger Rogers and Fred Astaire, on the screen behind her, began to smooch and croon.

Penny made no reply. "Pen, you alright?" Still no answer. She was definitely sleeping. Mocking his own sense of melodrama he noted that she was breathing. Without conviction he decided to leave her alone and withdrew to his own room, to unpack his case, tidy things up and call Charlie.

A quarter of an hour or so later he made tea and carried the tray with an extra cup through to her in the sitting-room. Penny had not changed her position on the floor. He placed the tray on the carpet beside her and gently tapped her shoulder-blade.

"Want some tea?"

A mute moan as she lifted her head from the floor. Her eyes were swollen and blank. "Jesus, are you alright?" She shook her head deliberately. It appeared to be as heavy as a cannonball.

"Want to talk about it?"

"Whatimeizit?" she drawled.

She had been crying and she was stoned on something. He had noticed an empty vodka bottle jettisoned in amongst the kitchen rubbish. He watched her now as he poured out two cups of Earl Grey tea. "No milk, I'm afraid," he said lightly.

"I haven't been out." She rolled from her stomach over onto her back and lay gazing mindlessly at the ceiling. "Want to come to a party?" she asked with a malevolent smirk on her face.

"Sure, why not?" He decided that to humour her might be his best option. He had no idea what she had taken or the quantity of it. "You want this?" He offered up the weak, honey-coloured liquid. Penny shook her head and covered her face with her outstretched arms but not before Bill had glimpsed a tear roll down her colourless cheek. Her body heaved silently and then relaxed against the floor. She began to sob. At first the sound was almost inaudible, but then it grew louder and louder until it crescendoed like some grotesque retching. Bill knelt on the carpet at her side and took hold of her limp body. "I'm calling the doctor," he whispered.

"Nooo!" she moaned as he stretched and reached across the room, dragging the phone across the floor towards them.

When the doctor left a few hours later he confided to Bill that Penny's condition had been caused by some form of shock, heightened by a lack of food and sleep, but that she was going to be fine. She had taken no drugs. "She hasn't taken an overdose you'll be pleased to hear. Certainly a surfeit of alcohol . . . Does she often drink so heavily?" Bill shook his head. "Perhaps she's taken one sleeping pill but nothing more worrying than that. I think she told me a few months ago that she's an actress?"

Bill nodded, refraining from adding that he too was an actor.

"Mmm. Highly strung. Give her this," he concluded, handing him a prescription for sleeping pills and tranquillisers. "She'll be right as rain in a few days. Happy New Year to you." He folded away his bits and pieces into his well-worn Gladstone bag and disappeared down the five flights of stairs.

"Bit of a climb this, eh?" he chortled as he

disappeared.

While Penny lay sleeping upstairs in her room, Bill, having cancelled his date with Charlie, sat watching *How to Marry a Millionaire*. He ate cold turkey and a limp salad, but he had lost his appetite worrying about what might have happened to her. The telephone rang. It was Penny's mother.

"Is she alright?" she asked. "Oi've been trying to get through to her for two days. She left in such a hurry."

"Yes, she's fine," he lied. "She's out tonight. I'll ask her to call you tomorrow."

"She must've made it up with Harry. Oi think they had a row. Thank you so much, Bill. Happy New Year."

"Happy New Year." He replaced the receiver.

So it was Harry, again.

"Will you guys come to the party or not?" Intensity hardened Penny's speech.

"I s'pose so, but I don't know why you want to go back there." Bill was perched across a great pile of cushions. They represented the furniture in the Kentish Town flat. Penny's emotions were volatile. He knew he was treading on broken glass. He felt a cautious amateur in her game. Although Penny had slept she still appeared to be weak and he felt wary of distressing her. The doctor had warned him to make sure that she remained calm.

Bill, his young Chinese friend, Charlie, and Penny drove together to the studio in Penny's Beetle, to the party given by Harry, presumably Helen, and Ches. Charlie drove. It was the only car they owned between them and not insured for Charlie, but Bill felt it was still a safer bet than Penny driving.

He was feeling mildly anxious. She had been a very long time in the bathroom, – getting dressed, she had explained – and anyway he was not convinced that this was the way any of them should be celebrating the arrival of a new year.

" . . . When the moon is in the seventh house . . . "

The soundtrack from the musical *Hair* vibrated through the empty streets and alleyways of London's dockland signalling a lively party in the vicinity. They parked in a deserted, dimly lit cul-de-sac – Penny had discovered it during her months of residence here – and they headed off in the direction of the music. Her spirits had miraculously lifted.

"And love, love will steer the stars . . . " She hummed and strode forward with purpose, a step or two ahead of the boys until she reached the source of the sound.

Outside the warehouse in the cobbled walkway, guests, all of them unknown to her, sprawled like lizards against the walls. Into the darkness they gazed, the polluted Thames a stone's throw in front of them. They talked and passed joints to one another and, careless of pollution, tossed their empties into the passing river. Penny peered at her watch. It was still early, not yet eleven. She thought of Harry somewhere overhead, of Helen, and the new year in front of her.

The studio above was already overflowing with people. Silhouettes packed tight against one another filled the open windows like sardines in tins. Empty wine bottles littered the stairway. Penny pushed on ahead of her two companions. She was dragging mercilessly on the remains of a spliff that an unrecognised person had passed to her at the bottom of the stairs.

She pushed open the entrance door which, although not closed, was jammed with people. Inside everywhere was blanketed by clouds of hazy smoke. Candles flickered here and there, creating balloons of whispered light. The huge space was awash with stoned bodies lounging about the floors, or walls, or hanging onto one another in movement. Several girls with flowing hair danced or writhed around the centre of the room. They were naked, their arms high above their heads.

"Where's Harry?" she shouted to a dark-haired male, someone whom she did not know but who seemed to be looking in her direction, smiling lewdly.

"Huh?"

"Harry Knowle, have you seen him?"

"Don't know 'im, man."

" . . . Aquarius, Aquarius . . . " The music spun and circled, echoing around the warehouse. Bill yelled into her ear that he and Charlie were going in search of something to drink. She nodded and watched them as they disappeared into the wall of people, Bill's arm around Charlie's petit Asian waist. She was reminded of her own loneliness. Her head was roller-coasting from the grass that she had just smoked. She pushed herself into a space and moved further into the room seeking Harry, or Ches. They were nowhere to be seen. She stumbled over a chair, it already housed a couple locked in one another's embrace, so she crouched beside them on the floor. A half-filled glass between their legs caught her eye. She picked it up and finished the contents in one gulp. Scotch. Ugh! She detested Scotch.

She peered blearily about her in search of Harry. She thought she should go and find him but remembered Helen and felt heavy, a vague inability to move. The music vibrated against the floor beneath her. It seemed to be getting louder. The bass sounded through her head in loops, whirling about her brain and then paused. Something softer. Someone had changed the disc. Roberta Flack sang out a number from her new album, *Killing me Softly with his Song*. Penny recognised it immediately. She spun on her buttocks, focusing indistinctly. On the wall behind her she recognised one of Harry's sketches. It was of her.

Suddenly in the midst of the throng she spied Ches, standing alone, weight balanced on his good leg, rolling a joint. She pushed her way towards him shoving stoned people out of her path. "Ches! Ches!" He heard his name and looked expectantly about him, grinning when he spotted her.

"Heyey, Pen, how you doing?"

"Just great, Ches," she shammed. "Seen Harry?"

"Greece. He and Helen left yesterday. They've gone to visit the Koumoulides family, to celebrate the new year with them. Melina telephoned to . . . "

The beat of the music swelled and people swirled about her. Ches continued talking, something about Nikos and his family but she heard nothing more. It couldn't be true. Harry had gone.

The stranger who didn't know Harry loped towards her and grabbed her by the wrist, wrapping her in a great bear-hug which lifted her feet from the floor. He began to swing her firmly about the room keeping time with the velvety sounds. He smelt of whisky and tobacco and sweaty cologne: the perfume of an unknown male. A tear fell from her cheek and landed in the hollow of her neck. She tasted its salt as it slipped past her lips and swiftly buried her head in the stranger's shoulder. Encouraged by her gesture he pulled her body towards him, pressing tightly and rubbing himself up against her, his hard sex pushing into her, turning her around the room unrhythmically, humming close in her ear, running his solid hand across her breast. She thought she might collapse, but he was her anchor now as she staggered directionlessly about the place, mourning Harry and the emptiness within her. He was hirsute, open-pored and without tenderness but she would be lost without him. She needed him and clung hopelessly to him. He could do with her as he wanted, she was his for the taking, and after him, any who wanted her. It hardly seemed to make a difference now.

13

Five years later. March, 1979.

"Apparently Miriam is a big fan of your work from way back."

"Yes, she told me when I went to see her for the part in *The French Lieutenant's Woman*, but Ben, I think she says that to all the girls." Penny leaned across her desk and closed the sash-framed window. Better no air than the bloody racket coming in from the main road.

"Don't knock it, Penny. She means it. I think she's really selling you. I wish all my clients had casting directors for fans. She sent your photos – the set that I gave her a couple of weeks ago – to the States and the producer Sam Schuster called her back, asking to meet you for his new picture. She said to warn you that they will almost certainly want to test you."

*   *   *

Jimmy Gaza momentarily lifted his pen from the paper, it remained poised in mid-air.

"I take it this is going to be me?"

"You were the one who said tell it the way it really is, Jimmy. No more sub-Hollywood."

He sighed and reached for a cigarette. "You take me too literally," he drawled.

Penny smiled ruefully and turned her sight away from him, the better to concentrate . . .

London. 1979.

The young Penny was perched at her desk, on the telephone, listening to her agent, Ben. Her head was

209

bent to one side, smiling, the receiver resting between her shoulder and chin, leaving her hands free to file her nails. "Great! Have they come back with an appointment?"

"Have you got a pen handy?"

"Sure have."

She was wrapped in a bath towel. Noting that she was in need of a manicure, she dropped the emery-board, picked up a pencil and turned the pages of her leather-bound diary.

"So the initial meeting is tomorrow afternoon, three o'clock. Grosvenor House Hotel. Ask for the film company, they have a flat there. Bellevue Pictures. Got that? B-E-L – "

Penny interrupted his spelling. "I have it, Ben." He had become such a worrier of late.

"Don't be late and phone me afterwards, let me know how it goes."

Penny printed the details for the following afternoon and against today's date – Monday, March 19th 1979 – she hastily scribbled the words: Nicky, hairdresser.

"Okay, Ben. Thanks. Talk to you tomorrow." Replacing the receiver she glanced at her watch, almost half past eleven and she was still not dressed. It had been a late night and she had promised herself that it would not be. She had a lunch meeting with a Dutch journalist for one of their national magazines. Hurrying through to the bathroom she remembered that she had intended to call the hairdresser, turned back to the desk, dialled the well-known number and made herself an appointment for later in the day.

Background music coming from a radio broke the silence in the living-room, Bob Marley singing *Satisfy my Soul*. Five flights below in Kentish Town Road a pair of navvies were digging up the road, the non-stop rrrrrr-rumming of the pneumatic drill had been driving her crazy since half past eight. "I've got to get out of this place," she had cursed in the kitchen earlier whilst making herself a *cafetière* of strong black coffee. And then out of the blue one telephone call from her agent and life was good again. The roadworks were almost lyrical.

A screen test for a film directed by the American, Jimmy Gaza. At the very least a meeting with him! She sang out the words, alone in her flat.

From the window she gazed happily down onto the fruit-stall erected outside the pub on the corner across the main road. Articulated lorries constantly swaggered past blocking her view. Five or six housewives were queuing for veg holding their shopping bags in front of them. Two young blokes, the stall-holders, cigarettes in their mouths, sang along to Capital Radio – the station she was listening to. They weighed up the fruit and vegetables, pausing only to exchange a word or two with the regulars. Penny admired them, up at dawn to buy the produce at Covent Garden, here by seven-thirty to set up the stall. They worked bloody hard. During idle moments she watched them from this window, impressed by their determination.

"Work hard and you'll get on." That was what her dad used to tell her. He would be proud now, if he were alive, to see all that she had achieved.

And would she miss all this, if she had the chance to get away, to really get on, to make it to America? No, she breathed steaming the glass in front of her, she certainly would not. She lifted her fingers from the receiver and the very next second the telephone rang again. "Hello?" As she spoke she positioned her face close to the art deco mirror on the wall in front of her, examining her skin for blemishes, wondering if she should book a facial for this afternoon as well as her hair appointment. Got to look my best tomorrow, going to do my damnedest, grab my chance, she promised herself.

It was Bill on the phone. "We're giving a house-warming party on Saturday. Do you want to come?"

"I'd love to." Mindlessly she turned the pages of her diary to Saturday, 24th and scribbled their names, Bill and Simon. "But don't tell me the house is finally ready?" she teased. "I can't believe it."

"No, of course it's not. But Heal's can't deliver the new carpets for another fortnight and Simon thinks we should give the party before they are fitted. I suppose he's right though it seems a bit dismal. Bare boards everywhere, what do you think?"

"William my friend, when is Simon not right?" She laughed, glancing again at her watch and dragging the telephone towards the bathroom.

"Yes, that's true. Okay then, better get on, I've got plumbers at the Saucer. That burst pipe has been dribbling again. See you Saturday. Shall I put you down as one or two?"

Such tact, she smiled. Bill knows Michael almost as well as I do. "Just lonely old me," she charmed. "Hey Bill, before you hang up, guess who I'm seeing tomorrow . . . and then we both must dash."

"Can't guess, tell me, who?"

Penny repeated the names of the director and the producer knowing that her dear friend would be more than impressed. "They are looking for an English actress to play opposite Robert De Niro. The film is being shot in Hollywood, to play his girlfriend, can you believe it!"

"Lucky you." She caught the tinge of regret in Bill's voice and bit her tongue for showing off in such a thoughtless fashion. It was difficult. She wanted to share her successes with Bill, more than anyone else (except perhaps one other) but she knew that so much of him regretted his decision to stop acting. Although, as she constantly reminded him, his tea-shop – The Flying Saucer, fondly known as the Saucer – was reputed to be the finest in London. "You're a star," she would tease. "Better reviews in the *Observer* than I receive," consoling him whenever he whispered to her of his pinings for the theatre. Simon had never really understood the actor's spirit in Bill. Charlie had, but Charlie had been in the fashion business – not so unlike show business. But Charlie was part of another life now. Personally, Penny had always cherished a certain fondness for Charlie. He had always been so discreet, and so generous towards her, during those difficult months. Months buried in her history and about which she never allowed herself to reflect.

"I'll tell you all about it on Saturday. Wish me luck."

"Of course. See you then." And they hung up, leaving Penny free to dress for her lunch-date, warning herself that she must not drink too much out of a sense of boredom. She loathed journalists but the BBC had insisted that she meet this one. Her new series was a smash hit in the Netherlands.

"Second floor and then all the way along the corridor. Last suite on the left." Penny thanked the porter and stepped into the lift. Her heart was pounding with nervous anticipation as she rang the doorbell above which were the numerals, 209. Moments later it was answered by a gangly fellow, all skin and bones, dressed in shirt-sleeves and wearing a chauffeur's hat. She announced herself, explaining in case he should doubt her that she was expected. With a broad cockney accent he invited her in and offered to take her coat.

"It'll be in the cloakrom there, when you need it."

She nodded, curious as to why he might be wearing his hat inside.

The apartment smelt of leather, fresh flowers and rich, musky French perfume. Everywhere had been designed in cream: thickly piled cream carpets, cream fuzzy wallpaper, cream silk drapes. A Lalique vase filled with extravagantly tall cream lilies stood on a small glass table just in front of her. They looked glorious, but the place had an uninhabited feel about it, just as though she had stepped into the cover page of a *House & Garden* magazine. A room that had never known a footstep. Everywhere felt strangely silent, demanding almost that one speak in muted reverential tones.

A sensation of ill ease began to suffuse her, exacerbating her nerves.

Miriam, the casting director, appeared from around a

corner looking over made-up and almost more nervous than Penny. A tight smile was fixed across her powdered face. Ironically she too was dressed in cream, and beige. The perfume was hers. A long string of imitation pearls dangled from her neck and reached to just above her waist. Penny smiled a hello. Lilies and pearls, a funeral parlour. The necklace gave the impression that Miriam was even shorter and dumpier than she actually was. She pulled and twisted at them in a rather theatrical fashion as though not quite knowing what she ought to be doing with her hands.

"Hello, darling, we're so grateful that you could make it," Miriam enthused loudly, no doubt within earshot of the Americans, and then a little more *sotto voce*, "They're crazy about your photos, longing to meet you. Sam's on the telephone to Los Angeles. He'll be with you in a moment, dear." And she turned vaguely about her as if searching for something but not knowing what. Inspiration. She spotted the chauffeur hovering by the front door, leaning casually, taking it all in, summing it all up.

"Ken, get Miss Morrison a glass of something, would you dear?" And with that Miriam was gone, disappearing back round the corner, her short thick calves sinking into the cream carpet.

Penny turned back to face Ken, who smirked, drew himself away from the door and languorously removed his hat, placing it on the surface of a bar which she had not noticed before − glass and gleaming silver tucked discreetly out of sight.

"I expect you're in need of a stiff one?" He was grinning lasciviously.

Smart arse, thought Penny, whose discomfort was making her tight and edgy. The last thing she needed was fifteen minutes with a lout like this. "Just a tomato juice, please." He poured the drink. From behind the bar − tall and thin, leaning slightly to one side like the tower of Pisa, large ears protruding from his worn skeletal skull − he watched her. A guy on the make.

"You an actress then?" His words were disparaging.

214

He might just as well have asked her if she were a whore.

"Something like that." Penny took the drink and moved away from him, burning him with a look which in other circumstances would have been even less pleasant.

Miriam reappeared smoking a menthol cigarette. "They're ready for you, darling, follow me. Don't be nervous. They're both so nice," she purred reassuringly. Penny noted that it was the first time that she had ever seen this casting director in a dress. Normally she wore slacks. Must be for the Americans.

And there they were, seated about ten feet apart, both in sunken, oversized velvet armchairs. Empty and unopened bottles of Schweppes tonic water, glasses, stuffed olives, an ice bucket, cocktail sticks and a virtually dead bottle of Gordon's gin rested on a glass table in between them, within arm's length of each of them.

Penny recognised the director at once. She had seen his photograph, a younger, more flattering impression of him, in the *Guardian* newspaper a few months earlier. He had given an interview during a retrospective of his work at the National Film Theatre. He was a highly regarded talent, and a bankable one, with two Oscars to his credit. Both award-winning pictures he had made with this same producer. They were a winning team. This new one was to be their third, or perhaps even their fourth, collaboration. If she could get this role it might secure her future, and it might make her, the prize and secret dream of almost every young actor, bankable, in other words, a star.

Both these men seated now in front of her were ancient giants of the film industry, both had lived and worked in Hollywood during its golden age. They had enriched the lives of such as the likes of Penny for many years. She recalled now having been seated with some long-forgotten boy in the back row of the scruffy dark cinema in her local town of Saxmundham. She would have been in her teens, dewy-eyed, watching movies that these two men had created, swept up by the passions and confusions of their working-class heroes, those fifties pin-ups. The rebel Brando, the misunderstood Jimmy Dean, the voices of a generation, she had dreamt of them, had loved and wanted them, Sellotaping their photos to her bedroom door and fantasising about her own chance to be up there on the screen with them.

Between them these two men had built and, she was later to discover of one of them, had broken careers.

As she stood wondering where to sit or what to do, waiting to be informed about what was expected of her, she took a deep unhurried breath and drew herself to her full height. She knew just what was at stake for her and she was as determined as she had ever been to win.

The producer rose to his unsteady feet. He couldn't be a day less than seventy. Miriam, lightly touching her arm with an encouraging nudge, introduced her with the gravity of a toastmaster and then slid humbly to the very edge of the room.

"Penny Morrison," said Sam, his head nodding in appreciation of her. "What a pleasure. We loved your photos, but you're even lovelier in the flesh," he flattered, rotating on the spot, apparently no longer very agile, to address his fellow American. "So Jimmy, we finally meet Miss Morrison. How about that? We talked about you already quite a few times, Penny."

Penny smiled, standing awkwardly in the middle of the exceptionally generous room, working hard to give the impression that she was thoroughly at her ease. "Hi," she said, with a strained casual air. Her voice was tight in her throat, her hands felt puffy and awkward resting against her hips (she almost wished that she had the distraction of Miriam's hideous pearls to fiddle with) and her blouse was damp and clung to her in what felt like unsightly patches.

Jimmy Gaza nodded curtly. He made no attempt to get up. Instead he poured himself a slug of gin, empty-ing the bottle, all the while appraising her, his eyes never leaving her, combing her up and down, committing every last inch of her to memory. He was a compact muscular figure, with half-moon glasses set in tortoise-shell rims resting on a beaked nose. Probably in his late forties.

"Sam, where would you like Penny to sit?" Miriam's voice from across the room attempting to be helpful, wanting to do the best that she could to put Penny at her ease. Penny's tension was mounting, her limbs felt rigid. These guys would serve me on toast for breakfast, she observed silently.

"Anywhere you like. You just make yourself at home, Penny. May I call you Penny?" cooed Sam.

"Yes, of course." A quick glimpse about her, sussing up the seating arrangements, before she plumped herself onto the sofa, probably the longest she had ever seen, regretting it instantly, aware that she was settling into the cushions, sinking as if in a quicksand and that this was no way to appear sexy and elegant!

"Why are you wearing trousers?"

"Why not?" she answered without thinking, a defensive response. The question had surprised her, caught her off guard.

"We can't see your legs."

"I'll roll them up if you like." It was a sarcastic retort which she had not intended to be quite so abrasive.

"Thank you, I'd like that."

Penny was speechless, a combination of anger and disbelief. "Sorry? You'd like me to roll up my trousers so that you can see my legs," she repeated.

"Thank you." Gaza without blinking, steely-featured, took a shot from his gin, waiting for Penny, who glanced swiftly about her as if expecting either Miriam or Sam to call a stop to the proceedings. No one said a word. Miriam puffed amateurishly at another menthol cigarette, legs wrapped over one another. Sam had reseated himself and was in search of the bottle of alcohol, craning his head about him like a tortoise, holding a glass which contained nothing but ice-cubes melting fast due to the central heating.

"Ken!" No response. "Ken!" he crooned with a gravel

217

twang after deducing that it was Gaza who had finished his bottle of gin. He spoke with an accent, something else besides the American. Viennese perhaps? An American Jewish émigré. There was not a great deal of power in his vocal chords. Sam was an elderly man with everything on his side except longevity.

The chauffeur appeared at the doorway, settling his jacket in place. "Yessir?" Smooth as butter Ken.

"Ken, bring us another bottle of gin and a glass for Miss Morrison."

With an obsequious imperceptible nod he disappeared.

Penny wondered if she should be rolling up her trousers now, while all this was happening, or should she wait until she had won her audience's attention. She almost wondered if anyone beside herself had taken Gaza's request seriously. She decided to play safe and do nothing, looking to Sam for a signal. He simply waved a mottled, Bermuda-tanned hand in her direction, craving her patience. She liked him instantly. There was a fierce intelligence and a middle European generosity about him, a compassion in his features.

Noticing a lull in the proceedings Miriam rushed to her feet and scurried after Ken, no doubt to hurry things along.

Left alone with the two moguls Penny coughed and then lifted and shuffled herself to the corner of the sofa, hoping to use the arm-rest as a de-sinking prop.

Sam watched her. He had kindly amused eyes. Penny guessed that they had seen pretty much all there was to see of life.

"I think Jimmy and I are ready to test you, Miss Morrison. Isn't that so, Jim?"

Gaza nodded, more a blink of acceptance than a positive movement of the head. Inscrutable and sharp behind his glass and glasses.

"How would you feel about that?" he continued.

The words were music to Penny's perplexed ears.

"Just tell me when." She grinned, hardly able to

contain her joy. "I'll be there."

On Saturday evening Penny sat alone in her flat. Michael had promised to 'drop by for a drink' around seven. Not unusually he had not shown up. Nor had he telephoned, but that too was not unusual. She was glad now that she had refrained from mentioning Bill and Simon's party. As it was she had been expecting to go unaccompanied.

She had placed two glasses and a rather excellent bottle of Chablis at her side around seven and had settled with a book to wait. It was ten to nine. She had already consumed two-thirds of the bottle. The telephone rang. It was Ben, reconfirming the details of the screen test which had been postponed a day and was now scheduled for Tuesday. "Ben," she laughed, "you sound more jittery than I am!"

She poured herself another glass of wine and relaxed back into an art deco sofa which she had purchased at a local flea market that very afternoon. Feeling confident about the outcome of the screen test she had been on a spending spree. In reality it was an expression of her nerves, always when she had the heebie-jeebies she went shopping, it was her way of forcing herself to win. "Going for bust," she called it.

She hadn't told Michael about the screen test because she had not seen him for over a week. The Chablis, a swish haircut for her and a silk tie for him were to have been her way of celebrating the good news with him. Her glass stained with lipstick hung from between her fingers while the other remained untouched on the tray. The bottle was almost empty.

"Damn you, Michael!" She lifted herself from the sofa and climbed the stairs to her attic bedroom to change. If he arrived now she would not answer the bell.

The party was in full swing when she arrived. Bill greeted her at the door. He was looking beetroot-flushed, mildly sozzled and wearing a navy-blue striped butcher's apron, the type they sold at Heal's.

"You're just in time to eat," he grinned. "Come on up, gorgeous."

Upstairs in the dining room – the house began on the first floor because the ground floor had been given over to The Flying Saucer tea-shop – the place smelt of pasta, pesto sauce and garlic. Someone shoved a glass in her hand. "Red or white?" the good-looking stranger enquired. In one hand he held a bottle of Chianti and in the other, Frascati.

"I'd better stick to white." Though why she was being precautious she was not sure because she was pretty certain that she was going to get plastered tonight, screen test or not the following week. For some inexplicable reason she was feeling blue. She put it down to Michael. Simon came swanning towards her, stainless-steel kitchen utensils in hand.

"Hello beautiful, glad you made it. Bill has been worrying, he feared you might not get here."

They both looked across the room in the direction of Bill, who appeared anything but worried. He was flirting outrageously and vaguely dancing with a group of young men who looked as though they had been freshly plucked from a sauna or gymnasium.

Penny leant forward to kiss Simon on the cheek. He reeked of herbs and Geoffrey Beene cologne. "The house is looking terrific. I love the Wedgwood-blue walls and, sorry, I forgot to bring a bottle."

"You can take us for a sumptuous spread at the Ritz before you leave for Hollywood," he grinned camply.

Penny raised her glass in acceptance and glanced about the room as Simon disappeared back towards the kitchen bustling with his friends, all chopping and screeching merrily. There were next to no women about, she noted, and less than a handful of straight men either. Fat chance for Mr Right! She giggled silently, sipping at her wine, vaguely wondering whom she could talk to.

Someone laid a hand against her bare shoulder and

above the beat of a Linda Ronstadt record shouted her name. She turned to find a face from the past. Her stomach lurched in shock. It was Nicholas Lockett, Harry's art agent. She took a deep breath and smiled ruefully.

"My darling, you grow more beautiful every time I see you," he charmed. He had begun losing his hair since they had last met. "How are you, my dear? I caught a fleeting glimpse of you on the box recently. Rather good, I thought. Harry says you're quite a celebrity these days. A household name, he claims."

"Harry?" So Harry still spoke of her from time to time. She had not been entirely forgotten by him.

She had often asked herself, one night or another, if he had been amongst an audience, sitting unknown to her in the theatre where she had been performing, or whether he might have switched on a television and by chance seen her there, or opened a magazine only to discover an article about her. From time to time when she gave an interview or a performance she thought of him, wondering if what she did ever reached him.

A tiny part of all of it, always, was meant for him.

It had been over five years now, Boxing Day 1973. Perhaps the remarkable part was that during these five years this was the first time she had heard anything of him. But then she had been careful to seal him out, or wall herself in. She had never answered Ches's calls in those early days, not since the New Year's Eve party until, finally he had stopped telephoning. Harry had never rung. She had kidded herself, believing until this moment that she had buried him, that she had built another life for herself but that had never been true. There had never been anyone else who had touched her soul as Harry had.

Nicholas rattled on, gossiping contentedly, oblivious to her silence, impressing her with his list of clients and artists, the success of his new gallery recently opened behind Piccadilly, his plans to open a second one in New York and informing her that Harry's work was beginning to find a market, albeit a small one. "He will be a big success in America, I'm sure of it."

"How is he?" she ventured as casually as she might, suddenly glad that Michael had not shown up tonight. Which paintings had he sold she questioned privately. Some that she had posed for?

"You know he has a son?" She shook her head. "They've christened the poor child Ziggy. Très hippy, my dear."

"He must be five or six now." Penny sipped her Frascati, picturing little Ziggy Knowle, wondering who he resembled.

"And Helen?" Penny hardly dared bring herself to ask.

"She's blooming. Well, you know Helen. Carries on like Medea, darling, but so resilient. She doesn't work, of course. Doesn't need to. They have a nanny for Ziggy and she takes off. Back to Greece now that things are liberated there or off elsewhere, freedom fighting. I think she's just left for California, some nuclear disarmament rally I believe, or perhaps it's Nicaragua this month. Harry doesn't seem to get involved with her flights of fancy. Well, you know him, he just gets on with his work."

"Yes, I suppose he does." He used to get involved, she thought. He cared for Nikos, helped Melina and the children escape. Penny peered into her glass. Empty. So Harry and Helen had stayed together after all.

Something within her had just been numbed, anaesthetised, just as though the very thing she had been working towards had been crushed. In the very deepest recesses of her heart a tiny part of her had prayed that he would not stay with Helen, that one day, one miracle of a day, he would forgive her and would return to her.

"I understand what happened, Pen." That was what she had been waiting for.

It was Harry that she had wanted to tell about her screen test for America, not Michael. Secretly, of course, she *had* told him, just as she always confided everything to him.

Crushed by crowds of noisy partying people she realised that that was what Harry had become for her, an inner life. He inhabited a consecrated place within her and from there he never hurt, or judged, or betrayed her, always loved her and had never left her.

Simon yelled from the kitchen door that supper was served. A loud cheer rang out and odd groups began to dribble towards the groaning table.

"Shall I get you another drink?"

Penny shook her head. "I promised to help in the kitchen," she lied. "My turn." She kissed Nicholas on the cheek.

"I'll send your love to Harry, shall I? He'll be thrilled to know I bumped into you."

Penny with her hand still on his shoulder nodded elegantly and slid away from him, melting into the gathering around the spaghetti, and then when all attention was on some over-sized dish arriving from the oven she grabbed her chance to flee. She would get drunk tonight, but not here. Her grief would be shed in private.

On her drive back from Regent's Park she stopped at a recently opened Late Nite Deli in Camden Town and picked up a bottle of Burgundy.

Back at the flat there was one message on her answer machine. Not Michael as she had supposed. Nothing from him, but an invitation from Jimmy Gaza to join him for dinner and asking her to call him at the Connaught when she got back. She glanced at her watch. It was already eleven-thirty. She had not left until nearly ten.

He's eating late, she thought wryly, speculating about why he had called and deciding not to return his call. Not tonight anyway.

She poured herself a drink and pictured Harry, alone perhaps with Ziggy and Helen in California. Was he still living at the studio? Without a second thought she leant across to the telephone and dialled their old number. The bell sounded several times before someone picked up the receiver. It was him. His voice was thick and lazy as though she had woken him.

"Hello?"

She could not bring herself to speak. It had been too long.

"Hello?"

Oh Harry, will I ever rid myself of you and the sin I committed against you, she pined, as deftly she replaced the receiver.

14

The following morning.

"Hello, is that Penny?"

"Yes, hello." Her voice sounded like something being suctioned through a Hoover nozzle. Her head was as heavy as a cannonball.

"I left a message for you on your Ansaphone asking you to call me last night. Did ya find it?"

"Yes, I did."

"I was expecting to hear from you."

"Yes, I was going to ring this morning . . . "

What the hell time was it? Penny rolled heavily onto her right flank, grappling for the clock, turning it towards her. It had fallen on its face on the bare wooden floorboards at her bedside. The glass was cracked. She must have knocked it with her arm searching for sleeping pills. Jesus, ten past twelve. With effort she lifted her pounding head and glanced towards the dormer window. She was lost, not knowing whether it was the small hours of the morning or the middle of the day. Beyond the curtainless window the city skyline suggested signs of day. A bleak toneless day. A blanket of battleship-grey clouds type of day. It was drizzling and it was afternoon. A wet Sunday afternoon, the city's worst, and she had slept right through.

"It was too late to call you when I got home," she growled, coughing like an early morning smoker. Something had congested in her throat. "Excuse me." She spoke with difficulty, eyes watering. She was feeling ghastly.

"Partying, huh? That's no way for a kid with a big screen test coming up to behave," Gaza chided lightly and then with a more deliberate, artful note in his voice

225

which Penny was unable to decipher – it read somewhere between concern for her well-being and worry that she may not be made of the right stuff for the film – he added, "Jeez honey, you sound terrible. I hope I haven't woken you."

Penny searched for nonchalance, pulling herself together as efficiently as she was able. "No, nooh of course not. I was miles away, buried in a book. What's happening? Has there been a change in the arrangements for this week?"

"No, no. Thought ya might like t' brunch with me today. Discuss the test, an' the rehearsal we have tomorrow. Get to know one another a little. Or mebbe you've eaten already?"

"No, it's a great idea. I'm starving," she lied, hauling herself from the mattress, knowing that it was more than she dare do to refuse him. From their one previous meeting she had sussed that he had the manner of one who always got his own way. However, to charm and fascinate him would take some doing, after the wine and pills she had finished the previous night and the way she felt this morning.

"OK, listen it's five after one. You wanna grab a cab and come directly here?"

"Five past one! My clock must have sto— ."

Oh shit! The hour had changed to summertime, and she had forgotten it. "Would you mind if we make it two o'clock?" she fudged feebly. "I promised to return some newspaper cuttings to a friend of mine before this afternoon. I could stop at her place and drop them in on my way." Buying the time she needed to put her act together. A little witch-hazel on the eyes, a cold shower, get herself in motion,

"Sure, take your time, honey, take your time." Of course he probably didn't mean that. "I'll call down to the restaurant and book us a table."

After the best kedgeree that she had ever tasted and the first few velvet mouthfuls of a bottle of Margaux '61 – a treat that Gaza had insisted upon – Penny was beginning to feel light, even pretty good about herself. She was less bruised, still a touch puffy around the eyes, but a little more able to cope. Harry, her longing for him, the unnourished pain and the crass stupidity of her cowardly behaviour, the late-night phone call to him, had been folded away like rejected wedding-linen, buried once more in a private bottom drawer.

Gaza was proving to be anything but dull company if a little on the disconcerting side. His eyes cool as marble were lasers which never left her, not for one second. Even when addressing the waiters and the sommelier he fixed her with his gaze, weighing up every word she spoke, every gesture she made. He was honing in, breathing down her neck, sitting close, almost inhaling her; it felt as if a microphone was recording every whisper of emotion, lingering upon each construction of thought.

To diffuse her sense of being pried upon she had been keeping him talking, throwing the ball constantly back into his court, asking enthusiastic questions about his films and about the people he had worked with. It was her method of keeping him at bay.

"And you?" She had smiled, hovering coquettishly on the safe side of flirtatious, playing fascinated by him.

And she had been doing fine, even scoring a point or two here and there, until she had asked him about his childhood and discovered that he had been born in Greece.

"I was born just outside Athens but I was brought up in the States. We fled to America in '41 – my parents, two brothers, me – when the Germans invaded the mainland. We were Jews – " he paused lost in subdued reflection, and then, "You know Greece?" He shot the question at her, probing her features whilst tapping the table with his stubby fingers as though habitually impatient.

"Just a little." Suddenly she pictured Nikos whimpering on the floor, a rifle at his head. His shrivelled drooping cock. Almost heard his cry. That night he died. Helen in bed with Harry. Waiting for their return, cold on the mountainside.

"Where?" It was Gaza doing the probing now.

"Amber, to complement your eyes." Nikos, tired, smiling, handing her his sandied treasure.

"Where what?" she whispered, closing her eyes. As though the darkness might erase it. What are you asking me? Where did Nikos die, is that what he's saying? She was momentarily lost, an unclear head, an excess of panaceas, too many memories, the discomfort of Gaza's determination to know her. She glanced towards him. Pity me, she seemed to say. Don't dig too deep. Don't disturb. It doesn't hold together. Gaza squinted those ruthless unrelenting eyes. And then he smiled, triumphantly. He had pierced into her. Not the details perhaps, what are those but story? But he had punctured her reserve, cracked the very shell of her.

The trolley arrived with their roast lamb. It smelt mouthwateringly good but Penny had long since lost her appetite.

Later – three heady glasses later – he offered her an Armagnac. She waved her hand as a refusal. "Calvados?" Once more she declined.

"OK, good! Let's go to work!" Penny was momentarily puzzled. "Let's go upstairs to my suite and take a look at those scenes. Give you something to think about overnight."

Cliché images of Hollywood directors, starlets and casting couches slipped through her mind but, aside from those, she could think of no acceptable reason why she should refuse him.

Upstairs, directly she was inside the door, he chucked a few pages of script at her, drew the curtains and switched on an insufficient table lamp thus insulating them both in a crepuscular world of make-believe.

"We'll start with the scene at the beach house. Late at night. Larky is walking Kate back, got it?"

She nodded. Suddenly, while clutching tightly at the

typewritten pages of dialogue, she lost her fear. Just listening to him, mesmerised by him, the director now, no longer focusing on her but on the creation of the world he was setting.

"It's the weekend, see. They're out of the city at the beach. Deserted. A moon overhead, the sound of the waves, her hair blown by the wind on the warm sea-water." He was conjuring up an image and she was bewitched by the intensity of the man at work. This Greek Jew who had fled with his family in fear of his life from his own country, who had risen to direct the likes of Brando, Jimmy Dean, Liz Taylor, a galaxy of others and now, Penny Morrison. Her distressed night and her thick head inflamed by the Margaux all began to dissolve. An energy from within her – born of her love of work, of film – began to flow, locking her into his narrative imagination, igniting her own. Nothing could take away from her the knowledge that she was here working with him, even if she didn't get the part. Here in front of her was one of the most perceptive directors of his generation and the one that she most admired and respected.

"It's one a.m., Penny. Kate's feeling real easy in Larky's company," he rhapsodised, "and Larky wants this woman. He's burnin' for the touch of her."

Penny felt Gaza's presence draw close to her elbow, coming to rest just behind her. Leaning over her shoulder, not quite touching the skin on the side of her cheek with his own, he pointed to the writer's directions on the script. He was a hair's breadth away from her. Penny edged herself unobtrusively to her left, putting them centimetres further apart.

Gaza continued, "He wants her so bad it's eating at him and she knows it. She feels her power over him and that's a real turn-on for her." He focused his gaze on the side of her face, lowering the level of his voice. "You understand what I'm telling you? You know this feeling?"

Penny nodded uncomfortably.

She smelt Gaza's passion coursing through his blood and she inhaled the tobacco on his hot breath. He was no taller than her – five foot six inches – and when she turned to him she could have touched the dark rough flesh on his dog-eared face. She felt overwhelmed by him, swamped by the power of his scruffy unshakeable energy. He took hold of her hand, speaking Larky's lines, which he knew by heart.

"Nice 'n' easy," he directed, before she, trembling, spoke the character's words. Kate's lines – a few simple well-chosen thoughts.

"When I was a girl . . . " her character began. Penny's voice was reedy and uncentred. Gaza eased himself from alongside her to in front of her drawing himself about her. His face was as close to hers as envelope to paper. Penny faltered and stopped speaking. She was feeling flushed and confused. The proximity of him disturbed her. Was this the behaviour of the character Larky, or the man Jimmy Gaza? And was it the man himself or the director working in some curious misunderstood way?

"Go on, don't be passive," he coaxed. "She wants this man. She feels the need of him in her groin. It's making her wet."

Penny said nothing. She lowered her head. "I can't see the script if you hold onto me like this," she muttered, head still bent in perplexity.

"Then improvise it!" he snapped, barely stifling his anger. Penny opened her mouth to continue. Nothing was forthcoming. Not a sound. She felt a sting of tears rise to her flushed face. None of this was what she had dreamed of. The man glaring centimetres away from her was a brute. This was not the genius. She could not reconcile this man with the artist who had told universal stories about ordinary folk trapped within themselves, strangled by their environment and their own small lives. Unexpectedly, the hand that he was holding, her hand, he twisted against her back and he lurched her towards him, pulling her against his breast. She felt his erect penis, hard and unrelenting like the man. Without a thought, with the free hand that still clutched at the crumpled sweaty script, she thrust him away from her. "Please don't!" she cried. He tottered back a step or two and then re-finding his balance, stood firm, speaking to her with a controlled bass voice.

"Where's your passion, Penny? You have great sexuality but you're tight with it. That's not good for an actress. That won't make you a star."

"I think I'd better go home," she whispered curtly and crossed the room to retrieve her handbag waiting where she had left it on the sofa. He remained rooted, watching her, apparently not fazed by her. As she walked past him he took her gently, but certainly, by the wrist.

"Learn those lines. If you were committed you would have done so already. Tomorrow we'll work on the passion." His words sounded like a threat in her ears. "See you in the morning. Get some sleep, and don't be late."

"Goodnight," she said, and made her way to the door, pressing it closed, like a seal, behind her.

The first message on the machine told her that Michael had telephoned. "Where've you been all my life, sweetheart?" One of his corny smooth-talking messages. Some nights, lonely nights, she was glad of him, of the attention that came with him (when it did), but tonight, angered by the impudence of man's basic self, it merely affronted her. He was suggesting lunch the following Sunday in Deauville. Saying he would hire a private plane. They could make up a foursome with Dennis, a financial partner of his and Angela, his wife. His very boring wife! Could she confirm with him before the end of the weekend if she fancied the idea because he would need to give notice for the booking of the light aircraft. "You've got a bloody cheek," she railed at the machine.

Not capable of simply apologising for having stood her up, Michael was offering this as a bait to re-ignite her and to dissolve the resentment he knew she must be feeling towards him. Michael hated scenes, hated any expression of commitment or emotion. "You think I'm putty in your hands," she warned angrily. "Well, not tonight, brother. You can go to hell. I don't want lunch with you or your unspeakably dull friends. Not even in France!" She spoke the rebuke aloud with a note of triumph in her voice while striding to the refrigerator in search of white wine. The next message caught her by surprise, jolting her in the pleasurable release of her temper. She had barely poured a measure when she was arrested by the mention of her name. "Hello Pen?" Glass in one hand, bottle in the other, she moved back to the machine, to listen more attentively, lured by the voice, only half believing what she was hearing.

". . . anyway I needed to reach you and had no idea if you were still at this number but I'm pleased to discover that you are and I sincerely hope you are not working out of town, in the theatre or something. If you could call me as soon as possible I'd be grateful. My number hasn't changed either. Hope to catch up with you again very soon and hope you're well. It's important. Oh, stupid of me. It's Harry Knowle."

Penny, still incredulous, played the message over again. Could he have guessed that it had been she who had hung up on him the night before? Surely not. Guilt suffused her. No, more probably he had spoken to Nicholas Lockett. Yes, that must be it. She finished pouring the wine and curled herself into the sofa, sinking deep into the cushions. She was trembling. His voice had sounded grave and distant, though that was not unusual. She sipped at the wine wondering whether she should call back right away or wait awhile. She would not be answering Michael's message, that was for sure. Let him stew, she thought. It was over. She decided to learn her lines for the morning and afterwards, when the work was settled in her mind, she would call Harry. Savouring the idea of the telephone conversation to come she went in search of her script.

About an hour later the telephone rang. It was Gaza's producer, Sam, apologising for the delay with the test and inviting her for dinner at the Grosvenor House Hotel.

"That's very sweet of you, Sam," she purred, containing her surprise, "but I think an early night is what I need."

"OK, honey. I'll call you tomorrow after the rehearsal. Sleep well." The call puzzled her. It had broken into the safe world of her imagination. What is this, she thought sarcastically, a conspiracy or a competition for my body? Had the old boy known that she had lunched with Gaza? Surely Gaza had not discussed with Sam what had occurred between them. She could almost hear the words, the tone of his brittle unrelenting voice judging her. Man to man. Two Americans who knew their business. "I tell you, this kid ain't right, Sam. She lacks passion."

Lacks passion, huh. OK, let's see. The very idea of such a call caused her flesh to chill.

It must be a coincidence, she consoled herself, or were all those lurid Hollywood myths a reality. Hollywood dreams and nightmares.

She poured herself another drink and settled back into the cushions, chastising herself for having bought the bloody sofa the day before. She had been impetuous, as usual. Things were not quite so hunky-dory as she had been kidding herself. She felt this film slipping away from between her fingers and turned dolefully to the next page of the script.

It was the beach house scene. The lines were already familiar to her. Her eyes flicked the length of the page. Words echoed through her mind and with them images of Jimmy Gaza, crude and overwhelming, hovering much too close. Carried on the tide of an exhalation of breath she muttered something vaguely obscene, chucked the script aside and reflected upon her afternoon. She was quite definitely ill at ease about where it was all leading, and what he might try the following day and how she should handle it. Working on her passion!

Bravo! It was foolproof, and pretty tawdry. She deliberated about whether she should call her agent and rejected the idea almost as soon as she had posed it. It immediately seemed feeble, crying home.

In any case Ben would almost certainly remind her that: "Sweetheart, this is Hollywood. You'd better learn to handle it." And he would have a valid point, but it was in moments like these that she chided herself for not having chosen a female agent who might be more sympathetic. Part of the curse of working in an industry dominated by men. Would a female director behave in such a fashion with a young actor? Recollecting one or two of the female casting directors she knew, pretty voracious women some of them, she decided that they might. Perhaps, after all, it was the nature of power rather than gender.

She decided to call Harry and poured herself another drink – Dutch courage – before dialling the number. As she did so, the telephone bell sounded again, startling her out of her wits. She was certainly nervy! She took a deep breath and a slug of wine, betting that it would be Gaza, preparing herself for him.

"Yes?" Her manner was icy. She was just about ready to tell him to get lost.

It was Harry. "Oh, goodness, it's you. I was expecting someone . . . well, long time no . . . " She was twittering. He had caught her off guard. She had wanted to be relaxed for this call, easy with him, with no sign of her present tensions. It had been a long time since they had spoken. She wanted him to know that she was getting along just fine.

"I'm glad I've found you," he began. His voice had a flatness to it and a distracted air. He didn't seem to have noticed her gauche ill ease. He continued, "I need to ask you a favour, I have some rather bad news."

Penny reassembled her head, changing tack, thinking of Helen or little Ziggy. Had something happened to his son? But why would he call her? The last thing that occurred to her was what she was about to hear.

"Ches is dying," he stated baldly. Pause, a long pause between them. "Look, I probably wouldn't have troubled you after so long but . . . well, the truth is, he's been asking for you, several times now. Once or twice when he was semi-conscious he mumbled your name."

"Dying?" she repeated blindly, closing her eyes and recollecting Ches, dear lame Ches. The news stunned her.

"I promised him I'd try and track you down." There was a silence while Penny assimilated the reality of what was being told to her. "Listen, I know it's been a long time and you . . . we've moved on and everything but I think it would make a big difference to him if you could manage a visit."

"I'll come now. Do you want me to come now?"

No answer. "Harry?"

"Yeah, yeah, I'm here. I'm just trying to find the . . . Shit, I must've left my watch at the hos— What time is it?"

Penny spun about. "Seven-thirty. No, wait!" She remembered the hour change the previous night. She still hadn't altered the clock. "Eight-thirty, yes, it's eight-thirty."

"It's too late tonight. He's in hospital, you see. Sunday visiting and all that. Could you make tomorrow morning?"

"I can't, Harry. Oh damn it! Listen, I'm working tomorrow. I've got this scr— What about the evening? I'll come straight after my rehearsal."

"Good, good. I'll meet you . . . let me think . . . yeah, I'll meet you at the hospital."

They made the arrangements – an hour and a location – speaking like strangers, efficient and without intimacy, their past distanced by time and the looming tragedy. When Penny replaced the receiver she breathed heavily, sucking for oxygen like an asthmatic. And then she wept bitterly, crying like a deserted or alienated child. There was no one to bear witness, to measure the density of her sorrow, or the extent of her loneliness which she had long stifled, and no one to comfort her in the dead of night, to hold and stroke her, to help her feel whole again.

The change of hour had delayed the dying of the light. Penny had grown used to the early wintry darkness. This evening she almost craved its isolating protection. Spring would soon be on its way and gentler weather, but not tonight. Tonight, through shafts of slow-fading day, the wind blew harshly. Coming up the street, heralding the growing darkness, wind whorls curled themselves beneath Penny's thin raincoat. They sliced into her insufficiently clothed flesh causing her whole body to tremble. Harry took her by the arm, more to support her than for friendship's sake. She was looking as drained as a corpse herself. A damaged stick-insect.

"Come on, let's find somewhere warm and welcoming and I'll buy us both a drink," he soothed.

The grey brick hospital towered behind them like a disused gas-works.

"Thanks." Her head was bowed, as if against the biting weather, but in reality hidden from him: the stranger at her side whose touch she recognised and cherished but whose face spoke of a steeliness, a maturity she had not figured on. His hair was darker and it had been chopped off – not short but no longer falling to his shoulders. His skin was untanned and scrubbed, still clean-shaven, but marked now by the first lines of age. They made him more handsome, a wintry, northern strength. His clothes were more orthodox, less flowing. But his eyes . . . they were as blue, they had not lost their intensity. She couldn't face him. Not yet. It was as though every memory, every past moment – those that she had held so dear and those that she regretted – were slipping away, lost behind the shocking mask and the dying eyes of Ches.

"I hadn't expected him to be . . . quite so . . . "

"He looked rough tonight but he was pleased to see you."

236

"How long has he got?"

"A couple of days, maybe a week." Bald facts spoken compassionately and with acceptance. Harry unlocked the passenger door of his car and shuffled her onto the seat before hurrying round to the other door, briefly checking for any approaching main-road traffic. An insalubrious part of London this: hurtling cars, winos, junkies.

Seated, he faced her. She was in profile to him, her expression still partially buried in her blue scarf. Blue skin, blue scarf. Hair darker, lacking sunlight. He had never painted her with such colours, never known her thus. Before it had been mellow, glowing shades. Voluptuous shapes. With both his hands, chilled against her cheeks, he eased her towards him. "Very fragile," he whispered. A tear toppled like a traitor from her hazel eyes and fell onto his finger. With his other hand he brushed the light bags beneath. "You look beaten," he acknowledged kindly. She simply managed a nod.

Gaza had behaved like a monster all day, relentless and dictatorial one moment and the next uncomfortably close, sweet-talking, sugary and greedy. She was feeling confused and dazed by him and had been stifling an angry desire to tell him to get lost. "You can keep your bloody film," she had been wanting to say, "I don't need this!" But of course she did need it, she did not want him to keep his film. She was desperate for the part and she was determined to soldier on, bite her tongue and prove to him that of passion, she had plenty and on screen, she could be sensational. Finally in the dying throes of an appalling day Gaza had received a message saying that the test had been postponed until the day after the following. Confusion over the studio-booking, the note explained.

"Well, it's a helluva bore, but it gives you and I another shot at the script tomorrow." And he had called her for yet another rehearsal the following afternoon. "Two o'clock sharp," he warned her as though she were in the habit of being late, which she certainly wasn't. Her baptism by fire was not over yet but at least she had the morning off. She had been exhausted. And now, the vision of Ches lying dying in his bed had chewed into her gut, had settled itself malevolently like some alien body chomping away within her viscera.

They cruised around Notting Hill Gate for a while. She was sufficiently vigilant to catch the ghosts of her past raise their disappointed heads. Harry turned the car into Kensington Gardens Square. They drove past the cramped bedsit she had once rented. The four-storey building had been renovated, a crisp white exterior bore the sign, 'Luxurious apartments for sale, Sole agents . . . ' Penny recollected the gas-metered room. Together they had crawled back to that welcoming single bed each night, shattered after gutting Harry's studio.

It had, after all, been his studio. Still was. His, his wife and his son.

"We'll plaster the walls with naked drawings of you," he had whispered provocatively. "And be immensely happy, you and I . . . " His promise to her; she had never forgotten those words, made such a distance ago, almost inaudible now. Blearily she recalled her dejection at the discovery of Ches on the studio steps, his unannounced arrival, unthinkable now, that she could have so resented his presence. Pre-Nikos. So long ago.

Moments from other lives, not these people. It could not be.

Lost tonight, somewhere between trauma and numbness.

"Listen, I think we'll head down Park Lane and find something over that way," he announced finally. She wondered silently if perhaps he too had remembered. Fleetingly he glanced towards her. "What do you think?"

"If you like," she mumbled. His hand found hers resting in her lap and lay across it. She felt its warmth on her chilled fingers, its strength all but draining the last breath of her resilience. "Soon be there."

He parked the car in one of the leafy squares behind Harrods and switched off the lights. Darkness had fallen while they had been travelling. Street lamps shone alongside them. Lasers of light through an obscure Scotch mist, settling for the night.

"Now, we have a few pubs, a pretty pretentious wine bar and several hotels. All within walking distance. You choose. What do you fancy?"

She shook her head, "Whatever."

"Or," he drew her gently towards him. His wool scarf brushed the white of her eye causing it to water. He pressed her close against him across the gearbox – an awkward and almost paternal gesture. "You could let me take you back home with me. We can be at the studio in fifteen minutes."

Penny hadn't the stamina to resist. Why would she?

Ziggy was sleeping. They were obliged to creep. She fell once or twice on creaking steps. It had been too long to remember which were which. Harry strode on ahead, opening doors, unlocking Chubb locks, paying off an awkward adolescent girl – the babysitter, a neighbour, who hurried past Penny shyly stepping down the stairs.

Inside, little of what she had helped to create re-mained intact. There were still the magnolia white walls, but now the place was furnished, albeit sparsely, with a few elegant well-chosen antique pieces. Helen's touch, no doubt. One or two tall dark wood sculptures poised in corners – of African or Egyptian origin she would guess.

"Helen's in the States," explained Harry, *sotto voce*. He pointed a finger towards the ceiling, the loft area that once had been his studio. "Ziggy's upstairs." Penny nodded as though all this might not have been new to her, masking her sense of intrusion. Almost an enemy spy, she declared herself silently. She glanced along the walls, still hidden by Harry's paintings. It was no longer her own face that stared back at her. He had found new models. Most of them clothed women. A host of women, different faces, older, coarser, more bleak. East London scapes and skylines. Foreboding colours. Wintry shapes.

Harry stepped towards her and removed her rain-coat, tossing it away from them towards a high-backed chaise-longue. It slid to the floor. Neither moved to retrieve it. He held his arms about her, standing firmly behind her, wrapped tight, binding around a parcel. She leaned in to him just as though without his heat she might perish.

"Thanks for making the effort. Ches often spoke of you and those early days here. He used to watch you on television. He's a loyal fan."

"I wonder why he didn't return to the States," she murmured, noticing that she was already referring to Ches in the past and that she was shutting out the implication of what Harry had just said.

"I guess he figures we're his family. His mother died a couple of years ago and his dad has been dead a long while." He paused. "Anyway, he's too sick to be moved." Releasing his long arms he gently took her hand and led her towards the kitchen. "Tea, brandy or chocolate?" he offered.

Penny smiled gratefully. "Chocolate. Thank you."

Harry busied himself about the space, shutting and opening cupboard doors with a consideration for the small being sleeping above them. A series of white units had been fitted. The room was pristine, the carpentry work fine and well-finished. Harry caught her glance. "Ches," he explained.

"Did this?"

He nodded. "Soon after he discovered he was sick Helen and he drew up the sketches. A couple of years ago, and then he built it. Pretty smart, eh? Said he got fed up with my promises of a kitchen."

"Does Helen know . . . ?"

"I haven't been able to get hold of her." His response was brisk.

"She'll be very distressed." Penny studied him, alerted by his curtness, grasping at a crack in her own despair.

"Can I see him?"

Harry glanced towards her, mixing milk and chocolate, not understanding. "If I tiptoe and promise not to wake him may I go upstairs and see Ziggy?"

Harry laughed without emitting sound. "Sure, come with me." And leading her by the hand – like children playing midnight truant – they stole through the main sitting-room and climbed the attic stairs. Ziggy's door was inches ajar, a bedside light remained illuminated. Harry pushed lightly against the painted wood, revealing the peeping head of a small boy across the room, curled sleeping like a squirrel. He eased Penny inside and as one body they crossed stealthily towards him. The boy stirred but did not awake, transported by his private dreams. Penny crouched to view him more thoroughly. His features were otherwise hidden by the shadow from an upper bunk.

He was tawny-skinned, like his father, with the same sleek locks. High cheekbones were visible even in his chubby unformed face. She saw little of Helen in him, but then she wanted him to resemble his father, Harry's creation alone, as if denying Helen's share in the making of him. The jaw, less angular, was Helen's, she conceded. Perhaps the colour of his eyes too, she could not judge those while he slept. Needing to touch him, to feel him alive she cautiously lifted her fingertips and lightly dabbed his soft damp cheek before wiping a light spittle from his chin. The small boy snuffled and rolled away onto his right side. Harry drew her back, took her hand and led her from the attic; it was she, not he, who lacked experience in these matters. She glanced swiftly once more into the room before he closed the door. No longer an artist's studio but a child's bedroom: bunk beds, adhesive cartoons on the walls, a blackboard scribbled upon with coloured chalks (would he grow up to be an artist too?), train set, double-decker buses, lorries scattered as debris about the floor and an indistinct perfume of damp bedding pervading all. A small person's world. A world she had never inhabited since her own solitary childhood.

Downstairs in the kitchen Penny drank the chocolate that Harry had made for her while he smoked a cigarette and enjoyed a glass of Italian red.

"He looks like you."

"One day, that little fella up there will re-create the world. Everything will change thanks to him and others like him."

She sat at the kitchen table, listening as he leaned against the sink. There was a slight ill ease or impermanence in their positioning yet it seemed they were alone at last. She unravelled her long scarf and rested it on the table. Harry watched her, sipping at his wine. "You've changed." He laughed. "Leaner, more hollowed out." She felt vulnerable under his scrutiny. With him her act felt empty.

"You alright?"

She nodded, apparently brightly. "Better, thanks. I'll just finish this and call a cab. Must be late."

"Stay, if you want."

The offer took her by surprise, warm and yet somehow formal. "I . . . uh . . . better not." Only the merest of hesitations, an inhalation of breath, might have betrayed her. "I've got a big day tomorrow. Work to do." Halfheartedly she reached for her scarf and rested it in her lap. Harry did not move. He dragged on his cigarette and sipped again at his wine.

"Have you got a local number?" she persisted. "For a taxi."

"What are you rehearsing?"

As he asked she rubbed at her eyes with the palm of her hand. She was weary and realised that she did not want to be reminded of or think about the following day. "I've got a screen test on Wednesday. It was supposed to be tomorrow but . . . it's been postponed. We're rehearsing again tomorrow."

"What time?"

"What?"

"Are you rehearsing?"

Suddenly she was feeling irritable, as if trapped by him or by her own emotions which she was unable to handle. "After lunch."

"Great. I'll give you a lift north when I go back to the hospital in the morning."

She rose to go, scarf in hand. "I think I should call a cab tonight, Harry."

"As you want, but no cab, I'll give you a lift."

From above them Ziggy called out. Harry strode purposefully from the room, glass and cigarette still in hand. Realising, he returned to the sink, ran water on the lit tip of the cigarette and threw it in a bin. Swiftly, conscious of the whining child, he downed the remains of the wine. "Give me a couple of minutes," he said, "and I'll be with you."

Alone in the kitchen – once upon a time her kitchen – Penny rose and wandered aimlessly about, glancing at this or that, not searching for anything in particular. Somehow, like a newly arrived beast, getting the smell of the place and wondering if any tiny sign of her past life here remained. Harry's murmurings drifted through the ceiling from above, soothing his disturbed son back to sleep again. Penny realised how jealous she still felt, both of Ziggy and Helen. She was startled by the sudden ringing of a telephone on the wall behind her and stared at it without answering, wondering stupidly what she ought to be doing. Glancing at her watch – almost eleven-thirty – she guessed it must be Helen in Los Angeles and decided not to answer it. Finally it returned to inanimate silence.

Harry returned. "Poor little fella had a nightmare."

"Someone rang," she said.

"Yes, I heard. Who was it?"

"I don't know. I didn't answer."

"Why not?" He poured another glass of wine. Clearly he was not thinking of her lift. She watched, but said nothing, deciding that she was in no hurry. It was good just being close to him.

"I supposed it must be Helen and thought I

shouldn't." Voicing the explanation it sounded faintly ridiculous. Her presence here was innocent enough, in any case she thought sadly, she was no threat, and Helen would understand when she heard about Ches. Ches. "Might it have been the hospital?" she asked weakly.

Harry shrugged. "Maybe." He looked concerned. "They'll call again if it was."

"Could I have a glass of wine?"

He smiled, stretching for a second glass. He was still leaning against the sink. Penny wished that he would sit down. He always used to pace or lean about when something was on his mind, or a painting lay unfinished and he was blocked. She sipped the wine wondering whether she should stay or leave, whichever was the easiest, not wishing to inconvenience him. "I think I'll ... " The telephone sounded. Harry lifted it almost instantly and Penny, carrying her glass, withdrew discreetly from the room.

She chose to sit on one of the Turkish rugs and lean against the base of the chaise-longue. She had always preferred sitting on the floor and wondered again what on earth had possessed her to rush out and buy her new sofa. From where she was now sitting she could more clearly view the gallery of paintings displayed before her.

Harry's style had altered almost beyond recognition, matured. His work was more sombre now. In the early days she had described it as Matisse-like with his open, sensual women exuding heat and promise. Even her own treasured 'Penny Reclining' was of that same school. Now, the women were distant, lost in their own preoccupations, disappointed, burdened. There was an alienation about his world. Still, his subjects, drawn or painted, were mainly of women, a spattering of landscapes, but very few portraits of men, although further towards the corner of the room she spied one that might conceivably have been inspired by Ches, looking aged, emaciated, Munch-like.

None of these figures lived on beaches. These were

inhabitants of Harry's adopted East End, but without the humour or devil-may-care that one might assume from sitting in a local pub. These people lived hard. Always pictured in isolation. Hookers, standing cheerlessly smoking cigarettes, on the look-out at tube-stations, street corners, or framed in windows. Housewives cleaning steps, huddled on bent knees, like underfed dogs, dying fags between tight lips. No one here resembled Helen.

Harry's voice, infrequently audible, drifted through from the kitchen. She could not have made out words but his tone was subdued. He was listening and responding rather than talking.

Concerned about eavesdropping she rose and wandered over to the opposite wall of windows, unhinged a lock on a recently fitted door and stepped onto a newly erected terrace to view the muddy Thames water and the skyline. A barge of some length was chugging past towards the inner city. The sky above hung low with barrelling threatening clouds. It was still lightly misty and too cold to be out here, particularly without a coat. She considered going back to the sitting-room to fetch hers but as she turned there were muted footsteps on the damp terrace and Harry was standing within arm's length of her. He looked grave. She smiled uncertainly.

"That was the hospital," he announced. Penny's stomach lurched as she resisted what he was telling her. "Ches is dead." His voice no stronger than a whisper.

15

Later that same night, very slowly, very deliberately with a neatness that had never been a part of her nature, Penny folded her scarf into a tiny tight square and placed it onto the seat of a bentwood chair. She was positioned in a corner, looking about her in an uncomprehending way as though she were not entirely clear what had happened or what events had led her to be here in this familiar yet curiously unfamiliar room. She stood for a while, almost as though she should not step any further, as though she mistrusted what might happen to her if she did, like a small Alice who had suddenly discovered herself in an oversized room. Finally she moved to the bed and collapsed in a heap, numbed by shock and exhaustion. She closed her eyes yet she doubted that she would be able to rest. In every sense ghosts appeared to surround her. Harry was on a couch in the next room, that was where he was spending the night and here she was, preparing to sleep in the very bed that they, accompanied by Ches, had bought together all those years previously. It seemed a risible irony that fate had brought her back to it under such paltry circumstances, certainly not in the manner she had once dreamt of.

The telephone resting alongside her sounded once more, intermittent tinklings. Harry was trying to contact Helen, his attempts were growing more frequent, he must be agitated. She lay back, disconsolate, limp with fatigue, still fully clothed, and rested her cheek against an embroidered linen pillowcase. Its fragrance was sweet and inviting, so alien to her present mood, freshly laundered, sprinkled with a rose cologne and aired alongside some ambrosial pot-pourri. She brushed her fingers against it, sliding them beneath it and touched

246

crisply pressed sheets, just waiting to be slept in. Somehow it surprised her, given Helen's absence. In the early days Harry had never taken much interest in domestic affairs although now he appeared content and proficient with the responsibility of Ziggy. They must have help, she reasoned. His life was noticeably more prosperous yet Nicholas Lockett had referred to him as no more than a modestly successful painter. Helen's money then. Perhaps it had always been Helen's money. How else had they lived so comfortably? She had frequently in those days wondered about it, supposing that the money had come from dealing dope and she had never dared to question it. How would it have been all those summers ago if she had been the wealthy partner? A pointless and painful reflection. She should try to get some sleep.

Commonsense told her that she should have gone home, crept back to her own celibate bed yet Harry's despair at the loss of Ches had been blindingly apparent. Strangely he had wanted her company, had asked her to remain by him.

"Please don't leave," he had said, "stay with me."

In times past — sweet irretrievable times — she would have taken him in her arms and held him tenderly, invoking her love for him as a balm against his bereavement, but the years that had slithered by stood between them, distancing them and immobilising her.

She conceded that it was Helen, not she, whom he would have turned to had she been here. Nevertheless she prayed to whatever divine forces might be listening — not since Nikos's death and her blundered confession to Harry in the Sibton pub had she considered herself a worthy recipient of God's mercy, but tonight she prayed — for the depth of understanding and generosity of spirit to best console him. For herself she begged courage, for to stand by him and keep her own delicate emotions intact was demanding a great deal.

So much had altered in Harry's life. She was merely an episode from his history and, had it not been for

Ches's request, probably a thankfully obliterated one. Not so for her, for her nothing had fundamentally altered. Her outer circumstances may have rejigged themselves, improved a degree or two – certainly her career was prospering – but in spite of various brief, or even in some cases extended affairs, and more than several stoned or insignificant one-night stands she had remained solitary, loyal to her memory of Harry, loving him as much as she ever had done. Meeting up with him again tonight had reinforced it. It was just as though she had travelled nowhere, had simply been dancing on the spot, and had never succeeded in distancing herself from him. It was a dispiriting realisation.

The telephone had become silent. Penny yawned, her eyes watered. It was ten to one. She had to get some rest, she had another hell of a day ahead of her before the famous screen test. Not unexpectedly the film's importance had diminished.

Without exerting any more effort than the stretching of limbs she began idly to tug at her clothes and peel them away from her, flinging them one by one to the floor at her bedside and without fully realising it to close her heavy lids. Within moments she had drifted from consciousness into dreamful, disturbed sleep.

It was barely daybreak when Harry crept into the bedroom wrapped in a grey herring-bone overcoat. He was returning from his atelier now situated a few hundred yards along the alley. Since Ziggy's birth there had been no place for his work in the studio. In his mind this warehouse had never lost the identity with which he had originally conceived and christened it.

Penny lay sleeping. He approached considerately, wanting only to regard her, to touch her softness.

"Where've you bin?" she asked as he drew near, her eyes gave the appearance of still being closed.

"I thought you were asleep."

"I heard you go out, heard the door closing, about three a.m. I couldn't get back to sleep again. Where've you been?"

"Working."

"I looked for you. I was worried."

"I didn't mean to disturb you. Thought you were out of it."

"I slept a couple of hours," she assured, opening her lids.

In the twilit morning darkness, a shaft of light shed from a lamp in the sitting-room crept through the door left partially open. Penny observed that Harry looked nothing short of wrecked. His face was contoured by unshaven growth, darker than his natural colouring and more marked by the shadowed light. It rendered him stricken, a tormented silhouette. She suspected by the slight burning around his eyes that he had been weeping although it might simply have been lack of sleep. Nevertheless she reached out a hand to touch him, resting it against his fingertips. Her nails chanced upon a wedding ring, she had not noticed it before. Harry bent towards the bed and stroked her long hair, pulling at it, covering her face with it as though kneading his pain, and then lowered himself towards her, greedily onto her, pulling back the sheets while at the same time wrestling with his great coat, thrusting it away from him as though it were on fire.

It was a violent coupling, rough and short-lived, rendering her empty. It caused her to shed tears that dribbled silent and hot across her burning cheeks ... when it was over, while he lay sleeping, oblivious to her, still wearing his shirt. She had not come. If she had stopped to consider the act, which she had not, she would not have expected to. This pairing had not been for her. She saw his need and had allowed herself to be his relief, his comfort. Because she loved him and because she believed she owed him at least that. And because although she wanted him, yes, certainly that, she was feeling too bruised to express herself sexually. Her libido was in hibernation.

His orgasm had arrived fast, been vocal, moaning

loudly, roaring out of his loins. He never mentioned her name or his love for her as he always had in the past. She recognised this kind of union because she knew it too well. The coupling of strangers. She might have been anybody. Any body before, a stranger afterwards. There had been many of those occasions in her life, rendering her empty, reminding her of a popular song she liked to listen to: 'Been too long in the rain . . . Taking any comfort that I can'. Elvis had recorded it, and Nina Simone. It consoled her. It frequently felt like that, life.

She disengaged herself from beneath the dead weight of Harry's splayed arm and picked her way across strewn clothes and discarded shoes towards the bathroom and then into the kitchen to make a pot of tea. It was a quarter to six. Beyond the walls of the studio she heard sounds that reminded her of her former existence here. Early morning traffic motoring towards the city humming with life, boats waking on the water, occasional horns, dawn choruses and seagulls screeching greedily, scavenging for breakfast. She put the kettle on and while seated at the table waiting for it to boil she heard another sound, unfamiliar to her studio history. A child stirring, and then calling.

Ziggy.

She lingered for a few minutes reluctant to interfere, in case Harry should wake. Perhaps he was gifted with an inner clock or something paternal that woke him whenever Ziggy called out. No one stirred. Someone, she decided, should soothe the little fellow and it might as well be her. She turned down the gas beneath the water, almost at boiling point, and mounted the stairs, to Helen's son. His face was in rage, contorted by discomfort as he stared mistrustfully at the strangeness of her; who was this answering his cry? His eyes, open now, alive with curiosity, were as blue and as penetrating as Harry's. "Where's Harry?" he demanded. "I want my dad."

Penny was sitting alone, cradling her cup, staring at

the frost on the kitchen windows when Harry appeared. He must have woken shortly after she had resettled Ziggy. He looked pretty frightful.

"Want some tea?" she proffered and without waiting for a response stretched for the pre-laid cup and poured the warm liquid into it. There was a certain awkwardness between them, born, no doubt, of their dawn coupling. Ches's illness had bridged time as well as everything else that had driven them apart. The shock of his death had drawn them temporarily together. In the light of day, their friend's spirit flown, nothing remained to bind them, bar a certain awkward politeness. Or that was how it seemed to her in that moment.

"Thanks for staying," he said, appearing to clear something in his throat as she, at the precise same moment, asked if he had managed to get hold of Helen. The comedy in such a moment, their mutual awkwardness, struck them both and caused them to smile, thereby easing their tension.

"I'll just finish this and be on my way," she said softly, gesturing towards the teacup. "Unless you need me to . . . "

He shook his head. "If you want to hang on, I'll give you a lift."

"No, I'll grab a cab. I'd prefer to. I . . . need to get on. Got rather a lot to get through before my rehearsal."

"What time?"

"One."

They spoke in a shorthand that both well understood, a throw-back from former days when little conveyed all that was required.

He asked her about the screen test. They were drinking a second cup of tea, luke-warm now. She was reluctant to discuss it. He sensed her discomfort.

"Why don't you want to talk about it?" he persisted. "Could be a big break for you, right?"

"Because the director is behaving like a shit," she blurted rather baldly. "He's forcing me towards a choice I don't want to make and right now I don't want to think

251

about him." She hesitated, and then said, "Harry . . . that weekend at Helen's . . ." A frown crossed his dulled features, dragging it back from memory. "I've carried it always, the guilt of what I did."

He shook his head, bent now, and reached out for her hand. "I think we shouldn't discuss it, not now, Pen. Never."

So you can't offer me some small respite from the burden of it, she thought. Even now you won't forgive me.

"Did you ever tell Ches that it was me?"

"We never discussed it," he assured . . .

*   *   *

"It was wet and windy that morning in March 1979. It felt like the end of something, a chapter of my life. Doors closing, all of that. Harry rang for my mini-cab and then helped me with my raincoat. The telephone rang. It was Helen. I sat in the living-room waiting in my coat as though at an unfamiliar station and when their conversation was over he came and sat with me.

"He said, 'If she can get on a flight, she'll be back tonight. She'll be here for the funeral.' His elation at the prospect of seeing her was apparent. I wanted to leave, just to get away from there and its wall of memories. The cab seemed to take forever. In passing, I think to make conversation more than anything else, he asked me your name and when I told him it was as though I had exploded a minor bomb in his lap.

"'You're right, keep away from him. Ches's dad gave him his first break in Hollywood and later when Gaza was winning he turned his back on him. It's a well-known story.'

"I didn't comprehend at first what he was telling me. I just stared at him blankly.

"'Jimmy Gaza.' He spoke the name with emphasis, as if to help me understand. 'During the McCarthy trials, writers, directors, technicians, all kinds of people

252

working in Hollywood were betrayed. Ches's dad was one of them. He was a communist all his life. Someone shopped him and the poor guy never worked again. Some time later he went to Gaza, begged him for work, anything, but Gaza wouldn't help him. Told him he was washed up. The injustice finally killed him. Ches told you about how he was out working at fourteen to support his family.'

"'But Gaza's a Jew!' I responded incredulously.

"'So?'

"'He fled Athens with his family when he was a boy. He knows about being hunted, about being the victim.' I had swallowed the idea, albeit bitterly, that as a man you might treat me − an insignificant nobody, a would-be-film-star − as little more than flesh, but to deny your colleagues, a man who had helped you, I couldn't conceive of it, couldn't take it in."

On hearing this Gaza made a sound, a vocalised scoffing, and beat his pen impatiently on his scribbled notes, striking at sentences as though he wished to tear them from the page.

"You lay too much at my door."

"You should have helped him."

"Penny, we've been through this. I was seventeen. The guy gave me a job, OK, but I owed him nothing. He was an alcoholic. Had been for years. You believed the painter because you needed someone on whom to vent your hurt and anger."

"You were my hero. Your films had inspired me, helped to structure my philosophy, guide my adolescence. I think eventually I would have slept with you just to get the part. Just gritted my teeth and taken it. It was patently obvious what the role meant to me."

"You seem pretty adept at rewriting your own history."

"That came later," she defended.

"Why are you denying us? You think it makes you less . . . whether we fucked because we fucked, or because you hated me, because you despised me for what *you*

253

judged me to be, or because your friend was gone, or just maybe because you wanted the goddam role badly enough to do anything. Who cares? It's history now. You always blamed me because you needed to make me the bad guy. You want to believe I abused you. It serves your picture of yourself. The self who has settled with Peter, the self who fled . . . "

She rounded on him. "I haven't said anything about how you telephoned my flat in the middle of the night, begging me to come over, begging to screw me. I haven't spoken of your womanising. Endless bitch after endless bitch!"

Gaza held his hand in front of his face, a defence or a gesture of peace. Pax, pax, pax. For God's sake! Not all that again. A weary truce.

"Let's drop it, the rage is fruitless. It's not in the film. What happened with the painter?"

Penny, shaken, sipped at a glass of water. She began to speak. Her voice was unsteady, reed-thin. "The taxi arrived, Harry and I said our farewells, 'good to see you after all this time, take care of yourself', all that sort of thing. Even the prospect of separating from him, losing him one more time had paled into insignificance. I sat in the back of the mini-cab feeling sick as hell. Ches was lying in a morgue somewhere in Notting Hill Gate – his body still warm. And I was battling with myself not to commit yet another act against my better nature, something else to haunt me and make me despise myself for all my days, simply because I really wanted to work with you. I had believed in you, but a fine film maker did not necessarily mean a fine human being. That much I was learning. You were no better than me. Somehow the whole thing seemed like the twist of a black tale."

Gaza tossed his scribbled notes, odd sheets of papers and the script across the crumpled bedding and rose, hands in corduroy pockets, striding to the window observed by Penny.

"I don't have to tell you what happened after that. You know it as well as I."

He nodded briskly, swinging his body as though agitated that she should remind him of that afternoon. "Whatever! You got the damned role and on your own terms. And the guy, this Harry?"

"I never saw him again. Never heard of him again."

He turned to regard her, to scrutinise the features in search of the heart.

"Did you write to him telling him your news?"

She shook her head.

"Did you try to find him?"

"Once I left for Los Angeles I forced myself to forget him. I had a new life, and then you, to contend with. I'd met my match. And then . . . by the time I returned to England years had passed. I figured it was too late."

"Never, not once?"

Penny hesitated, balanced on the edge of honesty.

"I want to know," he persisted.

"Alright, once, half-heartedly, after a late-night dinner party. I was driving my car back home. It was one of those hours before dawn. I suppose I was a little drunk, woozy and blue, bleeding loneliness. America was in the past. On an impulse I turned the car around, headed for the East End and coasted past the warehouse. It had been taken over, redecorated. A large boarding hanging from the brickwork announced the emplacement of a firm of young graphic designers. Harry had gone."

"Why did you go looking for him?"

"I suppose I was still thinking about him."

A knock at the door distracted them, the eye contact that had been held between them.

"All the while you were in California, you were still thinking of him?"

She said nothing, at a loss to answer.

"Were you still in love with him?"

Someone knocked again, tearing her away from Gaza, from the look in his eyes. She shrugged as though to explain that there was nothing more to tell, and crossed the room, leaving Gaza alone at the window standing with his back to the room regarding the horizon. David, the second assistant, was asking for the director. "They're ready for a full rehearsal."

Gaza nodded. "On my way," he said and patted the kid on the shoulder, sending him on ahead and then slowly he turned back to Penny. He looked like a man who'd lost at the track. "So, you never forgot him, huh?"

"Of course I did. It was the guilt . . . I couldn't root out the guilt, it felt like I couldn't get deep enough."

"Until Peter came along. And then what happened to you? To the girl who'd had violence in her soul. Passion. To the girl so riddled with jealousy that she betrayed and in so doing killed a man? You denied that violent creature, Penny. You didn't accept her, you smothered her. She has real honest beauty. Stand by her. Let her have her say. Don't bury her beneath success, beneath well-cultivated Italian vineyards and visits to the opera, or she'll come back to haunt you, to make you sick and drive you to an early grave."

Gaza held out his hand to her in a gesture of friendship, a declaration she had rarely witnessed from him. "Want to come and watch later when we're ready to shoot, play audience?"

She read a tenderness tinged perhaps with regret. He was hurt, or was that just her fancy. It surprised and for some quite inexplicable reason saddened her.

"Sure, why not? I'll see you there."

He nodded and gathered together his script and papers. It was clumsily achieved. They were pressed against him like so many old rags to be disposed of at the earliest opportunity. On his way to the door he paused and said, "You know something, what I despised, couldn't live with was your soft centre. You say I gave you hell on that picture. If it's true it was because I believed in you, believed in your potential, but you were weak, you were throwing yourself away. I hated to watch it. The picture may have bombed but you did pretty well out of it. It gave you the start you'd been craving and you made it. And another thing, a while back you asked me what I'm doing here. Why I came back to work on this one. Because I care for you. Always did." And he slipped from the room, saying, "I'll send young David to fetch you, when we're ready to shoot it."

The late afternoon was milky bright. These last moments of winter sun shone through a sky curdled with light fluffy clouds. Half a mile or so along the track, away from the house, groups of people, twos and threes, stood about in the cold mountain air, awaiting dusk, the gloaming hour, wrapped in coats and scarves, clad in boots and gloves and sunglasses. There was a sense of nervous anticipation and excitement milling amongst the team. An English accent hailing through a loudspeaker called for the drivers to prepare themselves, everyone involved to be in position. "Sixty seconds to action!" announced the loudspeaker moments later.

Penny settled herself on a rock, solitary, towards the cliff's edge, thereby gaining a view that swung the entire way down the mountain embracing the disappearing valleys beneath. It was a still evening. She watched her exhalations of breath float and disappear into the failing light, at the same time pulling her coat more tightly about her and turning around to admire the scape of mountain peaks jutting beyond the house. A silvery light from tiptoeing evening stars tempered by clouds and an early yellow moon highlighted the snow-capped mountains. They appeared crisp and forbidding, outlined against the sky, haughty with a glacial grace. She shivered and resettled herself.

She was worrying about why she still had not been able to get through to Peter and reasoned that he must have taken himself off again to Milan. La Scala, that's where he will be tonight. Someone down the hill called out her name and waved. She returned the gesture. An engine roared, anticipating its getaway. Pre-shooting. She loved these moments with a child's passion.

Lights had been positioned up and down the tumbling lane. They rose from the rocks, waiting to be illuminated, ready to flood the world of make-believe with an iridescent magic.

A firm hand came to rest on Penny's shoulder. She let out a startled cry. Its unexpectedness, its unremarked arrival, had given her a fright, caused her to jump nervously. She swung around to see who was there. It was Theo.

"Dear lady," he began with a smile, "forgive me, I had not intended to frighten you."

She shivered more from a release of tension than as a reaction against the falling temperature. "Shouldn't you be in your car?" she demanded, a touch too abrasively.

"I came to ask for your good wishes, a smile from you would encourage my luck." Before the sentence had been completed he had bent to her, leaning over her, breathing audibly and had taken hold of her gloveless hand which he lifted with a deliberate motion to his lips. "May I?"

Penny managed a nod, maintaining a distance, catching, could it be, the merest whiff of alcohol on his breath, reluctantly permitting his lips, his beard, to brush the back of her hand. "I'm sure it will go well." She smiled tightly. "Your skill will see you through."

The voice from the loudspeaker called to Theo, beckoning him from wherever he might currently be to seat himself in his car and prepare for the action. All were awaiting him. "You promised me a drink later," he called almost as an afterthought, a cavalier throwaway line as he departed, striding confidently down the track, crunching on stones and mountain grit, to where a myriad of folk and equipment awaited him.

"That's not so," she retorted fiercely but her voice was drowned by the roar of engines and yet another announcement reverberating within the mountain summits.

"I'll hold you to your promise, my Goddess of Good Fortune."

Oh no you won't, she thought sanguinely, and set off vaguely in the opposite direction to the action, but from where she would still be able to watch, to find herself a cup of tea and join the working crowds who were awaiting, more as spectators than crew, the drama of the car chase and the spectacular plummet of Nikos's burning car into the valley depths somewhere beneath them.

She caught sight of Chris Grange lolling against an olive tree, script in one hand, steaming tea or coffee in the other. He was looking weary. She approached, calling his name.

"Stand by," the voice from the loudspeaker.

A flood of light illuminated the mountainside creating giant shadows, curious black shapes born of trees and rocks, lighting up the sky with a crocus-yellow incandescence. Penny turned round to catch the impression. The scene about her possessed the solemnity, the suspense, the wonderful danger of a childhood Guy Fawkes night.

From somewhere behind her, further down the valley, the electric word, "Action," echoed. Gaza's command. A roar of engines first, then pistols began to fire. Take One was being filmed. Penny estimated from experience that it would perhaps be another two hours before they reached the moment which included the car bursting into flames as it spun into the air and over the mountainside.

"Cut!" The shot had been aborted. Something had not gone according to plan.

Might even be after supper at this rate, she gauged, walking stealthily towards her co-star, fearful of any distraction the tread of her feet might cause. He waved and welcomed her as she approached. The comradeship born of teamwork united them. He wrapped an arm about her, they were both smiling and he whispered in her ear.

"Theo's in love with you," he teased boyishly. "He's been telling the entire world."

They laughed conspiratorially, just as if they were o' friends.

"He'll mate you this very night." Bonded by common profession and another's prepos lubricity.

"Oh no, he won't!"

Penny's estimation proved not inaccurate. As the night became colder, the hours grew longer, the shadows more ominous, the expectant onlookers lost interest. It seemed that the entire sequence might not get shot before dawn. People dribbled towards the caterers' van in search of hot food, somehow hoping that their proximity might in itself bring about the supper break. Only two sequences had been completed in their entirety and one or two close-ups of cars, screeching tyres and firing guns.

"Cut!" Another brief sequence in the can followed by the long awaited words, "That's it folks, supper break. Back in one hour."

The announcement brought about a cheer or two from the electricians' van. Within what seemed an impossibly short time a queue had formed and folk were lining up with plates ready to take whatever was on offer. Penny considered sloping off to bed, she had lost her appetite an hour or so earlier, and looked about her in search of Gaza. In vain.

"Aren't you eating?" enquired Chris mooching towards her, carrying a plate laden with steaming meat and rice.

"Too tired. I think I'll call it a day."

"Lucky you," he said a touch camply. "I'm in the very last sequence of the night. I'll be hanging about until daybreak. Goodnight." He brushed a light kiss on her cheek. "But I'll tell Theo where he can find you."

She smiled, no longer really with the joke but nevertheless slapping playfully at his arm. She said, "Have you seen Jimmy?"

"He's there. In the jeep."

She turned round and spied him. He had just been back up the hill by the first assistant. He was intense discussion, appearing strained. No nging the remainder of the night's work. sidered interrupting him, or fetching

260

him a plate of food and then equally swiftly changed her mind. Better to leave him, just get some beauty sleep. Tomorrow, she'd talk to him.

"Hittin' the hay, gorgeous?" A little-known assistant from the design workshop called to her as she passed by him on her way back up the hill, trudging towards the lights and welcoming warmth of the house. She smiled a contented yes, knowing that very soon she would be curled up asleep. The thought was comforting. These last few days had been taxing.

It was twenty to four when Penny was woken. A scream pierced her subconscious and brought her back to earthly reality. She sat bolt upright, attentive, already clammy with presentiment. Beneath her window came cries from a gathering crowd. She rose from the bed dragging a dressing-gown with her across to the window and peered out. A woman was wailing while others — impossible from this distance to tell who — were running like disturbed ants every which way apparently anxiously seeking direction.

Without another thought she wrapped herself in the towelling robe, slipped her feet into the first pair of shoes she could find and hurried from the room, down the central staircase, out into the first blush of light in search of someone. Something uncomfortably familiar about this scene caused her saliva to dry up, her heart to pump faster.

What incident had caused that scream? The likely, or more accurately, unlikely, cause of the disturbance had begun to penetrate. A coincidence too weird and ill-conceived, a plot too bleak, and yet it had a ring of incredible possibility about it.

She ran the length of a stoned path, circumnavigating the house, past a fountain and cultivated rose garden to where she saw the first signs of life. Not the group she had spied from the window on high but another small group, huddled and still, talking furtively, smoking group in some way disconnected from the main of things, either through choice or their identiti could not tell which. She did not recognise any of them.

"Do any of you speak English?"

A woman nodded.

"Tell me," she said as she approached, "what has happened?"

The small stocky lady responded in unpractised English. "Hay man hass beeen killet."

"Who?" Penny's voice trembled with the fear of knowledge. Already she had begun to step away, to hasten her route down the hill to where the filming must have been taking place.

"I don't know." The words returned, ringing in her ears as her feet padded fast against pebbles and then dew-soaked grass. Her breath burnt in her throat as she ran, gathering speed, haring towards the large double-gated entrance, onto the skerried track, pounding, skeltering towards the clump of cars and equipment and folk bunched together as though for protection a way down the hill. The film lights had been switched off. There was little besides the aubergine glow of the natural rising morning light to guide her. Ahead a single moving beam of light shone out across the mountains towards the direction of the sea and then swooping into the great sweep of valleys, back up, out over the cliff-side, searching and turning like a sleepless soul. A soul in limbo.

As Penny drew closer she could make out silhouettes on the pathway and the distant flames of a small fire which burned way beneath her in the expanse of black, the cavernous hole that by the full light of day would be transformed into the villages and plateaux, the life of valleys beneath. She spied Jimmy marching and smoking, calling orders or information and unexpectedly her heart felt renewed, a sap revived. Thank God. It was a ...ion upon which she had not the time now to reflect. ...knew that she was more than simply glad to see

...t the man who had been killed. That, at ...ng.

It must be then as she had suspected. Not the two slightly known stunt men playing the police officers, no, not them. Somewhere in that burning car beneath her was the incinerated corpse of Theo. She felt certain of it. The death of Nikos re-enacted.

Her step slowed to barely a crawl. She was out of breath and her early frantic desire to be here, to in some way be of assistance at the scene of this dreadful accident had waned. She walked on, unnoticed, towards the solemn troupe but wanting in her heart to turn back.

It was Chris Grange, dark-eyed, reeking of Cognac, who confirmed her divination.

"He mismanaged a bend, skidded on the stones, lost control. The jeep exploded too early, burst into flames and went over the edge of the mountain before Theo had had a chance to dive out of it. We all witnessed it, all saw it coming. There was nothing to be done."

Penny, without a word, left Chris's side and the echoes of his slurred speech. She forged her way, through gangs of people, to Gaza. He was standing alone now leaning against something – she did not even notice what – smoking a cigarette, dragging hard, holding the smoke within him, deep down in his lungs, swilling it like liquid around his mouth, just as though his life depended on it, this drug, as though without it he would never breathe again. She approached soundlessly and stood at his side. Inadequately dressed and shivering from both the cold and the shock she leant against him, pressing against his hunched shoulder as though attempting to give him fresh life. He turned to regard her. There was a grimness in his eyes that suddenly appalled her. Small as pellets they beamed into her and equally as unexpectedly he wrapped an arm about her and whispered to her, "Two Nikoses, both sacrificed. Let us pray that the third is a redemption."

16

Cursing foully – there was no one to overhear – Giorgios Archimede stretched for the bedside telephone in his rambling untidy apartment in Kolonaki, Athens. As he did so he trained one partially open eye onto the alarm positioned on the pillow alongside his ear (nothing less could rouse him) and frowned with uncomprehending disgust.

"*Nai?*"

"Mr Archimede?"

"*Nai?*"

"*Mè léne David.*" It was impressionable young David trying out his Greek.

"Who?"

"I'm phoning from Crete – "

"*Kríti?*"

"*Nai* . . . from the location of *Akin to Love.*" A spattering of recently acquired phrases, points to remember; *Nai* was yes not no as David had originally supposed. His accent tripped him up but still he attempted to make himself understood, anxious to prove himself more accomplished and indispensable as the days of filming progressed. It was early in the morning; all the crew bar he had sloped off in search of sleep, oblivion.

"Do you know that it's only six o'clock?"

The Greek voice was articulate, tenor deep, masculine, furred by early morning listlessness and gravelly ⸺om late sybaritic nights. It sounded in contrast to the ⸺ 's reedy perplexity.

⸺ios was being asked by David to take the first ⸺ane from the capital to Iráklion.

⸺ing, why in God's name this morning? My ⸺ " Incredulity strained by irritation ⸺ he line, lifting the sleepy timbre.

"No one will be available to meet you due to . . . erm . . . unforeseen circumstances . . . "

"What?"

"An accident to be precise." David was precise, uncertain and stammering but precise. A helicopter had been arranged. It would deliver Giorgios directly to the location.

"An accident?" posed the Greek actor sighing, accepting that his sleep was over for this night, and trailing fingers along the marble floor in search of cigarettes. "What kind of an accident?" He listened as David recounted the tragedy, with eyes still halfway closed, naked muscular body still warm beneath the sheets and lungs expanded by smoke.

"Oh Jesus," he cursed laconically, "Theo was a friend. I hope someone called his wife."

Yes, assured David, he had already spoken to her – here he paused in uncomfortable reflection – and yes, it had been he who had broken the news to her. His speech jammed in his throat. He was stammering and distressed at the memory of Madam Theo's shaken tone, her rejoinder: "We have three small children. How ever will I tell them?" Her fearful words lingered in his head, persecuting David's callow sensibilities. It had been the toughest assignment in his vernal life.

Once assured that Giorgios would be on the plane by mid-morning David replaced the receiver. He left the deserted hallway, his footsteps echoing in the daybreak emptiness and wandered without direction until eventually he found himself hovering at the cliff's edge. Hands in pockets, scarf knotted inelegantly beneath his chin, he stood alone and stared out across the world. The sun had risen. In the valleys beneath life was creeping towards a fresh day. Life. The extinguishment of Theo's life was the first that he had ever faced. seemed an inexplicably unjust deed. Finally natu stunt, not Theo's. He had been close by the man in last moments before shooting, had smelt his bre spotted even earlier the bottle in his roo

265

swigging brandy, the fear in his eyes and he had asked himself: "Should I say anything? Should I tell someone? Make someone call a halt to the stunt?" But he had decided no, had decided to mind his own business, to keep quiet. Best not to interfere, he had reasoned.

The boy's tortoise-shell eyes were moist with tears now. He rubbed earnestly at them and at his running nose as though wishing to erase it, sniffing, cursing the sting in the early morning wind and considering whether or not he would ever rid himself of culpability.

It was impossible to call a halt to the film, even had anyone wished to. Once an early lunch had been eaten and the caterers had proficiently cleared all debris away, a meeting was called in the grand salon currently serving as the dining-room.

It was Jimmy Gaza himself, unshaven and seemingly half-clad, who rose to address the team. "Theo's death was an accident. There was no question of negligence on his part, or anybody else's. No mechanical fault that could be found in the wreckage. Theo was a brave man and his memory will be best honoured by the film."

Behind him someone entered: an unknown face with distinguished features. The man scanned the crowded room in front of him, taking it in, this space which was unfamiliar to him. He was a tall figure, possibly in his late thirties, with dark wavy hair, sympathetic observant eyes, clad in a camel-haired overcoat. Penny's attention was instantly drawn to him. He was unknown to her and as far as she knew unrecognised by anyone. In fact, to the Greek members of the team a face not only familiar but much loved and respected. A great actor.

Georgios Archimede acknowledged a seated figure, his direction, before he spied Gaza or had gravity of the address in progress. Swiftly out for a vacant place to sit, nothing he slid tactfully with briefcase in of the room where he could lean here, he lit up a cigarette and rubbed his left eye with the flat of his hand as though smoke had blinded him or he were too tired to focus correctly.

"Theo will be given a special mention on the credits of the film. It will state that his life has been lost in the pursuit of his work, dangerous work." Gaza paused, bathing in the silence he had created, theatrically, allowing the weight of his words to be taken on board. Only then did he continue, his ever-vigilant eyes roaming the room as though seeking to make personal contact with everyone, to reassure the first flicker of doubt that might creep across the brow of even the lowliest member. "Guys, in my opinion it is the finest epitaph for anyone working in our industry. It is everything I could wish for myself."

Penny watched him, his brusque unrelenting seduction, his reassurances, offered to the attentive, smoke-filled room. This small man, projecting his beliefs, calling upon his team, built like a wiry terrier, a hunting breed. Yes, she thought, it is true. He has given his life to his work, a life which includes his sins, his mistakes and his terrifying ambition. She supposed that they should hate him, at least despise him, should judge him harshly.

Yet it was she who had despised him. She who had spent time with him but had never ceased to silently accuse him. "You blame me because you need someone to despise," he had said to her.

Gaza called for the continued support of the picture. It was given without hesitation. His leadership was not in question.

It was blowing a gale outside the tall windows. During the late afternoon the weather had clouded over and it had begun to rain. By nightfall although the rain had been blown away the strength of the winds had increased. Trees were swaying and bending like fingers. A distinct air of relief pervaded the sharply lit upstairs room where the night shoot was taking place. Filming out of doors in these conditions would have been too

267

tough, almost too much to demand of a loyal crew considering all that had taken place less than twenty-four hours earlier.

It was already a "helluva difficult scene to shoot", Gaza's words before the evening's work had commenced. "Concentration, that's what's needed and a determined desire to put the past behind us."

Is that what he had succeeded in doing, putting the past behind him? Was it that which Penny had failed to achieve?

The filming had been in progress since half past nine. It was now after two in the morning. The wee small hours when tempers were becoming frayed or in some quarters outbursts of hysterical laughter were being used to challenge tiredness, to keep fatigue at bay.

Penny sat quietly, wrapped in a towelling robe, bunched in a corner observing the shooting. This portion of the scene did not include her. Someone offered her a cup of tea, she accepted it gratefully, dandling it between her fingers. Silence descended. A new take was about to commence: Nikos on his knees being harassed and beaten by the police. Everyone took their positions. The camera prepared to roll. Not for the first time this night did Penny find herself irresistibly drawn to the Greek actor Giorgios. He fascinated her. She watched as, crouched, ready to perform, he lifted his head and turned towards Chris Grange positioned on the bed, and to Beth, the beautiful young actress playing the screen Helen.

Beth had been having a difficult time. She had already forgotten her lines twice; the shooting had been forced to pause. In fact it had ground to a halt. Penny had been watching as Gaza battled to keep his cool with her, coaxing her courage, nurturing her as one would a child. A sign of his maturing years observed Penny with a secret smile. When she had been young, when they had worked together on their first film, on those occasions when she had forgotten her lines he had skinned her publicly. Tonight he was being patient. Impatience boiled beneath the surface perhaps but he kept its lid firmly in place. She wondered too if Jimmy had altered in another way. Had he found himself at Beth's door as he had so regularly at hers? She hoped not, though why, now, she was not sure.

Giorgios, head lifted from his position on the floor, winked at Beth who blushed and smiled weakly. It had been a gesture of encouragement, silent understated support from one fellow actor to another. Or had it? A rush of jealousy suffused Penny. She was once more that young woman who had watched from the doorway, who had witnessed Helen in the arms of Harry, who had stood by while two unknown figures had brutalised Nikos and brought him to his knees in pain and degradation; once more the young woman who had squealed, who had betrayed her friends and been responsible for death. She gulped at the tea, its warmth or the unexpectedness of liquid in her throat, something, caused her to cough, to splutter and make a noise. She had lived with that memory of Nikos on his knees, the police above him, menacing him, it had haunted her. She had never come to terms with it, with her responsibility in the creating of it.

"Cut!" The take had been aborted. Her coughing had disturbed? She searched about her for Jimmy's accusing eyes. "Boom shadow!" A voice from the sound department. Aborted through no fault of hers. She rose swiftly and slid from the room, slipping past lights, electricians and standersby, stepping over metre after metre of coiled black cable, out into the temperate corridor.

"You alright, luv?" A kindly enquiring shadow whispered from behind her who before she knew it was pressing a hand onto her shoulder, lowering her into a chair, offering to go in search of cold water. Penny shook her head. "No thank you." She smiled winningly, once again the actress, the composed leading lady.

"You look a bit rough."

"It's the heat, the lateness of the hour, that's all. I'm in great shape."

The scruffy well-meaning chap gave her a wink, brushed her cheek with the knuckles of his soiled work-beaten fist and whispered, "I know yer are. You're a beauty. We all adore yer."

It was almost five in the morning when they wrapped, called it a day and prepared to slope off in various directions to their bedrooms. The scene had gone well. Spirits had been lifted. Gaza, wrecked, unshaven, looking like something that had been washed up onto a beach after a storm, was smiling and joking with members of his crew, drinking whisky from a hip flask, slugs shared with other men, back slapping, the maleness of the industry. Bottles of locally brewed beer were being doled out. Beth crept towards Penny and whispered her goodnights, tiptoeing to offer her a brief kiss on the cheek: a moment shared between the women.

"Tired?"

The young girl nodded. She appeared a little more at ease, almost happy. Her pearly eyes might be fatigued but there was a quiet glow shining there. Must be because her portion of the scene had eventually turned out well. She had overcome her initial crippling fear. Gaza spied her about to step from the room and called out to her. "Get some sleep, Beth," he shouted. "You've earned it." The timid girl nodded, relieved to hear the compliment, the seal of his approval and then glanced back towards Penny who was thinking that she was a curious piece of casting for Helen unless . . . And it was then for the first time that it occurred to Penny that long before her conversation with Gaza, long before he had forced her to speak the truth about the death of Nikos, he had already created a different balance, a different truth. He had known her, had read her. She gathered her script and bits together in readiness for bed and threw a glance back towards him. He was watching her. Their eyes met. Surrounded by others, engrossed in discussion or weary dawn joke-telling he might be but he was watching her. Those eagle eyes never left her. She smiled and nodded a goodnight. He lifted his hip flask

270

almost as a toast and winked just as she disappeared from sight.

On the stairway she spotted Giorgios, a silhouette in semi-shadow. He was smoking a cigarette, lingering, as though waiting for something, someone, uncertain about where he was going to next. Smiling, Penny drew alongside him and brushed the palm of her hand against his shoulder. A warm easy congratulatory gesture, for the pleasure of his work, for having been introduced to him, for chancing upon him there in the darkness and yes certainly, something more inviting.

He took the upheld hand and latched onto it, toying with it, forestalling her with a firm grip, and then commenced to climb the stairs alongside her, never releasing the touch of his fingers. A delicious leash, it sent a light thrill through her, awakening her desire. They walked a step or two without speaking. The echo of their footsteps on the capacious marble stairway washed over her, cool and resistant in contrast to her own soft bait. His potency beat so close to her that submission strangled her breath. She was ahead, vibrating with the pleasure of passing the remainder of the night with him, being possessed by him, and lying ravished, sweetly sweated, in his arms.

"This Athenian painter," he said, "the revolutionary. Is he based on someone?" The question surprised her. She had not been expecting it. Had been anticipating something more intimate, more desiring.

"It's you, Giorgios who are creating him, you should know better than I." It flummoxed her. Such a statement.

"Yes, but you wrote him. Tell me his name. I would like to see his paintings, uncover a portion of who he was through his work. Has any of it remained here on the island?"

At that moment Beth appeared from her room along the corridor, apparently showered, refreshed, ready. Instantaneously Giorgios's eyes were upon her, appreciating her. So, it was her then that Giorgios had been waiting for. It was they who were promised, who were savouring their upcoming assignation. She had misread, misinterpreted! Such foolish presumption! The pleasure was to be Beth's not hers. Giorgios released his light hold of her fingers, his attention now lost to her. Reconsider me, a part of Penny was clamouring. To draw him back, pointlessly, albeit momentarily, she named Nikos. The real Nikos, spoke his name, the flesh and blood man.

"His name was . . . Nikos Koumoulides."

She suddenly felt fatigued. Throughout the long night, on the set, she had been seduced by Giorgios, had accepted his portrayal, almost to the obliteration of Nikos, she had almost forgotten his real identity, had to search for it while he watched her, patiently waiting. "And no," she continued, "I haven't seen his paintings here. I never thought to search for them. Maybe in Matala though you'll find them. More likely his widow, if she is still living, has kept them in Athens, or they have been sold. Silly, I have never thought to try to find her." She was loquacious, nothing would stop her mouth, or calm her foolish heartbeat, her drying sap.

Babbling, spilling out words and tumbling information she had regained his ear. But he was no longer at her side. She had lost his proximity. He had already moved on a step, hurrying to draw alongside his Beth, standing ahead of Penny now, looking back at her, amused and surprised. "Well, then there is nothing for me to discover! She lives," he said, "but not as Nikos's widow. Certainly not that."

Penny's expression communicated her non-comprehension, her confusion, her defeat and Giorgios, smiling, raised his hand to caress her flushed cheek. "You based this character on the artist Nikos Koumoulides?"

She nodded, feeling at a loss, vulnerable. Of course he did not know what lay behind the story, the source of her defencelessness, or her present fancy, or rather yes, he surely had guessed at that. But why was he laughing?

"I shall tell him when I return to Athens. Your Nikos is a close friend of mine. He will be most amused. I had not realised that it was meant to be him."

"Nikos is living . . . in Athens?"

"Yes!"

"Are you sure?"

"Forgive my gullibility, Penny. I had understood that it was based on someone who had really been killed." He was laughing. "Congratulations. Your story took me in."

"But . . . I don't . . . Where in Athens . . . ? Do his family know?"

"Of course! I shall give you his address. He has a gallery in Plaka." He turned as though to depart, ready now for his Beth.

"Wait! Giorgios, give me the address but please don't say anything. Let me call him, I'd like to . . . surprise him."

Beth drew alongside them and slipped her tremulous white fingers into Giorgios's hand, perched her chin against his upper arm, too short to reach his shoulder, ready for him, her moony regard spoke of anticipated seduction.

"Tomorrow. I'll write it out for you."

"Goodnight," said Penny and smiled to them both, stepping on ahead, leaving them to themselves, wanting nothing more than to be in her room, to breathe deeply behind the privacy of her closed door, to digest what had just been told to her.

If Nikos was still alive when was his body discovered, freed from the wreckage? Did Harry know? Had he always known? That morning, the morning after Ches's death, when she had asked Harry's forgiveness, confided in him her guilt, had he simply shrugged aside any possibility of absolution? Did he know then that Nikos was alive and living in Athens? He must have known! Both he and Helen had kept in contact with the family. So he must have deliberately kept that truth from her, forcing her to live believing that she had been responsible for Nikos's death?

273

She lay splayed, face pressed against the bedding, heaving. Had Harry been seeking revenge? During all these years had he been intentionally punishing her, to pay her back? Or worse, had she been of such paltry meaning to him that he had never even bothered to consider her emotions?

When the filming was over she would go directly to Athens in search of Nikos, she would delay her trip to Italy, to Peter. Just for a few days.

Gaza was drinking Scotch from a tooth-glass he'd hauled from the bathroom. His somniferous tipple, it rested on his stomach balanced loosely between the fingers of his left hand. The other arm was behind his head acting as a pillow. In spite of his exhaustion he was not ready or able to sleep. He lay watching the early morning light, a murky glow, a thick foggy mountain mist, stealing through the windows. His head ached. Weariness, booze, concentration, maybe even life itself. It didn't bear the contemplation. His thoughts circled around the film, the shape of it, the work achieved, the work ahead; to Penny and on, to the knowledge that he had not touched a woman since his arrival in Europe. Not true. There had been a chambermaid at the Connaught the week before. She had spent two afternoons with him in his suite. A pretty little Irish girl, soft dapple-fleshed. He took a sip of Scotch and recalled her face, the openness of it when she had been coming, cheeks pink, eyes blazing and blue.

He had not missed Giorgios's desire for Beth. Probably with the girl right now. Gaza lay supine on his bed asking himself why he had not attempted to bed her, but he knew his answer and cursed at the same time his too-long-in-the-tooth romanticism. He smiled. He desired but he knew that the object of his desire had never been Beth.

The knocking on his door came as a surprise, jolted him from his bleariness. He rubbed his face with his hands, an impatient gesture, a frequent habit and glanced at his watch. Who the hell could it be bothering him now? He would have left it, let them go away, come back later, closed his eyes to it as though that would erase it, but the knocking became more insistent, more determined, refusing to be ignored. He rolled the warm liquid in the glass, swilled it down and crossed to unlock the door.

"I need somewhere to be," was all she said as explanation for her presence there.

Penny's voice was quavery, she looked pinched, pathetic, quite changed from the proud woman who had left the set less than an hour earlier. Without speaking – just reflecting – his face screwed in thought which caused him to look badtempered, he opened the door and let her in, watching as she crossed the room making for the bed and then paced without settling.

"What's happened to you?" He was pouring her a Scotch into his tooth-glass. He could drink from the bottle. She was refusing and he insisted. Finally she succumbed, took hold of the glass and sank back onto the bed.

"I don't know what possessed me to begin this story," she whispered half-heartedly.

"To get it out of your system once and for all."

She shook her head, too weary to argue. "I thought I was telling a love story or something akin to love, but instead I've unearthed something much less palatable. Me. You've pushed me."

"No," he said, "you did. It's a process: cleansing of the spirit. We are all driven by it. Some of us deny it, others struggle on with it. It's a bitch but I guess for some of us it's got to be done."

Penny very silently, almost imperceptibly, began to weep. "I have just heard something extraordinary," she said. "From Giorgios." He listened patiently, watching, bottle in hand. She was sitting now on the very edge of the mattress with her head bowed. Her light was pale, very uncertain, like the last moments of a candle. "I never sent Nikos over the mountainside. He is living, painting, in Athens. You forced me to face something I have buried for almost twenty years – since that Christmas in the pub in Sibton – forced me to come to terms with what I did, and now after all, I was not culpable."

"Oh yes you are," he took a step drawing towards her. "You think it matters whether he's alive or he's dead. You pushed him, Penny, by the very act of your betrayal. His survival is immaterial. You killed him."

She began to shift uncomfortably, to shake her head, refusing to accept it. Quick as lightening he drew alongside her and grabbed her by the wrist forcing her to listen, and then softly with unexpected compassion he continued. "Live with it, Penny. There's nothing to be done. Stop running away. Find the courage to face yourself, your black self as well as your light self. Accept both, live with them. Be proud of yourself. Understand that they are both divine forces. You can't change them, so don't lie about them. Work with them, express them generously and with an honesty that's brutal, that's about as close to love as you are gonna get. For the rest, it's a passing fascination. We seek out others to reaffirm ourselves, the similarities, to give us comfort to continue."

17

"I frequently close the gallery on a Saturday afternoon for an hour or two and stroll up here. The gates to the Acropolis are locked so few tourists, thank the Lord! I can meditate upon my city in tranquillity. Shall we sit down?" Nikos pointed to a rock jutting like a great seal a few yards in front of them. Penny accepted. The climb had fatigued him. He was no longer a young man. They sat alongside one another in the crisp early April air. In spite of his breathlessness he reached into his jacket pocket in search of cigarettes which when found he offered first to her. She shook her head.

"So, what brings you to Athens?"

"I was shooting a film in Crete. It reminded me . . . " Not yet quite accustomed to the proximity of him her voice faltered. She inhaled the aroma of the almost luke-warm afternoon. Scents of pine, late-flowering almond blossom.

"From time to time I wondered what became of you and then I began to see your name outside some of the cinemas . . . so I knew you'd found what you'd been dreaming of. No . . . don't ask me. I never go to films."

She bowed her head. How would he consider her when he knew the truth? She was in the company of a living ghost. Nikos reincarnated. As though her story had given him flesh to live again and released her from her past.

Their view, coated in a powdery opaline light, fanned out across a basin of land to the sea, the southern aspect of the city and the port of Piraeus. Directly beneath their feet lay the Odeion of Herodes Atticus. Penny smiled. She pictured herself seated alone in that bleached stone amphitheatre, young, nubile, filled with expectation. That first summer before Red Beach, before Harry, before Nikos. She had been making a pilgrimage across Europe, an aspiring actress paying homage to the spirits of the great theatres. At Epidavros she had slept on the stage beneath the stars in her sleeping-bag and here at the Odeion she had watched the glittering bourgeoisie of Athens, decked in diamonds, congregate for a Sunday night performance of *Carmina Burana*. These days she considered it a poor piece but then she had been entranced. State police in dark uniforms (had they been navy-toned?) had lined the floodlit stone steps shoulder to shoulder, adding a minacious presence to the occasion. Her first taste of the dictatorship. Why, she had asked herself, are they here? And then, timed as though in answer to her question, at the last possible moment on that starlit night a hush descended. Silent as the grave. Papadopoulos, escorted by so many men in grey suits and tinted glasses, strode towards a predesignated empty row of seats. Athens society, on its feet, roared its support. Penny cut short the recollected ring of applause, shuddering to conjure it up from that lifetime ago. "Our artists are gelded." She remembered Nikos's words. He had risked his life for his opposition to the junta. And what of herself?

"I always believed you were dead, killed that night in the mountains."

"I might have been. My one chance was as dangerous. You see, the police would have hunted me, until they found me. They would have tortured my family. I had nothing left to lose. I drove into a bend. Mountain rock hid my car from view. It was an instantaneous decision. I leapt from behind the wheel, rolled into the dust and dragged my broken self to safety. I stayed hidden in the mountains for almost two days. Without food or water. When I thought it was safe I made my way to a village. There an old partisan family took me in. They fed and clothed me and found me a sympathetic doctor. I lived with them until early December and when I was well again I took a boat to Santorini. From there I contacted my mother in Athens. She told me that Melina, my wife, and my children were in *Kríti* mourning my death. Such an irony! Not six miles from where I had been in hiding. But I could not have told them any sooner, could not have eased their sorrowing. It would have been too dangerous. Finally I spoke to Melina and she contacted our friends in London . . . "

And Harry and Helen flew to Athens for the New Year she thought, but said instead: "Nikos, that night the police arrived because . . . "

"Because I set it up. In a manner of speaking. The bar we stopped at that morning, you remember I chose it, I went inside to drink. I felt the gaze of someone watching me, hatred burning in his eyes. He had recognised me: Nikos Koumoulides, painter and resistance fighter. At first I thought it was up for me and then it occurred to me: my one chance! I stood alone, conspicuously so. I prayed that the gods were on my side. One face recognised me. One face, to inform. They would come after me. No sense in fleeing. There was nowhere left to hide. I decided to stage my own death, or die! Exile would have left my family in danger. Of course it was madness but I had no choice. As I left I exchanged a few words with him. I left him in no doubt."

"But how can you be sure that it was him? What about the elderly woman who ran the café?"

"She was an ally. Most people in those Cretan villages were. Luck, so I perceived it later, had brought me face to face with an enemy. I had to turn it to my advantage. All that day I pondered on it. If it worked I could lie low. If not, I thought, if the worse should happen then God knows at least my wife and my children might finally be left in peace. I waited. I knew that at some point the police would come. I just didn't know when."

"The others, did they know?"

"No one knew. I could not take the risk. Our friends were generous young people but naïve in the business of politics. I could not endanger them further. When I spoke to my wife on the telephone that afternoon I knew there was no other way for me. I was on my own."

"What if I told you that it was not the man in the café who informed?"

"How else would the police have known of my presence there?"

"Until Giorgios Archimede told me of your existence, your life here, I believed that you had died, that I had sent you over the mountainside. Then, I knew I had to find you. You asked me a short while ago what brings me to Athens. I want to tell you what really happened." And so, beneath the angular shadows of the Parthenon overlooking the ancient city, Penny told Nikos her story. He listened, smoking incessantly while she spoke. And when the pale heat of the spring sun began to wane they walked to keep warm. Circling the Acropolis and then returning to the east, descending the corkscrew hills and narrow cobbled streets, returning to Plaka, to his home territory, to a café just yards from his gallery where they drank thick Greek coffee and brandy.

And when her tale was ended – to the final days of her film – Nikos leant across the table and cradled Penny's hand in his. "I am no priest who can absolve you of your guilt. I do not have the power but, as you said yourself, it was another life. That Penny was a frightened girl, a restless insecure creature. From what you tell me she has long since ceased to exist but she, like the rest of us, had her part to play in the grander scheme of things. I decided in that café to make my presence known so that I might 'die' and rid my family of their anguish. For whatever reasons, young Penny played her part. Unwittingly, she was a cog in my salvation. Perhaps I owe her my life. Who can say?"

"Thank you."

"You've grown into a beautiful woman."

"One more question . . . "

"What happened to . . . your Harry? Is that your question? We never meet these days. Our lives have taken us along different paths. He lives in Athens, in Kolonaki, with his wife . . . "

"Still . . . ?"

"Yes, after all, they stayed together. They have three children, a palatial apartment in Kolonaki and holiday homes constructed on several of the islands. Of course they are immensely wealthy. After her father died Helen inherited everything. She sold the shares of all his empires and built her own – a chain of interior design stores. She has her father's entrepreneurial drive, and dare one say it, his ruthlessness."

"Does he still paint?"

"Oh, I don't think so. He designs furnishing fabrics for her. I understand he's . . . content. And what of you, Penny, are you married?"

"Yes, and no, I live with someone else."

"Why haven't you married the man you live with?"

"Too much history, too many broken affairs."

"Children?"

She shook her head.

"A pity. I believe it would have suited you. Mother-hood."

Evening was descending upon the city spread out at their feet. Here and there a house shone with light, twinkling from out of the darkness. Another day folding across the ancient city. Penny glanced at her watch, rose and rubbed at her shoulders. The remnants of a winter chill hung in the evening air.

"I'd better get going."

"Let me leave word at the gallery and then I'll walk you to a taxi."

The streets were coming to life with hungry faces searching out suitable restaurants or tavernas. Penny smelt the juice of young lamb turning on the spit.

"So, no longer a resistance fighter, you are in the government now?"

"Yes, no ministry but that suits me. I have my painting and my gallery and they leave me little enough time to fight my cause." He stretched an arm towards the ancient city and its jaspered sky peeping back at them from between the walls of two ancient houses. "You see that yellowish light? Strangely beautiful streaked with

281

the evening sun. It's the smog cloud that hangs over us. We call it the *nefos*. Carbon dioxide. Pollution. It's corroding our lungs and our ancient monuments, stealing our history and asphyxiating our future. This is our oppression now and like the junta it continues its stranglehold of us because we are feeble in our attempts to oppose it and because we refuse to accept that it is of our own making. A man once said: 'As for our city, according to the will of Zeus and the thoughts of the serene, immortal gods, it will never be destroyed, since her protectress, ever so magnanimous daughter of such a father, Pallas Athene, has her hands over it.' Penny, sometimes I think of this and I look about me. I see no female reaching out in blessing above us. I see only the results of the *nefos* and I say to myself that someone has tied the hands of the beautiful Pallas Athene behind her back. Thank you for visiting me. Next time you are in Athens you must come to eat with Melina and I. Our children are adults now. We would welcome your company."

It was evening, Saturday evening, when Penny's taxi dropped her back at the Méridien Hotel in Syntagma Square. Waiting with her key was one message. It read:

URGENT, PLEASE TELEPHONE AS SOON AS POSSIBLE.

Beneath the words, a telephone number in San Gimignano. Must be from Peter. Our line out of order, but why, she thought, has he not left his name? Alone in her room she dialled the digits. An old friend of Peter's answered, "Known him since the ark!" Their local doctor.

"*Ciao* Claudio, *come stai*? What a surprise! Is Peter dining with you?"

Quite simply without fuss Claudio broke the news.

"He had a stroke. It was swift. Mercifully he suffered no pain."

"I'll be there as soon as I can."

Her plane to Rome had been booked for the following

morning. She rang the airport: nothing sooner.

She lay on the bed, perfectly still, thinking, blaming herself, listening to the incessant whine of the lifts; and then a choking need rose up within her; an elongated whimper, creasing her, giving vent to her loss, to escape the four walls, to breathe cold air, to mingle with the stinking traffic, to be a stranger lost in the darkness and drunkenness of night.

About midnight she found herself in Kolonaki, sitting alone in one of those bars stretching towards the heart of the square. She had been walking for several hours, was feeling numb and weary. It was crowded, noisy, fizzing with chic Athenian life. She was a solitary figure; in mourning, remembering Peter, how he used to pull at his hair as though it were old grass, how he had opposed her doing the film, how he'd feared her working with Gaza again . . . she was becoming maudlin, sentimental. It was time to get some sleep. She signalled for the bill. It was as she rose to leave that she spotted him . . . sitting with a group of men, Harry. In spite of the years she knew him instantly. He was plumper, with a beard, still handsome, no physical change could have denied the intensity of those eyes. For a moment or two she stood watching him, laughing with his friends, talking and listening, at ease with his own elegance, his maturity and then slowly she turned and retraced her steps back towards the hotel.

18

He had asked her where in London she would like to eat and she had chosen L'Escargot. He had booked a table for one o'clock. The reservation was for the upstairs dining-room. "There's less chatter there. We'll be able to talk."

He had walked from his hotel and arrived early, ordered a Scotch on the rocks and a bottle of Krug champagne and then sat smoking a cigarette, waiting for her. With one preoccupied eye he glanced at the other diners squeezed around the dozen or so tables: a couple barely conversing – he knew that all too well – two chic women lunching after shopping, sharing marital confidences; quartets of raucous men in dark business suits; a table of colourfully attired folk who looked as though they might work in advertising. They were ordering on expense accounts. No one who fascinated. He slipped on his tortoise-shell spectacles, fingered the corner of his *Herald Tribune*, gazed at the front page and then without having taken in one word of news glanced at his watch. One-fifteen. She was late. Taking her time. He finished his drink. It was unlike her to be unpunctual. He was worrying, becoming vaguely anxious, a sneaking fear suffused him. Mebbe she had guessed his game and would not show.

Perhaps this whole thing was a crazy bloody exercise anyhow. Why should it be any better the second time? How many variations of that damned question had been rolling through his thoughts these past few weeks?

He lit another cigarette and turned his head to survey the room, the soft-hued tones of the decor, warm unobtrusive colours. He spotted a photograph of her smiling down at him from the wall to his right.

The Krug arrived.

"Shall I pour a glass or will you wait, sir?"

"Pour," he confirmed and straight away took a swig, slaking a thirst. Her hair was a shade or two darker in the photo, longer, she was younger. He remembered her like that. It made him smile just as though he were looking at her. He bowed his head like a shy boy and sat playing with his lighter, smiling, thinking of her, remembering her, the way she used to grin. And then he saw her. Through the corner of his eye, through the glass, she turned the corner and entered the room. Someone spoke her name, a warm-hearted, grey-haired lady welcomed her. Good to see you again, Miss Morrison.

His ridiculous heart skipped a beat. She was dressed in black. Yes, of course, he had not considered that she would be. Was all this untimely?

A tight-fitting black suit, black stockings, high heels, slender ankles. It was warm outside. Summer was on its way, light fresh asparagus-greens in St James's Park, dogs barking, nannies wheeling pushchairs, all kinda out of date, the London he enjoyed. She must be feeling the heat in that outfit. She saw him, smiled and moved quickly, tripping elegantly, bypassing tables, heads turning at her neat figure, her vibrancy, her warm open smile. Her hair had grown. She was looking terrific. He rose to greet her.

"You're looking good," he said, "rested." She threw her bag onto the white linen tablecloth, leant towards him, kissed him briefly and perched herself opposite him.

"That's because I'm no longer working with you. How's the picture?"

"Finished. Final cut delivered."

"How is it?"

"It's OK. How was Italy?"

"Spring," she said. "Peter would have loved it." She felt a moment of loss, a regret settle in her eyes before she dismissed it and smiled again, looking at him and then lowering her head. "I've decided to hang on to it.

The farmhouse. As a gesture to him, his memory. He loved it there."

He watched her, sizing things up, wondering what this loss meant to her, then leant forward exhaling smoke and poured her a glass of champagne. Her eyes lit up with surprise and curiosity. "Are we celebrating?" she asked like a schoolgirl relishing the promise of a secret.

"Mebbe."

Suddenly she began to giggle, one hand against her mouth Asian-style, a friendly warm sound with eyes that loved and appreciated, young crow's-feet in a tanned well-cared for complexion, a hazel glow.

"What?" he snapped, detesting his vulnerability.

"You're wearing a bow tie. I've never even seen you with a tie. It suits you, Jimmy. Makes you look ... dapper."

The compliment calmed him. They lifted glasses, clinked them and smiled. "To the film," she said.

"Did you go to Athens?"

"Yes."

"And?"

"I saw him in a bar."

"Your painter?"

"Yes."

"Did you talk to him?"

"No."

A frown creased his features, disbelieving, mistrusting her.

"I walked away."

"Why?"

"You were right. It's a process, cleansing of the spirit."

A scurry of movement, someone arriving, joining the group of a neighbouring table, punctuated a silence which rested between them.

"Marry me," he said finally.

Her laugh rang out clear as a bell, not mocking laughter, carefree happy laughter, light clear notes, causing heads to turn inquisitively as she leant towards him and stroked his hand. "How can I marry you? . . . Anyway you said love was just a passing fascination."

"Well, divorce me then! But let's decide something! Your life is a string of men. One disaster after another."

"Seeking out a likeness to give us comfort," she pressed, only partially teasing.

"Jesus, you always take me literally! Mebbe I was wrong," he said, stubbing at his cigarette, dragging it across the tray, waiting for an answer. "What the hell! There's nothing else."

"It didn't work the first time, Jimmy." She sipped at her drink. "Anyway, before I left you, before I fled Los Angeles, I chucked your ring away."

"I know," he said wickedly. "Your parting gesture. An end to marriage!" and then with the dexterity of an accomplished magician he pulled a crumpled but freshly pressed cotton handkerchief from his breast pocket and held it in his fist. Drawn from it and clenched tight between his fingers so as to remain unidentifiable was a small object which he delivered theatrically to mid-air, Penny's eye level, and then swiftly, before she could clearly discern what it was, he plopped it into her glass of champagne.

The gold band plunged gracefully, settling contentedly in the curve at the base of her glass. "I was always a bit sentimental about it," he confessed. "Kept it all these years. Unlike you, my darling, I just couldn't bring myself to throw the damn thing away."

MORE TITLES AVAILABLE FROM HODDER AND STOUGHTON PAPERBACKS

HILARY NORMAN

☐	56635 3	Shattered Stars	£4.99
☐	41117 1	In Love and Friendship	£4.99
☐	49351 8	Chateau Ella	£4.99

CHRISTINA LAFFEATY

☐	56630 2	Where the Hills Reply	£4.99
☐	51582 1	Far Forbidden Plains	£3.99

ALEXANDRA THORNE

☐	56765 6	Past Forgetting	£4.99
☐	51335 1	Creative Urges	£3.99

All these books are available at your local bookshop or newsagent, or can be ordered direct from the publisher. Just tick the titles you want and fill in the form below.

Prices and availability subject to change without notice.

HODDER AND STOUGHTON PAPERBACKS, P.O. Box 11, Falmouth, Cornwall.

Please send cheque or postal order, and allow the following for postage and packing.

U.K. INCLUDING B.F.P.O. – £1.00 for one book, plus 50p for the second book, and 30p for each additional book ordered up to a £3.00 maximum.

OVERSEAS INCLUDING EIRE – £2.00 for the first book, plus £1.00 for the second book and 50p for each additional book ordered.

OR Please debit this amount from my Access/Visa Card (delete as appropriate).

CARD NUMBER .... EXPIRY DATE ....

AMOUNT .... SIGNED ....

NAME ....

ADDRESS ....

....